Blind in Granada

Blind in Granada

Tom Milton

NEPPERHAN PRESS, LLC
YONKERS, NY

Published by Nepperhan Press, LLC
P.O. Box 1448, Yonkers, NY 10702
nepperhan@optonline.net
nepperhan.com

Printed in the United States of America

Library of Congress Control Number: 2022944127

ISBN 978-1-7377413-3-6

For Marie

Give him alms, woman,
for there's nothing in life
like the pain of being
blind in Granada.

Francisco Alcarón de Icaza

Fort Snelling, 1995

ONE

As HE APPROACHED the counter the waitress exclaimed: "Senator Wyatt! Make yourself at home. Would you like some coffee?"

"Yes, please," he said, smiling. She was a nice-looking woman, probably in her late thirties and probably struggling to support her children without a husband—she wasn't wearing a wedding ring.

"How would you like it?"

"With milk but no sugar, please."

"Okay." She went and got the coffee for him with a dispatch that must have come from years of serving customers who had planes to catch. She placed the coffee in front of him, asking: "Can I get you anything else?"

"No, thanks. I'm fine."

"Well, I'm so glad I have a chance to thank you personally for all the wonderful things you've done. In fact, your health program—the one that covers people like me who don't have benefits—saved my daughter's life."

"Really?" Hearing this kind of thing from constituents made him feel that all his sacrifices had been worth it. "How old is your daughter?"

"She'll be twelve next week. She had a rare form of cancer, and I could never have afforded the treatment without your program."

"Is she your only child?"

"No. I have a son who's ten."

"I bet he's a handful," he said from experience.

"Ya, he is," she said with pride. She set a menu in front of him. "I don't want to be a pest, but could you autograph this for me? I can show it to my girlfriend as proof that I waited on you."

"Sure," he said, reaching inside his jacket for a pen. "What's your name?"

"Denise," she said shyly.

"Denise," he wrote, "thanks for being the best waitress I ever had. Your senator, Jim Wyatt."

"Oh, that's so nice of you," she said, reading it. "Thank you."

"Thank *you*," he said. "You made my day."

When he had paid the woman at the register he left a tip in cash for Denise and then headed for his gate. He was going to New York on a direct flight that departed at eleven-thirty in the morning and arrived in time for him to get settled in his hotel before having dinner. It was Sunday, and the Lindbergh Terminal wasn't yet thronged with the business travelers who by flying later could salvage a few more hours of weekend with their families. Living alone, Jim preferred to fly earlier and avoid the empty Sunday afternoon in his house.

At the gate he waited only a few minutes before they started boarding. They began with first class passengers, so he stepped aside and let them pass. Though he would have liked to, he never flew first class because it would give the impression that he was wasting taxpayers' money. And he couldn't go anywhere in the state of Minnesota without being recognized by someone.

"Senator Wyatt, please come to the desk," a voice said over the loudspeaker.

Assuming there might be a problem with his ticket, he went to the desk and presented himself to the young woman behind it.

"Senator Wyatt," she said, recognizing him. "We have two empty seats in first class, and we thought you might want a free upgrade."

"That's very nice of you," he said, "but why don't you give them to that elderly couple over there."

She followed the direction of his eyes. "Are you sure?"

"Yes. And thanks for thinking of me." He returned to where he had been waiting for them to call the economy passengers. Even though the upgrade wouldn't have cost the taxpayers anything, it still would have given the wrong impression, and it also would have made him beholden to the airline. After twenty-three years of being a state senator he knew the pitfalls.

Settling at last into his seat, he wondered if they were making the economy seats narrower. He knew he hadn't gotten any wider. In fact, he was the same weight as the day he graduated from college, thirty-four years ago. Maybe he had just erased the memory of how uncomfortable it had been the last time.

"Senator Wyatt," the flight attendant said. "Could I get you a paper?"

"I have one, thanks," he said, having bought the *New York Times* at a kiosk in the terminal. It was occupying most of his carry-on bag, which was on the floor now, soon to be shoved under the seat in front of him.

"Could I get you a drink?"

"Now, there's an idea," he said, joking. But even here he had to be careful. He didn't want to give the impression that he drank alcoholic beverages before noon on Sunday. "But I can wait until you bring the cart around."

"Well, please let me know if I can do anything for you." In her eyes was a look of hero worship that other men might have taken advantage of.

"I will, thanks." He was in the seat by the window, and he waited to see if anyone would occupy the middle and the aisle seats. He hoped not because it would be easier to get up and go to the bathroom without people sitting there.

A young man on his way to a seat farther back in the plane stopped to greet him. "Senator Wyatt? I want to thank you for your program that helps young people get jobs. When are you going to run for president?"

"President?" He laughed. "I don't know."

"Well, when you decide to run I'll work for you."

"That's very nice of you. Thanks."

As good as all this recognition felt, he was reaching the point where he hoped the person who sat next to him—if anyone did—was from out of state.

The middle seat was still empty when the plane took off, so after they served the minimal breakfast he could work in peace on his keynote speech, which tomorrow would open a conference of state legislators on the subject of health insurance programs. His state had arguably the most advanced, most comprehensive health insurance system in the country, and he had been the main creative force behind it. In fact, he had been asked to lead the team that the Clinton administration had put together in its ill-fated attempt to reform the national health insurance system. Based on advice from a colleague who had worked with the Clintons, he had turned down the offer, so he was still the brightest star in the firmament of health system reformers, as reflected by the large honorarium he was getting for his speech. He could have gotten more, but that was another thing that as an elected official you had to be careful of—getting honoraria that looked extravagant to some people. Little did they know of the expenses he had as an office holder, not to mention the expenses he had as a candidate running for office every four years. All his colleagues in the state senate had in addition to their government salaries income from businesses, law practices, and other professions. Jim had subsisted on his government salary and income from a trust fund, the origin of which was an oil business that his great-great-grandfather started in Pennsylvania. His grandfather sold the oil business at the top of the market during the Twenties, held the proceeds in cash and government bonds until the Thirties, and then assembled a well-balanced securities portfolio in a trust for his grandchildren. Not having the family fortune still in oil and not having control over the family trust relieved Jim of problems that he might otherwise have had in his political career because opponents were always trying to attack you for conflicts of interest. In this respect Jim was untouchable.

Where he was vulnerable, and where he had been repeatedly attacked, was in his personal life. Conservatives, who hated him for the social reforms he had implemented, kept reminding voters that Jim Wyatt had been married and divorced four times, which was almost true—his first wife had died in a car accident. They also insinuated that he had cheated on his wives, which was technically true but misleading because he had always been faithful until after his wives left him for other men. On advice from his campaign manager he never responded to these attacks, which in any case must have hurt his opponents more than him because he kept getting reelected by larger and larger margins. In his most recent election, running as an independent without a party to support him, he had received more than eighty percent of the vote against an opponent who had been a popular mayor of St. Paul.

He spent most of the flight to New York editing his speech. He was going to tell them that if you wanted to reform a health insurance system you needed a vision, you needed support for that vision, and you needed courage to implement it. Using his own experience as a case study, he would show them how it could be done and encourage them to try it in their own states and even in the federal government, which he knew was sending representatives to the conference.

As the plane began to descend on LaGuardia Airport the flight attendant stopped by his seat and asked him: "Do you have ground transportation?"

"I take the bus," he told her.

"The bus?" she said as if she couldn't imagine doing that herself. "We can give you limousine service."

"Thanks. I'll be fine."

He saw her walk by with the crew while he was waiting for the suitcase he had checked. She gave him a little wave for good luck.

Several people recognized him as they boarded the bus, and he could see from their faces how much they admired him for traveling as they did. He wouldn't have seen such looks if a limo had been waiting for him.

Once he got into the city he was lost in the crowd, and he could do whatever he wanted. From where the bus let them off he walked through Grand Central Station and out onto Vanderbilt Avenue. It was a hot day, unusually hot even for July, and the asphalt pavement felt a little soft under his feet.

He got a taxi and rode up Park Avenue to the St. Jerome Hotel, where he always stayed when he was in New York. Since the St. Jerome was luxurious, in reporting expenses for reimbursement from the conference sponsors he used the lowest rate of a respectable hotel in the city and paid the difference out of his own pocket, so no one could say he was milking them. And it was unlikely that he would ever run into a constituent at this hotel, so it gave him the freedom that he wanted.

Arriving at the St. Jerome, he was glad he had decided to stay here. It was always the same as he remembered, creating the illusion that not much time had passed since the last time he had stayed here. He checked in and took the elevator with the bellhop to his room on the sixth floor. Pleased with the room as well as the service, he tipped the bellhop generously. He unpacked and hung up his clothes, then gazed out the window over Park Avenue, remembering the first time he had stayed here.

It was Joe Marchi, the first of his four fathers-in-law, who had introduced him to the St. Jerome and other amenities of New York. That was the year after Renata died, when it seemed that Joe was trying to bond with him, trying to determine if he should adopt him as a member of the family in place of the daughter he had lost. The pretext for these trips was to meet with people at the New York bank that joined the local bank in St. Paul in financing Joe's construction projects. The meetings were unnecessary, but the bankers were always very friendly and they always knew where to have a good time.

Since then Jim had come to New York whenever he needed to get away and could find a plausible reason for the trip. What he liked most about New York was the anonymity it offered him. Back home, where everyone knew him, the only role he could play was that of the idolized senator who had done so much to improve the lives of ordinary people. There, no matter what he did, he always had an audience watching him and applauding him, though there was always one person who never applauded him, never gave him heartfelt approval, whose presence he felt deep within him but whose identity remained forever hidden from him. For all the recognition he got from everyone else, the lack of it from this unknown spectator made him feel invalid and empty. It made him wonder if he really was the man whom so many people admired. It made him want to disappear and never play that role again. But here in New York, where there was no audience other than a woman he might meet by chance, he could play any role he wanted—secret agent, mercenary, war correspondent, private investigator—and if she believed him, it validated his identity and filled the empty space within him.

After freshening up he went down to the hotel bar where he had spent hours with Joe Marchi envisioning projects and planning the future. He took a seat at the end of the bar, around the corner, so that he could see the whole room. He ordered a glass of red wine and idly surveyed the occupants of the room. Since no one caught his eye he gazed at the television above the long shelves of bottles behind the bar. The sound was turned off but captions on the screen informed him that Serbian troops were bombarding the city of Srebrenica. Though he had been following the story, it wasn't at the top of his mind. He was interested enough to have asked a college classmate, a journalist who had recently been in Bosnia, what was really happening there, and he had been told that it was an impending disaster, but he hadn't tried to do anything about it other than raise questions with the Minnesota representatives in Washington, who had politely told him to mind his own business. The captions said that the situation in Srebrenica, which had been under siege for more than two years, was catastrophic. The thousands of Bosniaks who had fled there from farms and villages around the city seeking a safe haven were short of food, water, and other basic necessities. Behind the captions were scenes of people gathered in the streets, preparing to escape before Serbian troops captured the city.

The story was followed by a commercial for a sports utility vehicle that looked as if it could traverse rivers and climb mountains. His interest lost, Jim turned and again surveyed the room. Two men in dark suits vacated a nearby table, and within minutes a young woman took their place. She was alone and facing him, no more than ten feet away, so he could see her almost as well as if she was with him. She had dark hair, parted in the middle and drawn back to reveal earlobes graced with green jewels that looked like emeralds—they matched her green dress. She had dark eyes and crimson lips. And she either had a perfect tan or was naturally the color of *café con leche*. He decided the latter, guessing she was from Latin America.

For a while he lost sight of her as the waiter intervened to take her order, and during that time he feared he might have imagined her. But then she reappeared, and he felt as if the sun had come out from a passing cloud that had momentarily hidden it. She was there, she was real, she hadn't been the vision of a lonely man.

The question now was what to do. He couldn't just stare at her like an idiot, but he didn't have the nerve to get up and sit down at her table. For one thing, she was almost certainly meeting someone who would join her in a few minutes. And he didn't know how to present himself to her. He couldn't tell her he was a state senator from Minnesota, not only because that might get him into trouble but also because she might not be impressed. For sure she had never heard of him, and she probably hadn't even heard of Minnesota.

He decided to wait and see what happened. Meanwhile, he might catch her eye and determine whether he had a chance. He recognized that the odds were against him because she was most likely in her mid-twenties—younger than his daughters—but if she was Hispanic at least he could bridge the cultural gap, and maybe the age gap wouldn't be such a problem because Hispanic women preferred older men. So he watched her out of the corner of his eye until she looked in his direction, then casually he crossed her line of vision and paused for a moment. When their eyes met he thought he detected a flicker of interest. It wasn't exactly an invitation, but it wasn't a rejection.

Encouraged, he wondered what to do next. If she was meeting someone there might be time to get her name and phone number before her companion arrived. He still had two more nights in New York. But what if she was waiting for her husband? At her age she could well be married, especially if she was Hispanic. Surreptitiously, he glanced at her left hand. She had a ring on the fourth finger, but it looked like an emerald, and he couldn't tell from that distance if it was accompanied by a wedding ring.

He finally decided to wait and if no one joined her to follow her out into the lobby, where he could find a pretext for making her acquaintance. If he couldn't think of anything better, at the very least he could ask her for the time. In preparation for that gambit he removed his watch and slipped it into the left pocket of his pants.

After about a half hour the woman got the waiter's attention and made a check sign in the air. Not wanting to miss this opportunity, Jim signaled the bartender for his check too. He noticed that the woman paid in cash, which suggested that she wasn't staying at the hotel, so she would probably go straight out the door. Without waiting for her change she rose from her table and glided out. Her dress fit snugly around her bottom, which undulated provocatively.

Jim was already on his feet when the bartender brought his check, which he quickly signed, having left a five dollar tip on the bar. And hoping he wasn't too late, he hurried after the woman in the green dress.

He found her in the lobby with a lean young man whose skin was a similar shade of coffee. In fact, he could have been her brother. With hands on her hips she was scolding him in Spanish: "*No me importa lo que pasó.* You were supposed to meet me at seven."

"I'm only a few minutes late," he said without the slightest hint of remorse.

"You're a half hour late. And you left me alone in a bar."

"It's not a bad place."

"It's still a bar."

"Well, if you couldn't wait for me, you could have picked up someone."

"*Boludo de mierda!*" she exploded. She yanked the ring from her left hand and flung it toward the entrance. "Go and fetch it."

"*Puta,*" he sneered before turning away from her.

She glared after him, then stormed into the elevator.

Jim pursued her, getting into the car before the door closed. She was leaning against the back of the car with folded arms, tightly compressed lips, and flared nostrils. Her dark eyes were smoldering.

He pressed his floor, observing that none of the other floors was lighted up. He seized the opportunity. "What floor do you want?"

"Eight," she snapped. Then after a long moment she said: "I am sorry. Eight, please."

"That's all right. I understand."

"You mean you overheard?"

"I couldn't help it."

"You speak Spanish?"

"*Por supuesto.*"

"*Dios mío,*" she groaned as if she wondered what else could go wrong.

"Don't worry," he assured her. "I've heard worse."

"You have?" She relaxed a little.

They reached his floor, but instead of getting out he held the door open. "If you want someone to talk to, I'd be happy to listen."

"That is very kind of you. But I do not want to bore you with my stupid problems."

"You wouldn't bore me."

"Are you sure?"

"I'm sure."

She hesitated. "Well, if you do not mind waiting while I freshen up—"

"I'll meet you in the lobby."

"Fine," she agreed. "In twenty minutes."

Amazed by his luck, he got out of the elevator and headed for his room. The problem now was finding a suitable place to take her. Given her status, it would have to be elegant. And given his intentions, it would also have to be romantic.

He stopped in his room only long enough to brush his teeth and smooth his hair. As he checked himself in the bathroom mirror he thought he looked good for a man his age. He could pass for under fifty.

Returning to the lobby, he obtained a restaurant guide from the concierge and looked under "Romantic Spots." He settled on the Café des Artistes, which he recalled from the time when his sister Anna had lived in the building above it. He hadn't eaten there in many years, but he trusted the guide.

He used a phone in the lobby to make a reservation for dinner. He was told that if he came in a half hour, when the Lincoln Center crowd was gone, there would be no problem. He was given the impression that by then the restaurant would be quiet.

The woman didn't keep him waiting. After the scene she had made with the young man she had to be punctual.

By now she had recovered her composure, and she moved from the elevator toward him like a fashion model. She hadn't changed her clothes, but she looked as if she had dressed for the evening.

"I've made a reservation for dinner at Café des Artistes. Is that all right?"

"Oh, yes," she said agreeably.

"Have you been there?"

"No. But I have heard good things about it."

"I hope you like it."

He put his hand behind her waist and gently conducted her out of the hotel.

As they rode in the taxi across Central Park their conversation was limited to such questions as where they were from, when they had arrived, and how long they would be staying. He found out that she was from Granada, which enhanced the romantic aura about her. She didn't find out where he was from because he evaded the question, saying only that he lived overseas.

Sitting beside her, he was conscious of her exotic scent and of the fact that her short dress revealed as much of her smooth thighs as it concealed.

When they arrived at the restaurant they had to wait a while at the bar before the table was ready, but that was all right—it was another stage for getting acquainted. And she was stunning perched on a barstool.

"Have you lived all your life in Granada?" he asked her.

11

"Yes. Except for the years when I was at college."

"Where did you go to college?"

"Mount St. Vincent."

He knew the college. "So you were allowed to come here as long as you went to a Catholic college for women?"

She smiled. "Yes. But I really liked it. I met some nice girls, and we could go into Manhattan whenever we wanted. It was fun."

She talked as if she had graduated only a year or two ago, and he concluded that she was even younger than he had first thought. "Was it hard going back to Granada and your family after all that freedom?"

"Yes. A little. But I wanted to go back to Granada. I did not want to live here."

"I don't blame you."

"Have you been to Granada?"

"Yes, of course." He had gone to Granada for the first time during his junior year in Spain, and since then he had been there many times. "I lived in Málaga for a while, and it was only a short trip from there to Granada."

"You lived in Málaga?" She seemed delighted. "What were you doing there?"

"Oh—" He paused while deciding what to tell her. "I was working on a project."

"Are you an engineer?"

"No. Do I look like one?"

She laughed. "No."

"What do I look like?"

She studied his face. "You look like an actor."

"Oh, damn," he said as if his identity had been exposed. "I should have worn my dark glasses so you wouldn't recognize me."

"I thought you looked familiar."

"Well, now that you know what I do, what about you?"

"Me?" she said as if she wouldn't have expected anyone to be interested. "I work for a foundation. It was started by my mother, so I had no trouble getting a job there."

"What kind of foundation?"

"Our purpose is historic preservation. Our main concern is the Albaicín, the old Arab quarter of Granada. We are trying to control development so we do not lose this treasure from the past." She sounded like she was quoting from a fund-raising piece.

"A worthy objective," he said sincerely. He remembered the maze of narrow streets, the white-plastered houses, the black iron grillwork, the flower pots, and the tiled courtyards with fountains in them, shaded by the leafy canopies of lemon, fig, or almond trees. "Does your family live there?"

"We have a house there. We also have a house in the country, where we own a lot of land. But it is too hot there. I prefer the Albaicín."

"So what are you doing in New York?"

"I came to see the Rockefellers. Not them personally, but their foundation. The one that is involved in historic preservation."

"To learn what they're doing?"

"Right. I think we are doing a pretty good job, but we can always learn."

At that point their table was ready, and they went into the dining room. The restaurant, whose walls were decorated with light-hearted nude women painted by Howard Chandler Christie, looked the same as he remembered. It was indeed a romantic spot, and he was glad he had brought her here, especially when the headwaiter sat them at a very private corner table.

At that point he finally asked: "What's your name?"

"Zoraya. What is yours?"

"Diego," he told her, giving the Spanish equivalent of his name. "Or Santiago, if you prefer."

"So it is James?"

"Yes. You can call me Jim."

"Jim," she repeated, softening the consonants and lengthening the vowel. The way she said it, the name even sounded sexy. "Are you really an actor?"

He decided to play the role that had worked before, only now he would be more subtle about it. He glanced around as if to make sure that no one was listening and then confided: "Actually, I work for the government."

13

She raised her eyebrows. "You do? What area?"

"International," he said glibly, hoping she would know what this meant. But to make sure, he added: "Covert operations."

"You work for the CIA?"

"Yeah, but please don't tell anyone."

"Do not worry. I will not tell anyone," she said, gazing at him with admiration. She was evidently more impressed than if he had really been an actor. "It must be interesting."

"At times it is. But most of the time it's just like any other job."

"Oh, I do not believe that."

"It's true," he insisted modestly.

When they had ordered he felt it might be a good time for her to talk about what happened in the hotel lobby. By now there was no vestige of her anger, and he could have avoided bringing up the subject, but she might want to talk about it, and if she did then he would learn more about her. "Was that your *novio*?"

"No," she said, making a face. "He would like to be, and that is why he gave me the ring. But it was only a birthday present."

"You don't like him?"

"No. I do not."

"Then why did you accept the ring from him?"

"Because his father is a good friend of my father."

"And your father wants you to marry him?"

"Right. His family owns land next to ours, and if we got married," she explained, "we would own a lot of land together."

"Are you the only child?"

"We both are."

"So a marriage between you would be like Isabel and Fernando getting together."

She smiled. "Not quite. But that is the idea."

Jim was satisfied, but he still wondered: "What's he doing in New York?"

"He is getting an MBA at Columbia."

"Then you haven't seen him for a while."

"No. And I have not missed him," she added. "He may come from a good family, but in spite of that he is *mal educado*."

"Well, if you don't intend to marry the guy, then what's the problem?"

"My father," she sighed.

He understood: she loved her father, and she wanted to make him happy. Given this evidence of filial affection, Jim saw how he might help her as well as advance his courtship of her. "You know, I have three daughters, and as a father I can tell you that what your father wants above all is for *you* to be happy."

"Then why does he keep promoting this marriage?"

"He must think it would make you happy. Have you told him how you feel?"

"No. I cannot." With glistening eyes, she bit her lip as if she was trying to restrain her emotion. "I do not want to disappoint him."

"But you'll have to tell him sooner or later, and the longer you wait the more you *will* disappoint him."

She pondered this. "I guess you are right. I should have told him the first time he proposed it. Then I would not have raised his hopes."

"If you're not engaged, it hasn't gone too far."

"It has not gone anywhere," she said. "So when I get home I will tell him."

"You might mention," he suggested, knowing how much fathers worried about their daughters, "that the guy made you wait for him alone in a bar."

"I will," she said, looking grateful for his advice.

They lingered in the restaurant until the waiters began to hint in various ways short of putting the chairs on the tables and sweeping the floor that it was time for them to leave.

As they rode in the taxi back across the park Zoraya laid her head on his shoulder, tacitly reminding him that she was still on Spanish time, so for her it was five-thirty tomorrow morning.

He put his arm around her shoulder, inhaling the scent of jasmine that emanated from her dark hair. It conjured up a night in the Alhambra, a courtyard of the Serrallo, with only the light of stars flickering in the deep sky and only the sound of water plashing from the fountains. A vision of earthly paradise, within his grasp.

When they got out of the taxi he could see that she was tired, but he still had hopes of getting her to come to his room. These hopes were reinforced when as soon as the elevator door closed she put her arms around his neck and lifted her face to kiss him.

The message from her yielding mouth was unambiguous: the rest of her was available and was being offered.

He opened an eye to find the button to press for his floor, and as they rode up they continued kissing. When the elevator stopped he expected her to get out with him. But she held back, saying: "I am too tired. It would not be any good tonight."

"We wouldn't have to do anything."

"No, but we would. We can wait until tomorrow."

"Do we have a date?"

"We do if you are free."

He was holding the door, which was trying to close. "Yes, I'm free. Could you meet me in the bar at six?"

"Okay. And do not be late," she added, smiling.

"Don't worry."

She gave him a reprise of that first kiss with the same clear message. Then with her hand on his arm she murmured: *"Buenas noches."*

"Buenas noches."

After the elevator door had closed he headed for his room. Of course he wished she had come to his room, but he couldn't complain. He could look forward to tomorrow night, and the next night, and maybe beyond into the future.

Entering his room, he noticed that the light on his telephone was flashing, indicating that someone had left a message for him. He sat on the bed and picked up the phone. The message was from Thea, his third wife and the mother of his fifth child, Matthew. It was only a little after ten-thirty in St. Paul, and he knew that Thea would wait for him to call or would call again later if he didn't, so he got an outside line and dialed her number, lying on the bed with his head propped up by two pillows.

Thea answered before the first ring ended, which meant that she had been sitting by the phone, waiting for him to call her back.

"I got your message," he told her.

"Where were you?" she demanded as if they were still married. She had left him almost thirteen years ago for a doctor at the institute where she was working.

"I was having dinner," he said, resisting the need to give any further explanation.

"Well, I was waiting for you to call. I have a serious problem."

"What is it?" he asked, guessing.

"I don't have money to pay the rent."

"I gave you money. What happened to it?"

"I don't know what happened to it."

"Well, you must have spent it on something," he said patiently, wondering if she was back on drugs.

"I don't know what I spent it on," she screamed. "Okay?"

"Okay." He paused, counting to ten before saying: "But you have to learn how to manage your money."

"The problem is, you don't give me enough money."

"I give you more than we agreed on."

"It's still not enough."

"I'll see what I can do, but I don't have an unlimited amount of money."

"You have money to go New York and have a good time."

"This trip is paid for. And I'm not here to have a good time. I'm here to give a speech at a conference."

"I've been to conferences. I know what they're like."

He could see how this conversation might go on all night, so he said: "Look. I'll call your landlord and tell him there's a check in the mail. And from now on I'll pay him directly."

"You mean you don't trust me to pay the rent?"

"I trust you," he said, avoiding the argument that this question might have provoked. "I just want to make it easier for you."

"It'll enable me to keep mismanaging the money. That's what you always did in our marriage—you enabled me to avoid dealing with my problems—and now you can see the consequences of your behavior."

"Thea," he said calmly, "it's almost midnight in New York, and I have to get up early in the morning and give a speech to a roomful of state legislators."

"So you want to avoid dealing with *your* problems?"

"I'll call your landlord, and we can talk when I get back."

"Go to hell," she said, hanging up the phone.

As always he was bewildered by the intensity of her anger. The therapist he had seen while he was married to Thea had explained that she was directing her anger at him only because she was afraid to direct it at the real object. That was plausible, but he still had trouble accepting her behavior. He just felt it wasn't fair for her to take out her anger on him when it had nothing to do with him.

Suddenly tired, he got ready for bed and asked the operator to call him at seven.

As he lay in bed with his eyes closed he reran the sequence of events with Zoraya, pausing at the highlights: the flicker of interest when their wandering eyes met in the bar, her swaying bottom as she left the room, her half-revealed thighs in the taxi, her look of gratitude in the restaurant, and her open-mouthed kiss in the elevator.

For a long time he stopped at the kiss, and then he continued, imagining what would have happened if Zoraya had come to his room that night.

TWO

THE NEXT MORNING, in anticipation of what would happen that evening, he called the desk of the hotel and changed his room to a suite. It cost a hundred and ten dollars more, but he didn't care. He could pay for it with his honorarium.

As he had breakfast in his room he watched the news on television. The Serbs were bombarding Srebrenica, and thousands of people were fleeing the city. A Bosniak leader was criticizing the UN troops for standing by and doing nothing. He said that the Bosniaks in Srebrenica had disarmed themselves in accordance with the UN resolution, assuming that the UN would protect them. The commander of the UN troops, who were far outnumbered by the Serbian army, had requested NATO air support to defend the city, but so far NATO had done nothing. There were scenes of people leaving the city, moving slowly in endless columns on side roads to avoid the Serbian tanks, taking only what they could carry.

The sight made Jim angry at the government in Washington for not intervening, and he made a note in his pocket calendar to call the U.S. senator from Minnesota who might listen to him. Congress was back from its July 4th recess, so he could probably reach the senator later in the morning.

It was too early to call Thea's landlord, so he made another note to call after his keynote speech. He packed his bags for the bellhop to carry to the suite, and then after leaving instructions at the desk he left and walked over to the Sheraton, where he found a number of state legislators with identification stickers on their lapels hanging out in the lobby. He recognized several of them from previous conferences, and he made the rounds, greeting them and introducing himself to the ones he didn't know.

He then went to the enormous meeting room where they were going to assemble for the opening session. He easily spotted the events coordinator, a young woman in a tight blue suit who looked as if she had a million things on her mind. She recognized him and rushed toward him with a welcoming smile, indicating that with his arrival she was now relieved of her biggest worry. From years of experience Jim knew that the worst thing that could happen to an events coordinator was for the keynote speaker not to show up. Once, while traveling to Phoenix for a conference at which he was the keynote speaker, his flight was delayed by equipment problems, and he didn't arrive until six in the morning, just three hours before his speech. He knew enough to call the events coordinator as soon as he got off the plane in Phoenix, and by then she was so far gone that when he assured her that he would be in time to deliver his speech, all she could say was: "Thank you, God. Oh, thank you, God."

"Senator Wyatt!" this one said. "It's good to see you."

"I'm happy to be here," he said, shaking her hand.

"Did you have a good flight?"

"Oh, yes. I got here yesterday."

"You're the kind of speaker I love. You know, I have speakers who fly in at the last minute. It drives me crazy."

"I did that once, not intentionally. So I know how you feel."

"Well, you know the routine. We have the opening remarks at eight-thirty, and then you'll come on at nine."

"Sounds good."

She paused before turning to attend to other matters. "I heard a rumor. Is it true that you might run for president?"

"What's wrong with the president we have?"

"I don't like the way he treats women."

"Well, a large majority of women voted for him."

"I know. I did. But I would have rather voted for you."

"That's nice of you to say. Thanks."

Momentarily alone, he pondered the irony of this conversation in which he had been compared favorably with the president in terms of his relationships with women. Since it was public knowledge he assumed that the events coordinator knew he had been married four times, so she evidently didn't count that against him. But he wondered what she would think of him if she knew about his covert operations.

By eight-thirty the meeting room was filled, and there were people standing, including members of the press. When the master of ceremonies introduced him the room exploded with applause. Standing at the podium, he looked around the room, and he felt that he was in command of this audience. One of his strengths as a politician was his ability to deliver an effective speech. It was a skill that he had been developing since grade school when every student was required to give a five-minute speech on Friday, and he had honed this skill in high school and college, where he had been president of the debating society. So the audience was in the palm of his hand from his very first words, and they followed him every step of the way. His goal was to give them the confidence that in each of their states they could do things to improve the health insurance system, as he had done in Minnesota, so that they would go away with a commitment. As he approached the end of his speech he could feel the momentum building, and when he closed with an exhortation they jumped to their feet and cheered him as if he had hit the winning home run in a World Series.

In the break after the opening session the master of ceremonies and the events coordinator complimented him on his speech, and the legislators swarmed around him, thanking him for the inspiration and asking for his card so that they could call him. By any measure his speech had been a complete success, but as always he felt there was one person in the audience who hadn't applauded, and for all the recognition he got from everyone else, the lack of it from this unknown spectator made him feel invalid and empty. It made him want to stop playing this role.

During the break he called the office of Thea's landlord, which was open by now. He verified their address and told them he was mailing a check for this month's rent as well as the rent for the following months. The woman thanked him, sounding relieved and saying: "I told Mr. Olson not to worry. I told him you would pay the rent if your ex-wife didn't. But he's a Republican."

"I know."

"Still, he admits that he voted for you."

"Well, maybe he trusts me more with public money than with private money."

The woman laughed. "I know he doesn't trust your ex-wife."

He didn't comment, he just said: "Please tell him that from now on I'll pay the rent directly to him."

"That'll make him happy."

He then called Washington, but the senator wasn't available. Jim left a message for him, expecting a long game of phone tag.

He spent the rest of the morning in a breakout session where a state senator from Oregon was leading a workshop. It was very good, and he got mentally involved in the process. Out of deference to the workshop leader he didn't contribute until he was asked to. Then he made a few suggestions that were well received.

He had lunch at the table with the presenters, and then he wandered out of the hotel and took a walk. He went into a bookstore and found a guide to New York where he looked for a place to take Zoraya for dinner. As he went through the restaurant section of the guide his eye landed on La Grenouille, which he remembered from the days when Joe Marchi had introduced him to the city. It wasn't far from the St. Jerome, so they could stroll back and have an after-dinner drink in his suite. From a public phone back at the Sheraton he made a reservation for dinner.

The speaker after lunch talked about health insurance plans. He was from the industry, and his presentation could have been more dynamic, especially after lunch when people were drifting into a food coma, but it was filled with hard information that they used in the afternoon breakout sessions. Jim could have snuck out early without being noticed, but he wanted to show support with his presence, so he stayed until five when the last session ended.

He walked briskly back to his hotel, got a new key at the desk, and went to his suite. It was perfect for what he had in mind. It had a mini-bar, stocked with beverages including brandy and two splits of champagne, so he wouldn't have to call room service, which might have interrupted the natural flow of events.

After showering and changing into a linen suit he headed for the bar. He was ten minutes early, just to make sure that he didn't keep Zoraya waiting. Above all he didn't want this evening to end prematurely.

Zoraya was punctual: she appeared while the chimes for six o'clock would have been sounding in a bell tower. With her entrance she turned a lot of heads. She was wearing a blue dress that was just as short as the green one she had been wearing yesterday, and she swayed across the floor as if there was a Latin rhythm playing in the background.

Jim rose and greeted her with a kiss on the lips which she reciprocated. For him this exchange was not only a way of resuming physical contact with her, but also a way of confirming at its source the offer she had made last night in the elevator.

After pulling out a chair for her and seating her at the table he asked: "What would you like to drink?"

"Campari and soda, please," she said.

The waiter duly noted this and left them.

Jim noticed that the jewels in her earrings matched her dress as they had last night, and he wondered if they were sapphires. "Well, how were the Rockefellers?"

"They were fine. In fact, I met one. A young one," she added as if he was therefore of no consequence.

"Did you learn anything?"

She considered. "Yes. I learned that historic preservation requires more money than I thought. At least in this country."

"It costs more to restore something than it does to build it."

"I guess that explains why in this country you have so many new buildings and so few old buildings."

"It does," he agreed, impressed by her grasp of the situation.

The waiter brought her Campari and soda, which she sipped through a straw with pursed lips.

Watching her, he said: "I've made a reservation for dinner at La Grenouille. Is that all right?"

"Oh, that would be lovely," she said with enthusiasm, holding the now red-tipped straw. "You know, it is my favorite restaurant."

"You mean in New York?"

"In the world," she told him.

"Well, there're some very good restaurants in Spain."

She shook her head, still holding the straw between her thumb and forefinger. She had perfect nails, painted red and just long enough to accentuate her tapered fingers. "There is nothing in the world like La Grenouille."

Though he recognized that at her age she had limited culinary experience, he was glad he had decided on this restaurant. A lucky choice.

During dinner, since things were going so well, he told her a little about his work as a CIA agent. He had expected her to ask him about it, but she hadn't made any reference to it, evidently because she accepted the fact that he couldn't talk about it. And maybe it was her absolute respect for his secrecy that induced him to reveal at least something about what he did.

After explaining unnecessarily that he couldn't tell her anything about what he was doing now, he regaled her with a story about how he had foiled the plot by the hard-liners against Gorbachev. He could have gone further back into the past, but he knew from experience with his children that events which occurred before they were old enough to vote had no reality for them. Assuming that Zoraya was in her mid-twenties, he figured that at least she would have heard of Gorbachev.

"Oh, yes," she said. "I remember him. I was a freshman in college at the time. I was taking a course in political science, so we talked about Gorbachev."

"Then you know that what Gorbachev did was a turning point in history. If the hard-liners had stopped him, we'd be living in a different world now."

She nodded, acknowledging this.

"Anyway, I heard about the plot, and I was going to warn Gorbachev when the conspirators caught me." In harrowing detail he related how they had held him in a dacha and tortured him, trying to find out if anyone else knew about the plot. They didn't crack him, and they decided to accelerate their plans before

Gorbachev could preempt them. They left him in the dacha under armed guard, but he escaped and warned a general who was loyal to Gorbachev. Meanwhile, the conspirators were holding Gorbachev and his family as hostages, claiming power. The general surrounded them with troops, and they finally gave up.

"So while we were talking about it in class," she said, gazing at him with awe, "you were involved in it."

He shrugged. "Yeah."

After a long silence she said: "We are taught that women are equal to men, but I do not think a woman could have done what you did. I know I could not have."

"You never know what you could do until you're in the situation."

"Maybe. But still—" She shook her head definitively. "I could not have done it."

Holding hands, they strolled back to the St. Jerome.

In the elevator she kissed him as she had last night, reaffirming her offer. And tonight, with her hand on his arm, she came to his room.

"Would you like a glass of champagne?" he asked, not wanting to rush things.

"Oh, that would be lovely."

While he got a split out of the mini-bar she sat in one of the armchairs and kicked off her shoes. She crossed a leg over the other, which had the effect of making her dress even shorter.

He handed her a glass half filled with champagne, and then he sat in the armchair opposite her. Leaning forward, he extended his glass toward her.

She held out her glass and touched it to his.

"*Salud*," he said softly.

"*Salud y amor.*"

He gazed at her, ready to abandon his life for her. Whatever time he had left on earth he wanted to spend with this woman.

As she sipped her champagne she sat back and uncrossed her legs. He caught a flash of white panties, and from then on he couldn't think of anything else—he kept seeing the flash as if someone had taken his picture.

25

Unable to restrain himself, he moved to the arm of her chair and kissed her.

She welcomed him with an open mouth.

As they prolonged and deepened the kiss his hand found its way under her dress to the edge of her panties.

She eased her legs helpfully.

He was almost there when suddenly the phone rang.

He tried to ignore it, but whoever was calling—probably Thea—wouldn't give up. After ten rings it finally stopped, but then after only a few moments of blessed silence it started again.

"You better answer it," she said, motionless. "It might be urgent."

He realized that she was alluding to his occupation as a CIA agent. "Oh, it's not business. They wouldn't call me here."

They waited for the phone to stop ringing, but it didn't stop.

"You'd think someone at the desk would tell them I'm not in my room."

"But you *are* in your room."

The ringing stopped.

He moved back toward Zoraya, hoping to pick up where they had left off.

But then the phone started ringing again.

"I think this is not a good time," she said, straightening her dress.

"No, wait. I'll ask the desk to block all calls."

"You should answer it, and when you are done you can come to my room. We will not get any phone calls there."

That sounded like a good idea. "Okay."

She gave him a kiss that still promised everything, and then she left, saying: "*Hasta pronto.*"

He waited a few minutes to control his anger at Thea for interrupting things, and then he answered the ringing phone.

"Hello?"

There was nothing but a click as the caller hung up.

It was the kind of thing Thea might do to annoy him. She might have guessed that he had a woman in his room, and she was trying to spoil his evening. He could call her to find out if she had called, or he could let the matter rest and go to Zoraya's room.

He decided to let the matter rest.

As he headed for the door he realized that in his excitement he hadn't asked for the number of Zoraya's room. He only knew that she was on the eighth floor, and he couldn't very well march up and down that floor knocking on doors until he found her, especially at this time of night.

After thinking about the problem he finally came up with an idea. He called the concierge and said: "This is Jim Wyatt. I know it's late, but someone just slipped an envelope under my door."

"An envelope?" the man repeated as if he didn't know what the word meant.

"Yes. An envelope," Jim told him. "A manila envelope, which judging by its weight has documents in it."

"Oh, I see. Well, I don't know who delivered it."

"I don't either, but it's addressed to a person named Zoraya."

"How do you spell that?"

He spelled the name for the man and said: "She must be staying in the hotel. And instead of delivering the envelope to her, they delivered it by mistake to me."

"All right. I'll send someone up to get it, and we can give it to her in the morning."

"It could be urgent, so it should be delivered to her now."

"What's her last name?"

"It doesn't say."

"Then how can I have it delivered to her?"

"Zoraya is Spanish, so you can look at the register for Spanish last names and see if any of them have Zoraya as a first name."

"What if she's registered under her husband's name?"

"Then that would be a problem. But see if you can find Zoraya. As I said, it could be urgent, and we're wasting time."

"I'll send someone up to get it."

"I'd be happy to deliver it to her if you could just tell me what room she's in."

"Well, that would take a while. I'd have to scan the whole

register for Spanish names, and you'd be surprised how many there are."

"I can narrow it down for you. When I was in the elevator tonight a Spanish woman got in and pressed the button for the eighth floor."

"You remember that?"

Jim almost said he remembered it because the woman was very attractive, but that might have revealed his motive for wanting to know what room she was in. So he just said: "Yes, I remember it was the eighth floor."

"All right. The eighth floor."

Jim waited tensely, aware of the fact that he was losing time. By now Zoraya might have given up on him and gone to bed.

"Excuse me, sir," the concierge said a few minutes later. "I have to put you on hold now. I have another call to attend to."

"Okay," Jim said, having no choice.

When the man got back on the line he said: "I have an emergency on the third floor. A man had a heart attack, and his wife is hysterical. She didn't even have enough sense to call the paramedics. So your matter will have to wait. I'm sorry."

Before he could say anything the man hung up.

By now it was more than a half hour since Zoraya had left. Remembering how she had reacted to the young man who had kept her waiting for a half hour, Jim was afraid that he had lost her. And even if he hadn't it was probably too late for anything to happen tonight.

He was ready to go up and sniff for jasmine under all the doors of the eighth floor, crawling on his hands and knees, when the phone rang.

He assumed it was the concierge, calling to give him the vital information.

"*Buenos días*," said a low melodic voice.

Relieved, he said: "I was going to come up, but I don't know your room number."

"I know. I realized that as soon as I got back here. I have been trying to call you, but your line was busy."

"I was talking with the concierge."

"Well, he could not help you," she told him. "You do not know my last name. And anyway, he should not have given you my room number."

"He didn't. So what's your last name?"

"Ramirez de la Vega."

"Zoraya Ramirez de la Vega. It sounds like the name of a princess."

"It does. And that is why I do not like to give my last name to people. As soon as they hear it they treat me like royalty."

"And you don't want to be treated like royalty?"

"No. I do not. I want to be treated like an ordinary girl. And that is what I liked about living here. The name meant nothing to my friends at college."

"It means nothing to me," he assured her. "Though it does sound impressive."

"Please do not be impressed."

"Okay. I won't be."

"Now, where were we?"

"I think we were about to get to know each other," he said, remembering the point at which the phone had rung.

"I think we were," she giggled softly.

"Do you want to pick up where we left off?" he asked hopefully.

"Of course I do. And I have an idea. It is very late, and I am still not adjusted to New York time. I also have a meeting at nine in the morning. But I could meet you tomorrow afternoon."

"What time?"

"Would three o'clock be all right?"

"That would be perfect."

"I hoped it would be. It is *siesta* time."

"I hadn't thought of that," he admitted happily.

"I will come to your room," she offered. "Unless you think we will be interrupted."

"We won't be. I'll tell the concierge to hold all calls."

"Okay. I will meet you at three."

Before going to bed he called Thea to see why she had called him, but she said she hadn't called him, and she acted as if he had interrupted something important, so he ended the call, wondering who had called him. It couldn't have been Inga or Keira, his other ex-wives, because they would have kept calling until they got him. So he decided that it must have been a wrong number.

Lying in bed, remembering how far his hand had gotten, he ached with desire for Zoraya. He wished there was some way he could speed up the hours between now and three the next day. In all his life he had never wanted a woman so badly.

The next morning, as he had a late breakfast in his room, he watched the news on television. While the Serbian forces were consolidating their position around Srebrenica, more and more people were fleeing the city. At least twenty thousand refugees were crowded into the nearby hamlet of Potočari, where the UN troops had their compound. NATO had finally taken action and bombed Serbian tanks advancing toward Srebrenica, but they had stopped intervening when the Serbs threatened to kill the UN troops they were holding as hostages and to shell the UN compound. Women and children were being loaded onto buses, while able-bodied men were trying to escape through the woods or across country to Tuzla, Zepa, or other towns that might be safe. Already there were stories of women being raped and men being executed.

Jim tried again to reach the senator in Washington, who had returned his first call. He waited at least ten minutes for the man to come onto the line.

"Hey, Jim," the senator said heartily. "What can I do for you?"

"Are you aware of what's happening in Bosnia?"

"Oh, yeah. I've been following it."

"Is our government going to do anything about it?"

"We've been trying to, but the Europeans aren't pulling their weight on this."

"What do you mean? Are you talking about our allies in NATO?"

"You know how they are, especially the French. Whatever we want to do, they're against it."

"How could they be against intervening? This is happening in Europe."

"That's what we say. But their definition of Europe depends on the situation."

"You mean these people aren't in Europe because they're Muslims?"

"They wouldn't put it that crudely."

"France has a lot of Muslims. Aren't they worried about how they'll react if their government does nothing to stop these Muslims from being killed?"

"They're worried about that. But they're more worried about Russia."

"You mean they believe that Russia will start World War III to defend the Serbs from our intervention?"

"No, but there are other things Russia can do short of starting a war."

"Yeah. They can cut off the vodka pipeline."

"I wouldn't joke about them."

"I wouldn't take them too seriously."

"Well, we finally did get some action out of NATO."

"Not enough," Jim argued. "Is it true that NATO stopped intervening when the Serbs threatened to kill the UN troops they're holding as hostages?"

"It's true," the senator sighed. "The UN troops were useless. They didn't protect the safe haven, and now they're in the way."

"You blame the Europeans, and you blame the UN, but what about us? Aren't we to blame for doing nothing?"

"We have no strategic interest in Bosnia."

"I don't agree. I think we have a strategic interest in any part of the world where civilians are being raped and murdered."

"So what would you do? Resume the bombing and let them kill the hostages?"

"Doing nothing won't stop them from killing the hostages. And since when," he asked bluntly, "are we willing to negotiate with terrorists?"

"They haven't been classified as terrorists."

"What does it take to be classified as a terrorist these days?"

"It takes a decision that they're a threat to us."

"Meanwhile they're what?"

"They're Serbian nationalists."

"And what are the people who are being exterminated?"

"They're people who unfortunately are in the wrong place."

"Well, even if we don't care about them," Jim said, still hoping to influence the senator, "we should stop them from being exterminated. If we don't act now, we'll pay for our failure. Believe me."

"I'll do what I can," the senator promised.

He took a shower and walked over to the Sheraton, where he made the rounds of the breakout sessions, killing time.

For lunch he went to a French bistro on the West Side. He had to eat something, but he didn't want a heavy meal, so he ordered a filet of sole with butter and capers, which came with parsley potatoes and green beans. He left the potatoes untouched.

It was only two when he returned to the hotel, which gave him ample time to change his clothes. He decided to wear the jeans and the polo shirt he had brought along. He checked his appearance, standing in front of the large mirror in the bathroom. Thanks to his weekly visit to a woman who had a way with scissors and color, his hair had just the right amount of gray in it. And he was proud of his flat stomach, which didn't even show the temporary consequences of his recent lunch.

As he waited in the armchair where Zoraya had been sitting the night before, he imagined what might have happened if the phone hadn't interrupted them. He was roused from his revery by her arrival, right on time. In fact, she knocked on his door when the digits of the clock on the table were exactly at three. Though he was somewhat mystified by her strict compliance with appointments, in the present situation he appreciated it. He couldn't have waited much longer.

"*Buenas tardes*," she said brightly. She had tied her hair up in a ponytail, which made her look even younger. She really could have passed for a college student.

They greeted each other at the door with a hug and a kiss, and then she came into the room.

She was also wearing jeans, which fit her perfectly and revealed every contour. On top she wore a white tee shirt with the letters AVE, and he could tell she wasn't wearing a bra.

"Would you like some champagne?" he offered.

"No, thank you. I have a better idea," she told him excitedly. "How would you like to spend a few days in the country with me?"

"Where?" he asked, interested.

"The house of my uncle. It is only about an hour from here, and my uncle is in Spain. We will have the house all to ourselves."

"No servants?" he joked.

"No, none at all. I will cook for you."

Having lived with four successive women who refused to be demeaned by cooking, he welcomed the prospect.

"I am done with my work, so I can stay there as long as you can." With a smile she added: "My uncle will not be coming back until September."

That left a fair amount of time.

"Do you like the idea?"

"I love it," he said, ready to go. He was thinking far beyond the weekend. "How do we get there?"

"I have a limo waiting for us."

He should have guessed. If your name was Ramirez de la Vega you didn't go to Hertz and rent a mid-sized Japanese car. You rode in style.

While she waited he packed only what he thought might be useful in the country and left the rest of his clothes in the room. If he decided to prolong his stay, which seemed very likely at this point, he could always call the hotel and check out by phone, asking them to hold his things until he returned.

Carrying his bag, he followed Zoraya out of the room, unable to keep his eyes off the back of her jeans. He was mesmerized by her swaying bottom.

33

When the elevator door opened in the lobby she seized his hand and hopped out like a schoolgirl who had finally gotten permission from her parents to have her best friend stay for a sleepover. But no matter how young he looked for his age, anyone seeing them at that moment would have concluded that he was her father. Painfully aware of their age difference, he began to have some second thoughts—until she bounded ahead of him in her skintight jeans.

A black, stretched limousine was parked in front of the hotel, with a man in livery standing by. The driver was a thickset man with a stolid face, but he smiled happily at the pretty young woman.

"Señorita Ramirez," he said in Spanish, "it's so good to see you. It has been a long time."

"It has been," she said, patting his arm with obvious affection. "Manuel, this is Mr. Wyatt. He's going to be our guest for a while."

"It is a pleasure to meet you, sir," the driver said in English, inclining his head.

"*Igualmente*," Jim said, shaking his hand.

"Oh, I should have told you," Zoraya said, smiling. "Mr. Wyatt speaks Spanish."

"*De verdad?*" Manuel said as if he never would have guessed it.

"He even lived in Spain for a while."

"Then you are especially welcome, sir."

"*Gracias*," Jim said, with a warm feeling.

Manuel took his bag, which he ceremoniously deposited in the open trunk of the long car. Then, turning to Zoraya, he asked: "Where are your bags?"

She laughed. "*Dios mío.* I almost forgot them. I left them in the lobby."

"I'll get them for you. What do they look like?"

"They're red," she told him.

"How many are there?"

"Three," she said.

"You're traveling lightly."

"Well, I didn't expect to be here long. But now I think my plans have changed." She snuggled up to Jim, with her arm around him. "Of course, that depends on Mr. Wyatt. I have no idea what his plans are."

"No idea?" Jim said, continuing in Spanish.

"Not the least," she said innocently.

Manuel smiled as if he was glad to see the young heiress having such a good time, and then he swaggered off to fetch her bags.

When he had put them into the trunk he held the door open for Zoraya, who slid into the limousine as if she was used to this mode of travel. Then, careful of the traffic on Park Avenue, he edged around the car and respectfully opened the door on the other side for Jim, who having rejected the offer of a limo at the airport got into the car and stretched out his legs and enjoyed the luxury of all the room.

Zoraya, who was on his right, found his hand again and joyfully squeezed it, making him feel as if she was sealing a pact with him.

They headed over to the West Side and up the Henry Hudson Parkway to the Saw Mill River Parkway. Since he had traveled this route a number of times, Jim recognized the parkway and remembered most of the towns as far as Tarrytown, where his brother Stephen lived. He had called his brother a week ago from St. Paul to let him know he would be in New York, and they had agreed to get together for dinner at a Spanish restaurant where they had been going for years. He was supposed to call Stephen and confirm the date, and when he saw the exit sign for Tarrytown he decided to call him as soon as they returned to the city.

As they rode north on the parkway Zoraya lay down with her head on his lap, slipping a hand under his thigh and putting the other hand on his knee.

"Are you still on Spanish time?"

"No. Riding in a car makes me sleepy. I hope you do not mind."

"I don't mind at all," he told her, completely relaxed.

By the count of ten she had dozed off as only the pure of heart could do.

He watched over her with his left hand idle on the seat and his right hand resting on the edge of her hip, where he could feel its breathtaking swoop down to her waist.

The smell of jasmine drifted upward from her dark hair.

They got onto another parkway, which Jim didn't recognize. It was wider than the Saw Mill, and the driver accelerated, though in the limousine it still felt as if they were doing only thirty.

An hour later they exited from the parkway and headed east on a winding road. From the white-painted fences and the sleek animals grazing in the lush pastures, Jim could see that they were in horse country. The houses all had long driveways, and many had the name of the farm posted at the gate.

When they turned into one of those driveways Zoraya raised her head and looked around drowsily. "Oh, good. We are here. I hope you like it."

"I'm sure I will," he said, seeing no reason why he wouldn't. The main house wasn't yet in sight, but they passed a caretaker's house that was bigger than his house in St. Paul. He wondered what the uncle did for a living.

Zoraya sat up, staying close to him. "There used to be a lot of horses, but my uncle no longer has time for them. He is so involved in his business. But he keeps a few horses just to ride, and if you want we can go riding. I assume you ride."

"Of course," he said as if everyone did. He had taken lessons as a teenager because his mother had believed that knowing how to ride a horse was one of the requirements for the social status she wanted her children to maintain. He hadn't actually been on a horse in more than forty years, but he was confident that he could fake it.

"Oh, I am sorry," she said, noticing a little wet spot she had made on his pant-leg. "I must have done that while I was sleeping."

"It's perfectly all right," he assured her. In fact, her secretions were more precious to him than the emeralds and sapphires she had worn in her earrings. Or the delicate pearls she wore in them today.

They finally approached a white mansion that looked as if it had been built during the colonial period. It had dark green shutters and red brick chimneys, which must have provided a fireplace for every room. It easily could have accommodated all the guests on a floor of the St. Jerome, so it would be more than adequate for the two of them.

Manuel stopped in front of the mansion, then got out and opened the door on Zoraya's side of the limousine. Before he could come around Jim followed her out and stood with her in the driveway while Manuel went to get their bags out of the trunk.

"I used to come here when I was in college," Zoraya said, looking fondly at the mansion.

"Did you bring your friends?"

"Girlfriends," she said. "Never a boyfriend. You are the first."

Jim was flattered but also curious. "Where did you go with your boyfriends?"

"I did not have boyfriends while I was in college."

"I don't believe it. There must have been a thousand guys after you."

"If there were I did not notice. I was not interested in them. I came to this country to get an education, not to find a husband."

"Then you must have had boyfriends in Spain."

"No. I was too young. I mean, before I came here to college. And I have not met anyone since I went back. The only man in my life is Ramón."

"Who's he?"

"The man my father wants me to marry."

"But you haven't ever—"

"Slept with him? Of course not," she said, making a face. "I told you, I do not like him."

Since she hadn't had any boyfriends, Jim wondered where she had learned how to arouse a man so effectively. Had she learned the art from having affairs with married men? Had she been born with it?

Zoraya led him into the house and up a grand stairway while the driver followed with their bags. They went down a long hall, passing several open doors, and then entered a large bedroom that overlooked a formal English garden. The bed was king-sized, with a mahogany frame and a canopy.

After setting down their bags Manuel asked: "Is there anything I can get you, Señorita?"

"No, thanks," she said, dismissing him.

Discreetly, he withdrew.

"This is the room for important guests," Zoraya said, looking around. "I have never stayed in it. I usually stay in a smaller room, at the other end."

Jim felt honored, among other things.

"I hope the bed is made up." She went and checked, drawing back the white spread and exposing the lavender sheets. "Oh, good."

He waited, willing to place himself in her hands.

"Excuse me for a minute," she said, heading for the bathroom. She closed the door behind her.

After several minutes he heard a toilet flushing and then the sound of water running into a bathtub.

When she came out she politely asked: "Do you want to use the bathroom?"

"Yeah. I guess." He went in and closed the door behind him. The bathroom was enormous, with a tub that was big enough to hold at least four adults. It was gradually filling, and a pleasant scent of lemon rose from the surface.

Having relieved himself, he rejoined Zoraya in the bedroom, where he found her sitting on the edge of the bed untying her sneakers. She slackened the laces as if she had all the time in the world.

"I hope you do not mind taking a bath with me," she said shyly.

"I don't mind at all," he said, conscious of having said this before.

"Then you should undress."

He hesitated because he didn't want to miss a single moment of her undressing.

She removed her sneakers, and then still sitting on the bed she untucked her tee shirt and carefully lifted it, revealing her breasts.

He gaped at them with unbearable longing.

She pulled the tee shirt over her head, momentarily hiding her face and exposing her hairless armpits.

Jim was still gaping.

With head bowed she looked up at him as if she was afraid that he might not like what he had seen so far of her body. Apparently reassured by his eyes, she rose from the bed and unbuttoned her jeans.

As she peeled them down he saw that again she was wearing white panties, which after a few heart-stopping moments were the only garment she still had on.

"Are you going to join me?" she asked ingenuously.

"Yes. Of course." He began to undress, following her progress with ravenous eyes as she glided into the bathroom. He stripped to his briefs, out of delicacy not going further than she had gone, and he joined her at the tub.

By now it was filled, and she leaned over to turn off the water, presenting her scantily clad bottom to him as if she was totally unaware of its effect.

Still bending over, she tested the water and declared: "It is ready now."

"Okay," he said hoarsely.

With one hand on his shoulder to steady herself she used the other to take down her panties until they dropped of their own accord, enabling her to kick free of them. She had no tan lines, the absence of which virtually confirmed that this lovely shade of brown was the natural color of her skin.

She stepped into the spacious tub and with closed eyes lowered her body into the water, emitting a long luxurious sigh when she touched bottom.

"How is it?" he asked, scrambling out of his briefs.

"It is absolutely perfect," she crooned.

He joined her in the tub with room to spare.

For a while they lay side-by-side in the water with their heads resting on folded towels that she had arranged at the end of the tub for that purpose. Then she washed him, starting at his neck and ending at his toes. Between those two extremes her stroking fingers didn't miss any part of his body.

Gratefully, he reciprocated, sitting behind her with his legs extended on both sides of her. As she had done he started with the neck, but he had trouble getting past her breasts, which filled his hands and grazed his circling palms with erect nipples. He might have lingered there indefinitely if her wet body hadn't proffered other alluring areas.

When they finally got out she reached for a towel that was ample enough for both of them, and they wrapped themselves together in it, rubbing each other's back with it while the fronts of their naked bodies touched. They took as long as possible to dry each other.

Then she reached back and undid her hair, which tumbled like a curtain of night over her bare rounded shoulders and extended down as far as her navel.

He buried his face in that darkness, smelling jasmine.

"Come," she said softly.

He was more than ready to go with her.

Along with a fresh towel she took a bottle of something from the bathroom and led him to the bed.

He watched as she set the bottle on a night table, drew the spread the rest of the way, and laid the towel over the sheets as if she was preparing a banquet.

"Lie down," she said, picking up the bottle. "I will rub you with oil."

He did as she bade him, with his face down.

She straddled his hips and began to rub his back with oil. It smelled of almonds.

"Oh, that feels good," he told her.

"Relax," she said. "Enjoy it."

She straddled him, rocking back and forth as she massaged him. Gradually, she worked her way down, and when she had finished with the heels of his feet she asked him to roll over, which he gladly did. After rubbing his chest with the oil, she worked her way down to his toes, not missing anything. Then, wanting to reciprocate, he pulled back from her and told her: "It's your turn now. Lie down."

She looked as if she hadn't expected anything from him, but she lay down, and she let him rub her with the oil, starting with her neck and ending with her toes. With the tips of his fingers he paid tribute to her body, he anointed her as if he was performing a ritual in her coronation as a princess.

Her eyes closed as she succumbed to his tender ministrations.

In a series of steps he took her up the mountain and into the dazzling open sky where she let go and soared on her own, whooping in amazement and exultation. Then with a sigh she glided down, nuzzling his throat and kissing him thankfully.

They went to sleep in each other's arms. He dreamed of the Alhambra, the reddish towers of the Alcázar and the ornate arches of the Nasrid palace. It was night, and they were swimming naked in the long pool at the Court of the Myrtles. The moon was rising over the Sierra Nevada. He could smell jasmine.

"Wake up," a man commanded in Spanish.

He opened his eyes and saw three people, including Zoraya, who had put on her jeans and tee shirt. Even in his stupor he noticed that now she was wearing a bra.

The other two people were familiar: Ramón, the young man her father wanted her to marry, and Manuel, the driver.

"What's going on?" he asked, confused.

"We're holding you hostage," Ramón informed him.

"What?" he sat up. "You've got to be kidding."

"We're not kidding," Ramón snarled. He raised his arm and pointed something at the center of Jim's forehead.

It was a gun.

THREE

AFTER A LONG uncomfortable silence he looked at Zoraya and summoned enough courage to say: "You said we'd have the house all to ourselves."

"We did for a while," she reminded him.

Reflecting, he acknowledged that they could have seized him the moment he had entered the house, and he wondered why they hadn't.

Zoraya stooped and picked up his clothes and laid them on the bed, saying: "You better get dressed."

He got out of the bed and took his clothes into the bathroom. He found his briefs on the floor where only a few hours ago he had hastily discarded them before sinking into the tub. As he stepped into them he tried to understand what was happening. Evidently, it had all been planned from the moment their eyes met in the bar. She had strolled out, swaying her hips in order to make him follow her, and like a fish in search of a meal he had fallen for the lure. The tiff in the lobby with Ramón had been staged for his benefit, to give him an opening. And the rest had been easy.

The kiss in the elevator, the flash of panties, the tee shirt without a bra, and the bottom displayed by the tight jeans—they had all been used to lead him into this position, to blind him from what was really happening. Even the annoying phone call last night had probably been timed to interrupt them and stoke his lust by deferring the moment of gratification. And she had skillfully taken advantage of his confusion by leaving his room without telling him the number of her room. She probably hadn't been staying at the hotel. After parting with Ramón in the lobby she had gone into the elevator knowing he would follow her, and now he understood why she hadn't pressed a button for her floor: she was waiting to see what floor he would press so that she could pretend to be staying on a higher floor. If she had been on a lower floor he might have followed her out of the elevator there, and that would have complicated matters.

Pulling on his shirt, he understood why they had selected him. She had believed his story about the CIA, just as he had believed her story about the foundation. Despite the gravity of his situation, he had to laugh. There was a kind of justice to it: they had duped each other. At some point he would have to explain that he really wasn't a CIA agent, but then what would he tell them? In this situation he couldn't pretend to be someone else, so he had to admit that he was a state senator. They would find that out anyway when they saw the news of his disappearance. And where would that leave him? For their purpose did a state senator have as much value as a CIA agent?

He zipped up his pants, feeling a sudden tremor of fear as he confronted the fact that he had seen their faces and could easily identify them. Surely they wouldn't want to leave a live witness.

When he returned to the bedroom he found Zoraya and Ramón waiting for him. They were speaking Arabic, which he understood because at college he had minored in Arabic while majoring in Spanish literature. He had written his senior thesis on the Arab poet Ibn al-Khatib, who had lived in the Emirate of Granada during the 14th century. Though his Arabic was rusty, he could easily follow what they were saying.

"I still think we should tie him up," Ramón insisted.

"It won't be necessary if we keep him on the third floor," Zoraya argued. "He can't escape from there. It's too high for him to jump out the window."

"Well, if there's a room with a good lock, then I'll go along with you. But we have to watch him."

"I'll take care of that," she said.

Jim pretended not to understand because their not knowing that he could follow their conversations in Arabic would give him an advantage.

"*Ven*," Ramón ordered, waving the pistol toward the door.

"Before we go any further," Jim said in Spanish, "could you tell me what this is all about?"

"Would you explain it to him?" Ramón said to Zoraya.

"Sure." She was still the pretty girl who had lured him here, but there was a new expression on her face that conveyed the message that she was a force to be reckoned with. "As Ramón said, we're holding you hostage."

"You mean for ransom money?"

"No. We don't want money," she said with scorn. "We want your government to release a prisoner."

"Could you tell me who?"

"We don't have to tell him," Ramón said in Arabic.

"We have to tell him eventually," Zoraya said.

"All right. Then tell him. We're going to kill him anyway."

It took an extra measure of control for Jim to keep his face from revealing that he had understood that last sentence.

"The prisoner we want your government to release," Zoraya told him, "is being held unjustly. He's a Muslim cleric, a holy man, and he has done nothing but preach—as you say—the gospel of peace."

"So why is he being held?"

"They convicted him of inciting violence in connection with the bombing of the World Trade Center, but they had no evidence. His trial was a sham. If his name had been John Smith they never would have arrested him."

"What *is* his name?"

"Abdullah ibn Hasim al-Qahtani."

As best he could remember, the name meant Servant of God, Son of Hasim from the Qahtani tribe. He racked his memory but the name didn't ring any bells. "I don't know anything about him."

"I told you," Ramón said in Arabic. "He's an ignorant infidel."

"Let me handle this," Zoraya said.

"Have you tried using the legal process?" Jim asked them in Spanish.

"Yes. We have," Zoraya said. "But it hasn't gotten us anywhere. The judges keep refusing to let us appeal."

"The judges are Jews," Ramón said nastily.

"Well, maybe you don't have a good lawyer," Jim said.

"We've tried a number of different lawyers," Zoraya said, "and all they do is take our money."

As a member of the small minority of politicians who weren't lawyers, Jim didn't feel compelled to rise to the defense of the legal profession. He just said: "If this man is innocent, and I'll take your word for it that he is, then you can get him released through the legal process. And I can help you do that."

"Don't listen to him," Ramón said in Arabic.

"How could you help us?" Zoraya asked, ignoring Ramón.

"I have some influence in my position." Having said this, he realized that he had just offered to use his influence in return for a gift, which he had never done before. But no one could blame him in this situation for accepting the gift of his life, not even the person who never applauded.

"I can't imagine the CIA helping us," Zoraya said. "You're the ones who catch our people and claim they're terrorists."

"I'm not a CIA agent."

"You see?" Ramón said in Arabic. "He's lying to us. He's trying to make us think he's someone else."

"Why would he do that?"

"Because he wants to trick us."

"If you're not a CIA agent," Zoraya said, "then what are you?"

"I'm a state senator."

"*Mierda*," Ramón said.

"It's true. I can prove it." He reached into his back pocket and got out his card case. He found his ID card and handed it to Zoraya.

She examined it, then handed it to Ramón.

"This is his cover," Ramón said in Arabic, shaking the card at Zoraya. "Of course he wouldn't have a card that says he's a CIA agent."

"Prove that this isn't a cover," Zoraya told him.

"I can't right now, but if you show my picture to anyone in Minnesota they'll tell you I'm a state senator."

"Where's Minnesota?" Ramón asked.

"It's in the Midwest." He tried to think of something from Minnesota that they might have heard of, but they obviously weren't baseball or football fans.

"I know where it is," Zoraya said.

"They'll see your picture," Ramón told him after a silence, "so we'll find out if you're telling the truth."

"How will they see my picture?" he asked, curious.

"We're going to make a tape of you and send it to CNN."

He understood. "So I'm going to say that if our government doesn't release Abdullah you're going to kill me?"

"That's right," Ramón said.

"Do you really believe that a stupid stunt like that will work?"

"It better work, or you're a dead man."

"Listen," he said, thinking fast. "Up to this point you haven't committed any crime, at least that they know about."

"We're holding you hostage," Zoraya said. "Isn't that a crime?"

"I came here voluntarily," he reminded her.

"You did," she said with a straight face.

"And no one but the four of us knows that for the past hour or so you've been threatening me with a gun."

"That's true," she agreed.

"So we'll make a deal. I'll agree to use my influence to get our government to release Abdullah, and you'll let me go. Of course," he added, "I'll promise never to say anything about the gun."

"You won't keep your promise," Ramón said.

"I always keep my promises," he said firmly. "I'm probably the only politician in the world who can say that."

"He's not a politician," Ramón told Zoraya in Arabic. "He's a CIA agent."

"But what if he's telling the truth?" she said. "This could be a chance for us to do things legally."

Ramón scowled. "He's not telling the truth. He's using his cover as a state senator to trick us into releasing him."

"Well, let me see his ID card." She took it from Ramón and examined it again. "I don't know much about these things, but I don't see how a state senator would be a good cover for a CIA agent. It's a public position."

"They're a lot of people in public positions who are CIA agents," Ramón said.

"Maybe there are, but a state senator from Minnesota?"

"Forget the cover. If he's not an agent, then why did he tell you he was?"

"That's a good question." In Spanish she said to Jim: "If you're not a CIA agent, then why did you tell me you were?"

He hated to admit it, especially in front of Ramón, but to save his life he could swallow his pride. "I wanted to impress you."

She looked puzzled. "But you didn't have to pretend you were a CIA agent. You're an attractive man."

"Well, that's why I did it."

She looked at the ID card, then back at him as if she wanted to believe him but couldn't understand why he didn't say he was a state senator if that's what he was.

"I thought I had to impress you," he said, realizing that the situation was turning against him, "because of the big difference in our ages."

"I prefer older men," she said. "I would never be interested in someone Ramón's age."

Ramón didn't seem to take offense.

Jim remembered his first impression of Ramón in the lobby, that he could have been Zoraya's brother. Maybe he really was her brother.

"And why did you think I would be impressed by your being a CIA agent?"

"Other women have been," he said truthfully.

"You mean you've done this kind of thing before?"

"Yes," he admitted. "I mean, not often."

She shook her head. "I just don't understand why an attractive man like you would feel he had to pretend to be a CIA agent to impress women."

"Well, that's how I feel."

"Don't believe him," Ramón told her in Arabic.

"But why would he admit such a shameful thing if it's not true?"

"He'll say anything to save his life."

She sighed. "Okay. We'll operate on the assumption that he really is a CIA agent. But I hope you understand that once we make a tape and send it out, there will be a public record of what we've done."

"That's the whole point. We want the public to know about the injustice that was done to Abdullah."

"I know, but from then on we'll be criminals."

"Only under their law. Under our law we'll be heroes."

"Or martyrs," she murmured darkly.

"I have an idea," Jim said as if he hadn't understood their conversation. "You can call my office in Minnesota. They'll confirm that I'm a state senator."

"That won't prove anything," Ramón said.

"Why would they lie?"

"They wouldn't be lying. They wouldn't know you're a CIA agent."

He could see the problem. No matter what evidence he offered them, Ramón could always say that it proved only that he had a cover. And the CIA would always deny that he worked for them even if he did.

By now he regretted not staying with the role of actor.

"You can call my ex-wives," he said in desperation. "They'll tell you I really am a state senator."

"The wives of agents don't know what their husbands do," Ramón said.

"Of course they know. You can't hide something like that from your wife."

"How many ex-wives do you have?" Zoraya asked.

"Four," he said. "Three of them are living."

"You've been married four times?"

"None of them would know what he really does," Ramón argued.

"Are you married now?"

"No. I was divorced three years ago."

"Well, if you were a CIA agent," Zoraya said after a moment, "I think you could have hid it from your wives."

"No, I couldn't have. I couldn't have hidden a thing like that from my wives."

"I think you could have," she insisted.

"You don't know anything about it," he said, challenging her.

"You mean because I've never been married?"

"Yes," he said. "And because you've never had any experience with CIA agents."

"We're wasting time," Ramón told her in Arabic. "There's no way he can prove that he doesn't work for the CIA."

"You're right," she agreed. "But there's no way we can prove that he does."

"So let's make the tape and see what happens."

"Okay," she agreed reluctantly.

Jim could see that he wasn't going to get anywhere with them by arguing further. When they went public they would find out that he was telling the truth. Or maybe they would. Ramón might keep insisting that the evidence proved only that he had a cover as a state senator. Zoraya was his only hope.

"*Ven*," Ramon ordered.

Zoraya led the way and Ramón came behind him.

Having no choice, he followed her out of the bedroom where he had briefly attained his vision of earthly paradise, and going upstairs close behind her, even with a gun pointed at his back he couldn't help admiring the contours of her bottom in the skintight jeans.

She led him into a small bedroom, which must have been a maid's room. It was furnished simply, with a dresser, a table, two chairs, and a single bed. It had one narrow window that overlooked the garden in back.

Ramon came into the room after him, and Manuel came last, toting his bag as if he was still playing the role of a driver.

Zoraya settled into one of the chairs, and Jim sat down on the edge of the bed.

Ramón and Manuel remained vigilantly on their feet.

Appraising them, Jim attempted to sort out their respective roles. It was easy to see that Manuel provided brawn and Zoraya provided brains, but between her and Ramón it was hard to determine who had more power. Zoraya had made the decision to go ahead with the original plan, but Ramón had influenced her. Jim believed that if Ramón hadn't been there she would have accepted his proposal to help them get Abdullah released through a legal process.

"So what's your relationship with Abdullah?" he asked them in Spanish.

"He's our brother," Ramón said.

"Your biological brother?"

"No. Our spiritual brother. We're all brothers under Islam."

"What about sisters?" he asked, looking for a wedge between him and Zoraya.

"Unlike your women, our women know their place."

"Do you know your place?" he asked Zoraya.

"My place is with my family."

"Is Ramón your brother?"

"All Muslim men are my brothers."

"I mean your biological brother."

"Yes," she said. "Can't you see the family resemblance?"

He could see a little but not much. "Are your parents living?"

"Our mother's in heaven, and our father's in hell."

"Do you believe that you'll go to heaven if you get killed doing this?"

"I don't care about going to heaven," Zoraya said. "I only care about getting Abdullah out of prison."

"You're willing to sacrifice your life for him?"

"If necessary, yes."

"What's so special about him?"

"He's holy."

"Okay." He took her word for it. "So what's your plan?"

"As we told you, we're going to make a tape of you and send it to CNN. You're going to ask your government to release

Abdullah, and you're going to tell them that if they don't you will be killed."

"Are you going to give them a deadline?"

"Yes. It's next Tuesday."

"At sundown," Manuel said.

"That only gives them a week," he protested with a spasm in his bowels.

"It only gives *you* a week," Ramon corrected him.

"To do what? You're not letting me use my influence."

"We're letting you use your powers of persuasion," Zoraya said. "If you really are a politician you should be able to talk them into releasing Abdullah."

"I haven't been able to talk you into anything."

"You talked me into something."

"Okay. You're right. So when do we start making the tape?"

"We'll come back in a while and get you," she told him, rising from the chair.

The two men followed her out, with the last one closing the door and locking it.

Finally alone, he rose from the bed and went to the window. It was partly open, and there was nothing to prevent him from going out—except that it was fifty or sixty feet above a brick patio. There was no way to climb down, and even if he managed to jump without killing himself they would catch him as he attempted to hobble off.

He looked beyond the extensive garden, hoping to see a neighboring house that he could signal to, but there was only an apple orchard, then a pasture, and finally woods. There were no other houses in sight.

Discouraged, he went and checked the door. It was locked tight, with a dead bolt that could be opened from the inside only with a key—the kind of lock that stopped burglars from breaking through the panel of a door, reaching inside, and simply turning the knob on the lock to let themselves in.

He paced the room, retracing in his mind the steps that had led him into this predicament. He looked for points where he might have figured out what was happening, but he had trouble finding them. Zoraya had played her role so well that she hadn't flubbed a single line or even a word to make him suspicious. True, she had been very impressed when he told her he was a CIA agent, but she was supposed to react that way. And she hadn't asked him any questions about his work.

With grudging admiration he recalled how well she had played the scene in his room last night when the phone had rung. She had let the call interrupt them and used it to defer his gratification, so that he would jump at her suggestion the next day that they go to her uncle's house, where there would be no interruptions.

He wondered what she would have done if the phone call hadn't been timed so well. He supposed she would have found ways of deferring him until the phone rang because she was really the one in control.

As he paced back and forth he wondered what would have happened if he had told her the first night that he was a state senator. From what she had said downstairs, she might have been interested in him anyway. She said she liked older men, and she found him attractive. They might have decided that for their purpose a state senator was as good as a CIA agent, but they might have been more likely to accept his offer to help them by using his influence. At least they would have believed that he was a state senator, and they might have been more likely to trust him.

Looking for a source of hope, he returned to the fact that they could have seized him the moment he had entered the house, but they had let him have sex with Zoraya. Obviously, she had made that decision, and he still wondered why. Because she liked him? Because she felt that having promised him something she had to deliver it? And could she have faked the whole scene? Though he had never been with a prostitute, he knew from hearing other men talk that prostitutes were capable of making you feel that they really loved you. But Zoraya wasn't a prostitute, at least not in the usual sense. She might have been willing to contribute her body for a cause, but it took practice to fake a scene like that, and she couldn't have done this sort of thing repeatedly. So there must have been something real about it.

He paused at the window, resolving not to think about how he had gotten into this predicament but to think about how he might get out of it. The only two ways he could see now were to take advantage of any opportunity to escape or to convince them that their best chance of getting the holy man released was to let him use his influence as a state senator. But he couldn't do the latter until he convinced them that he really was a state senator.

There was of course the remote possibility that once it was known that he had been kidnapped the police or the FBI would find him. They would trace him to the St. Jerome, where he was still a registered guest, and they might pick up the trail from there. Though he could see how skillfully Zoraya had led him out of the hotel, avoiding the use of a bellhop, he reckoned that someone must have observed them leaving together, and though limousines were a common sight in New York, someone must have noticed them getting into the long black car.

But from the hotel they could have gone in any direction, and if people passing them on the Saw Mill River Parkway could have seen through the dark-tinted windows they wouldn't have spotted a man and a woman because she had been lying out of sight. Again, her behavior may have served another purpose.

Still, the police would surely be able to compose some good descriptions of the woman and the two men. Zoraya, especially in those short dresses, must have attracted the wandering eyes of other males. Seeing her with a man at least twice her age, they must have looked at him enviously, wondering what he had to offer her. She would be the prime suspect, while Ramón and Manuel could be tied to her: the scene in the lobby as well as the meeting beside the limousine must have been witnessed, and once the story hit the media people would come forward with details that they remembered.

With good descriptions of his captors the police would eventually locate them because they couldn't operate in this area without being noticed, maybe by a gas station attendant or a supermarket checkout girl. They would be conspicuous in such an area, where people—far removed from the inner city—were typically white.

But how long would it take the police to find him? The deadline was only a week. And what would happen if they found him in time? Would his captors use him as a human shield to make an escape? Would they hijack a plane and take him to Libya or wherever they were from?

As the light fell outside in the garden his chances of survival looked bleak.

He was lying despondently on the bed when he heard the door being unlocked. He sat up, preparing himself. If he was alert he might see a way to help the police track them down before the deadline.

The door opened and Ramón entered, holding the gun and saying: "*Ven.*"

He left the room ahead of Ramón and walked down the hall to another room as directed. It was unfurnished, except for a floor lamp, a table, and a chair. A folded blanket had been nailed up over the window, and a white sheet had been hung up on the wall. From the lamp a photographer's light was directed at the sheet, which provided a backdrop for the table and chair.

Zoraya and Manuel were standing across the room from this set, the former holding a legal pad and the latter holding a video cassette.

"*Siéntate*," Ramon ordered.

Without protest Jim installed himself in the chair behind the table. Squinting, he said: "That light needs to be adjusted."

"We didn't ask for your advice," Ramón said.

"I think he's right," Zoraya said, approaching the floor lamp. "If there's too much light it will ruin the picture."

"Then adjust it."

She did, pointing the lamp a little away from the set. "Is that better?"

"Yes," Jim said. He wondered if he should tell them he had a lot of experience at making video tapes, but decided to wait and see what happened.

"Here. Read this," Zoraya said, handing him the legal pad.

It was a script, which she must have written. Her penmanship, with its clear rounded letters, suggested that she had received a Catholic education, which gave him some hope: like other women who had undergone the process and rejected the content, she might not have expunged all traces of its influence.

"My name—" she prompted.

"My name," he read slowly, "is Jim Wyatt. I am an agent for the CIA. I am being held hostage by the Islamic Human Rights Movement. They are giving you until Tuesday, July 18, to release their religious leader, Abdullah ibn Hasim al-Qahtani, who was wrongfully convicted of inciting violence. If you do not release him they will kill me. But first they will torture me to extract information that you would not want in the hands of your enemies. So I am pleading with you as a faithful servant of my country to meet their demands. They mean what they say, and I believe that if you do not meet their demands they will do exactly what they say."

"Read it again," Zoraya told him. "You didn't sound very convincing."

"I need to rehearse it. But I'd like to make a few suggestions."

"Go ahead."

"For one thing," he said, trying again, "you're not giving them enough time. It takes the government forever to do anything."

"It didn't take them forever to arrest Abdullah."

"Well, a week just isn't enough."

"We can extend the deadline later if they need more time."

"If you do, then they'll push you to keep extending the deadline."

"So we won't extend the deadline at all," Ramón said.

"It's better to give them a realistic amount of time to begin with," he argued, "so you don't have to extend the deadline."

Zoraya consulted with her partners in Arabic: "What do you think?"

"I think a week is enough time," Ramón said.

"The more time we give them," Manuel pointed out, "the more time they'll have to find us."

"All right," Zoraya said in Spanish as if they had confirmed her own position. "They have enough time. Now, what other suggestions do you have?"

Though he had lost that critical point he had at least gained the knowledge that she was the leader, which would be useful. "You should take out the part about torturing me. It's bad enough that you're threatening to kill me, but they really won't like the idea of your torturing me."

"You mean you don't like the idea," Ramón said.

"Trust me. It would be bad for your image."

"We don't care about our image."

"Well, you should care. You want to make a deal with them, and if they don't like you they won't do business with you."

"I think he's right," Zoraya said in Arabic.

"I think he's just trying to get out of being tortured," Ramón told her.

"Whatever he says, we can still torture him," Manuel said.

"Take out the part about torturing you," Zoraya said.

"Okay. And if you don't mind, I'll also use contractions. It sounds stilted for me to say 'I am' instead of 'I'm.' No one speaks that way."

"Foreigners do," Ramón said.

"I'm not a foreigner."

"We aren't either."

"So you're residents of this country?"

"It's none of your business."

"Come on," Zoraya said. "Let's make this tape."

He edited the script, then read it again.

"You still don't sound very convincing," Zoraya said.

"Maybe it would help," Ramón said, "if I aimed the gun at his head."

"Or at his balls," Manuel said.

"Read it again," Zoraya said, ignoring them.

Jim did, and whether or not they had goaded him into it, this time he gave a better performance. It just took practice.

Zoraya was apparently satisfied, and she told Manuel to tape the next reading.

Jim by now was cooperating fully. He had adopted the goal of his captors, the release of Abdullah ibn Hasim al-Qahtani, in return for which his life would be spared. To achieve that goal he wanted the tape to be effective, so he gave an even better performance.

"We're going to watch it," Ramon told him.

"Let me go with you," Jim suggested. "So I can improve it."

"All right," Zoraya agreed as if she had sensed the change in his attitude.

She led them down to the second floor, with Jim behind her, still admiring the contours of her bottom, and Ramon behind him, still pointing the gun at his back. Manuel was at the end of the line with the cassette.

They went into a bedroom where there was a television set with a video player. It was positioned to be watched by people lying in the bed, which happened to be wide enough for three of them to sit on the foot, so with Zoraya in the middle as a buffer between him and Ramón, he watched his performance as a captive pleading for his life.

"What do you think?" she asked her partners in Arabic.

"It's all right," Ramon said.

"It's a very good recording," Manuel said.

She turned to Jim to get his opinion.

"I think it's fine. But I have a question. How are they supposed to respond?"

"By making an announcement on television."

"Will they understand that?"

"Of course they will," she said. "I mean, everything happens on television."

"Okay," he said, acknowledging that she was right.

He went back upstairs to his room, with only Ramón behind him and no one in front of him. Alone in the room, with the door locked, he went and stood by the window. He couldn't see any lights out there, but now he could see another way out of his predicament. The chances of his being rescued by the police might have diminished, but the chances of his being ransomed by the government might have grown. Having just given the performance of his life, he felt that when they saw that tape they would have to respond positively.

A half hour later, as he was lying on the bed, he heard the door being unlocked. He sat up, wondering what they wanted now.

Zoraya entered the room with a tray, accompanied by neither of the two men. She obviously believed there was no risk in her being alone with him. Shutting the door, she said in Spanish: "I've brought your dinner."

"Thanks," he said warily.

"I promised I would cook for you."

"Yeah, I remember."

"And I always keep my promises," she said, setting the tray on the table.

"I think you just answered a question I had."

She faced him. "What question?"

"Well, I was wondering why you had sex with me. They could have taken me prisoner the moment I walked into this house."

"They could have."

"But they didn't. You didn't let them. And now I think I understand why. You promised me something."

"That's right. I did."

Recalling the extent to which she had kept that promise, he marveled at her. "I must say, you have a highly developed sense of honor."

She evaded the compliment, saying only: "I hope you like tagine."

"I do," he said, still marveling at her.

She lingered as if she wanted to see if he liked her cooking.

Jim got up and went to the table, feeling hungry. He pulled up a chair, sat down, and tried the tagine. "Mm. That's good."

"I'm glad you like it."

He chewed and swallowed. "Are you really from Granada?"

"No. I'm from Ceuta."

Ceuta was the Spanish enclave in Morocco on the southern coast of the Strait of Gibraltar. "So that's how you know Spanish and Arabic."

"Yes," she said. "I'm a Spanish citizen but we prefer to speak Arabic."

He took another bite of food. "Did you live in Granada?"

"Yes. For a while."

"What were you doing there?"

"I was a maid for a rich family. I went there when I was fourteen," she said as if it had been fifty years ago.

"What happened there?"

"How do you know something happened there?"

"I don't know. I just have a feeling."

"Well, I don't want to talk about it," she said, turning away from him.

"Okay." He resumed eating. "From the way you speak English, you must have lived here for a while. Did you really go to college here?"

"Yes, but I didn't go to Mount St. Vincent. I went to Hunter."

"Did you graduate?"

"Yes. I got a degree in history."

"Did you plan to teach?"

"I didn't know what I was going to do, but I liked history so I majored in it. Ramón went to Baruch," she continued. "He majored in business. We came here as international students."

"What's your status now?"

"We're illegal aliens," she said derisively.

"Like millions of other people." He could have told her about his program to deal with that problem, but he figured that now wasn't the time. "So what's the Islamic Human Rights Movement?"

"It's just a name we decided to use."

"Then there isn't a movement?"

"There isn't yet, but we're trying to build one."

"What's your purpose?"

"To end discrimination against Muslims in this country."

"You believe that Muslims aren't treated fairly?"

"We aren't. Abdullah didn't get a fair trial. And whenever there's an act of terror we're the prime suspects."

He couldn't deny this. "But don't you see that by taking me hostage you're only reinforcing our image of Muslims as terrorists?"

"I considered that. But I decided not to worry about your image of us. All that matters is achieving our goal."

"You mean getting our government to release Abdullah."

"That's right. Your image of us is your problem."

"But it's your problem too. Unless our image of you changes we'll continue to discriminate against you."

"No, you won't. You'll realize sooner or later that your behavior has consequences."

"Like your kidnapping me."

"That's right."

He stopped eating. "I just want to clarify something. You said you always keep your promises. I assume that if the government releases Abdullah you'll keep your promise to let me go."

"That's right," she said. "But if they don't I will keep my promise to kill you."

From the serious look in her dark eyes he knew she meant it. Quelled by that knowledge, he pushed the plate away, saying: "I'm done."

FOUR

STEPHEN, HIS YOUNGER brother, had talked him into going to the party. Jim was home for Christmas vacation during his junior year at college, and for some reason this year there wasn't much for him to do. He wasn't dating anyone, and he was growing apart from most of the people who had been his friends in high school. So even though he didn't want to go to the party with Stephen, he had no other social engagement that he could use as an excuse not to go.

The party was on Summit Avenue in an area where the mansions built by the old wealthy families were still in private hands. The house that now belonged to Joe Marchi, who had made his fortune from construction only after World War II, had originally belonged to a family whose fortune dated back to the days of fur trading. It had been built with local limestone by masons brought from Italy, among them the great-grandfather of the current owner, as Jim would later learn. And it was still an impressive monument to success.

The people at the party were friends of Angela, the second oldest daughter, who was Stephen's age. Jim didn't know any of them, not only because they were four years younger but also because the girls went to Visitation and the boys to St. Thomas Academy, and that was a different world from the private nondenominational schools that the children in his family went to. He wondered how Stephen had met Angela because the paths laid out by parents for children in these two worlds seldom crossed. But that was the whole attraction for the children—to meet people outside of their approved range of social interaction.

Stephen introduced him to Angela and to her father, Joe Marchi, who was present as if to make sure that nothing irregular happened at the party. Jim's initial impression of the man who would become his first father-in-law was mostly favorable—as they shook hands Joe clapped him warmly on the shoulder and said: "It's a pleasure to meet you. I've heard a lot about you from your brother."

"I hope you don't believe everything he says," Jim quipped, not knowing what else to say. It would have been presumptuous to say that he had heard about Joe from his brother, especially because he hadn't.

Joe laughed, evidently liking his response, and clapped him on the shoulder again. "Don't worry. I don't."

Of course no alcohol was being served, and after getting a glass of punch, which tasted like orange juice spiked with sparkling grape juice, they went into a large room and mingled. Stephen introduced him to girls with Irish and Italian names, some of whom were very pretty. These girls were obviously impressed by the fact that he was a junior in college, being at an age when high school boys were beginning to seem too young for them. But none of them made an impression on him, and after a while he wondered what he was doing here.

He was on his way back to the punch bowl in the other room when he saw a girl coming down the stairs. She had dark flowing hair and dark glowing eyes, and she had an aura that struck him like a force of nature. He stopped in his tracks while she kept coming down the stairs, oblivious of him.

Turning in his direction, she finally noticed him.

"Oh, hi," she said brightly. "Are you here for the party?"

"I'm here with my younger brother," he told her to make sure that she knew he wasn't among the boys whose voices they could hear.

"Are you Stephen's brother?"

"Yes," he said, caught off guard.

"I've heard a lot about you from him," she said, appraising him to see if he lived up to the advance promotion.

"That's exactly what your father said."

She smiled. "Well, it looks like your brother has been talking to my whole family about you. Do you think he's trying to fix us up?"

"I have no idea what he's doing."

"Did he mention that Angie had an older sister?"

"No. He didn't. Maybe he wanted it to be a surprise."

"Was it?" she asked playfully.

"Oh, yes," he said. "A pleasant one."

She looked as if she was happy to hear that. "Then maybe we should introduce ourselves. I'm Renata."

"I'm Jim," he said, extending his hand.

Her hand was soft and delicate but her grip was firm, and there was something about her handshake that evoked her father.

"I was going to join the party," she said, "but I'd rather talk with you, so we could go into another room and get away from them."

"That sounds like a good idea."

She led him into what looked like a family room, where they sat down in easy chairs, obliquely facing each other. After an awkward silence she said: "I'll tell you what I know about you. Okay?"

"Okay." He waited in suspense.

"You're a junior at Princeton, and you're getting a degree in Spanish literature with a minor in Arabic. You plan to have a career with the government working overseas."

"That's right," he said, wondering why Stephen had told her all this.

"How do you know you'll get a job with the government?"

"I already have an offer from them."

"How could you? You're only a junior."

"I passed the tests, and I interviewed with them."

"So when would you start?"

"Right after I graduate."

"And when would you go overseas?"

"In about a year."

"I wish I could do that," she said with envy.

"You do?"

"Yes. I wish I could get away from St. Paul and live in a country where no one ever heard of me."

63

He waited for her to explain why.

"You have no idea what it's like," she quietly confided, "being a daughter of Joe Marchi."

"Are you the oldest?"

"Ya. He has three daughters, no sons, and guess who has to make up for the fact that he never had a son."

He nodded, guessing. "Are you in college?"

"I'm a freshman at St. Catherine."

"It's an excellent school."

"I know. But it's not the college I wanted. I wanted to go away to college, but he wouldn't let me. So I wanted to go to the U of M, but he wouldn't let me. He would only let me go to a Catholic college for women."

"Where did you go to high school?"

"Visitation," she told him as if he should have known.

"So you've never been in school with boys?"

"No. Always with girls."

"Well, I've never been in school with girls," he told her, hoping that would make her feel better.

"You went to St. Paul Academy."

"Right. And the only school activities we did with girls were chorus and drama. With girls from Summit School."

"Of course. They wouldn't want you to mix with Catholics."

"I thought it was the other way around. A friend of mine's father wouldn't send him to SPA because he didn't want him to mix with Protestants."

"You're right," she admitted. "It goes both ways."

"Yeah," he said. "Our parents want to keep us in familiar waters."

"Mine want to keep me in a wading pool."

"Your mother goes along with your father on this?"

"She goes along with him on everything. He's a powerful man, so I don't blame her for not standing up to him."

"Do you stand up to him?"

"I try to," she said, "but he still won't let me do what I want."

"Well, after you graduate from college you can do what you want."

"In theory, yes. I just don't know if I can wait that long."

"What do you want to do?"

"I want to work for a newspaper. If possible, I want to be a foreign correspondent."

"Are you majoring in journalism?"

"We don't have a journalism program, so I'm majoring in English."

"That's fine. The important thing is knowing how to write."

"I know how to write. And I like my courses," she added, "so I can't complain. At least he let me go to college."

"What does he expect you to do with your life?"

"He has two things in mind for me—to have grandsons and to take over his company after he retires."

"He expects you to do both?"

"Ya. He expects me to do both."

"That doesn't give you much room."

"It doesn't give me any room. And I want room," she said passionately. "I want room to grow and become my own self. I don't want to be a daughter of Joe Marchi all my life."

"Well, maybe you'll get the room you want," he said hopefully.

"Maybe," she said as if she doubted it.

They were sitting in silence when her father suddenly appeared in the doorway and said: "I wondered where you were."

"We're here talking," she told him.

"What about?" Marchi asked, entering the room and standing before them.

"About colleges," she said after a pause. "We were comparing St. Catherine and Princeton."

"St. Catherine's as good as Princeton, right?"

"Right," Jim said. "It's excellent."

"You see? I wouldn't send you to a bad college. Though," he added, "I don't see the value of college. I didn't go to college, and look what I've done."

"If you'd gone to college, you might have done even better," she said.

"How could I have done better? I'm the top dog."

"You're the top dog in St. Paul but not in the world."

"You see what happens when you send your kids to college," Marchi said, appealing to Jim. "They stop showing respect for you."

"I respect you," she assured him.

"Then you better show it," he said testily.

"You want me to lie? You want me to say you *are* the top dog in the world?"

"I want to you mind your mouth, young lady."

The tension between them was palpable, and Jim was looking for a way to break it. But unless he said the right thing it would be like sticking his hand between two animals whose teeth were bared.

"Jim was offered a job by the government," she said, changing the subject. "He passed all the tests and the interviews."

"That's good," her father said, welcoming the change. "What kind of job are you going to do for them?"

"I'm going to work at our embassies," he said, providing a cover for his real job with the CIA.

"So you'll live overseas?"

"Most of the time."

"Why would you want to do that?" Marchi asked as if he was crazy. "You were lucky enough to be born in the greatest country in the world."

"We still have to deal with other countries."

"We don't have to deal with them. We can bomb them if they get out of line."

"Well, some of them have the capability to bomb us back."

"You mean the Russians? Oh, we don't have to worry about them. They don't have anything that compares with what we have. I can tell you about the Russians from personal experience," Marchi continued. "You know, we met them in Germany. We were coming from the west, and they were coming from the east. You should have seen their soldiers. They were dirty and sick and covered with lice."

"My father was a war hero," Renata said proudly, making up with him. "He got a Purple Heart and a Silver Star."

Marchi waved his hand as if these awards meant nothing to him. "What matters is that I learned a lot from the war. It was better than a college education."

"I'm sure it was," Jim said respectfully.

"When are you going to graduate?"

"A year from this spring."

"Well, maybe by then you'll change your mind about living in foreign countries. There are a lot of great jobs in this country." He glanced at Renata, who ignored him. "There are great jobs right here in St. Paul."

When he had left the room she said: "I'm sorry."

"About what?"

"About the way I talked to my father in front of you."

"That's okay. After what you told me I wasn't surprised."

"It's happening more and more often," she said, "and I don't like it. I always feel like shit afterward."

"You shouldn't. He started it."

"He did? I don't remember how."

"He said he didn't see the value of going to college, meaning that for you it's a waste of time and money."

"You're right," she said, nodding. "But I didn't have to strike back."

"You didn't have to, but he made you feel like striking back."

"Well, I could have done something else with the feeling. I could have channeled it into something positive."

"Like what?" he asked, not knowing what she had in mind.

"Like this," she said, getting up and coming over to him. She put her hand under his chin and lifted his face and kissed him with a warm, wet open mouth.

He saw Renata as much as possible during the remainder of Christmas vacation either at her house or out on a date for dinner or the movies. When they came home in the late evenings Joe Marchi was always waiting for them, always making sure that his daughter got home safe and intact. He would go upstairs and leave them alone in the family room, but he never really left them, and even in their long all-out kisses Jim was always conscious of the possibility that Marchi would appear in the doorway to check on them. One night they tried making out in the car, but he was still present in their minds, so they decided that as long as they were under his surveillance they might as well be in a warm, comfortable place.

From the first letter she wrote to him when he was back at college he realized that she did know how to write, and he had to raise the level of his own writing to meet the standards she set for their correspondence. Mostly they wrote about the minor events in their lives, but there was always something about how they missed each other, and in her case there was always something about her father. The recurring theme was that her father gave her no room to grow, and that she couldn't wait to get away from him and have the freedom to find herself.

He went home for spring break, and during that short week they saw each other often, renewing the long all-out kisses but still constrained by the presence of her father as well as by the indoctrination she had received from a lifetime of nuns. Once, as they were catching their breath between kisses, she remarked that what they were doing with their tongues was a venial sin. And she smiled as if she was pleased with herself for being so rebellious.

His mother kept asking him about this girl whose family she didn't know, so he agreed to invite her for dinner and introduce her. His mother wasn't sure what to serve because she assumed that Renata, being Italian, ate spaghetti and meatballs, which the cook didn't know how to prepare. She finally settled on roast beef and mashed potatoes, which everyone would like.

Before the occasion Stephen promoted Renata, talking about how beautiful and talented she was—to a point where Jim wondered if Stephen was in love with her but knew he didn't have a chance because he was two years younger than her. In any case his campaign may have predisposed their mother to think well of Renata, or at least not to think ill of her because she was Italian.

The dinner went well. His father, who generally loved women, took to Renata immediately. Of course it helped that Renata was attractive, but more than that his father seemed to appreciate the very quality that her own father wanted to quell—the scrappy independence that was struggling to break through the walls that had been constructed by her family, her church, and her schooling. Though she had just met his father, by the time he started to carve the roast they were already sparring in a playful, respectful way over local political issues. Like her father, his father was conservative, and Renata was liberal, but instead of quarreling, as she would have done with her father, she made a game of it like tennis hitting him a shot with spin on it, which he hit back reversing the spin. At one point they both laughed like amateur players after an incredible rally.

His mother, when she had a chance, asked her where she lived, what her father did, where she went to church, where she went to school, and so on. Renata answered these questions politely, but Jim could tell she would have liked to say that these things weren't relevant. It must have annoyed her that his mother was trying to define her in terms that she was trying to reject.

When Jim returned after taking her home his father patted him on the back, saying: "I like that girl. She has spunk."

They talked for a while about Renata, and then he went to find his mother.

She was in the sunroom, picking dead leaves off a plant. With her eyes still on the plant she said: "An interesting girl. Where did you meet her?"

"At her house, at a party. Stephen knows her younger sister."

"Oh, yes. They live in the Carbonneau house," his mother said, pronouncing the name correctly in French. That was a family whose fortune dated back to the days of fur trading. It was more than fifty years since a Carbonneau had lived in the house, but people like his mother still called it the Carbonneau house. "Her father must have made a lot of money to buy that house."

"He owns a construction company."

"Well, that's all we know about him."

"I know him," Jim said, thinking that he did.

"You don't know him," his mother said, turning from the plant. "He comes from a different world. He's Italian."

"What does that have to do with it?"

"It has everything to do with it. He's also a Catholic."

"But you're a Catholic," he pointed out.

"I'm not a practicing Catholic," his mother said with a tinge of regret. "Just think about how your grandmother would feel if you married a Catholic."

His grandmother, who had grown up in Prague, had become an enemy of the Catholic Church when they refused to give a proper burial to her younger sister, who had killed herself after being jilted by her fiancé. When his grandmother immigrated to America she brought her hatred of the Catholic Church with her, and when her youngest son told her he wanted to marry a Catholic girl she refused to accept her into the family unless she became an Episcopalian. So to placate his grandmother Jim's mother had become an Episcopalian. "I'm not thinking about marriage yet."

"You will soon, and then you'll have to deal with your grandmother."

His grandmother, Iveta, was a tiny woman who by some mysterious force was able to rule and even at times terrorize her family. "Well, what if I did want to marry her?"

"If you did," his mother said, "I would advise you not to."

"You don't like her?"

"Of course I like her. But it's not a question of liking her. It's a question of whether a marriage between you and her would ever work."

"If we love each other it would work."

His mother shook her head as if he had a lot to learn. "Love isn't as strong as you think, especially when it's up against differences in the way people were raised. For one thing, you don't know what it's like being a daughter in an Italian family."

"Maybe I don't, but how could *you* know what it's like?"

"My roommate at college was Italian," his mother said, doing what parents so often did—pulling an experience out of their past that you had never heard about before, just when they needed it. "I saw what she went through."

"But that was a generation ago. Times have changed."

"They haven't changed much as far as I can see."

"Well, don't worry. I'm sure her father doesn't want her to marry me any more than you want me to marry her."

"You mean she wouldn't go against her father's wishes?"

"No. I didn't mean that. I just meant that there are reasons on both sides for us not to get married."

"I'm glad you see that," his mother said.

As he went upstairs he wondered why he cared so much whether his mother approved of his marrying Renata. He didn't need her approval.

By the end of the summer he and Renata decided to get engaged, but following his mother's advice he had a meeting with Joe Marchi before he even bought a ring. They met in an office that Marchi maintained in his home. Marchi sat behind an ornate desk, while Jim sat in the supplicant's position in front of it.

Jim was nervous, so instead of leading up to the subject he jumped right into it, saying: "Renata and I would like to get engaged."

Marchi nodded as if he had expected this. "Engaged to be married?"

"Yes. Of course."

"And when would you get married?"

"In June, right after I graduate."

"I'm sorry," Marchi said, shaking his head. "I can't let Renata marry someone who's not a Catholic."

Since he and Renata had discussed this problem he was ready with a solution. "I plan to convert."

"You do? What are you now?"

"Episcopalian."

"Well, from what I hear that's not too different from our religion."

"It's not," he said. "I've compared the services, and they're very similar."

"How would your parents feel about it?"

"They wouldn't have a problem. My mother's a Catholic," he added for good measure.

"She is? So why weren't you raised as a Catholic?"

"My grandmother wanted her grandchildren to be raised as Episcopalians."

Marchi smiled wryly. "You mean because it was higher class?"

"I don't know why. I wasn't involved in the decision."

"Okay," Marchi said as if that problem had been solved. "But I still have another problem with you marrying my daughter."

He waited, knowing what it was.

"I don't want her to live in a foreign country."

"What if she wants to?"

"She doesn't know what she wants. She's just a kid."

"She's old enough to make decisions about her own life."

"Maybe she's old enough, but she doesn't know enough. If she thinks she'd be happy living in a foreign country, she's in for a big surprise."

"That's possible," Jim allowed.

"Have you ever lived in a foreign country?"

"I lived in Spain for a year."

"What were you doing there?"

"I was a student."

"Well, that's not the same as living in a foreign country as an adult."

"It's probably not," he conceded.

"I spent two years in Italy," her father said. "And except for the parts that tourists see, I can tell you from personal experience that it's a dump."

"I probably wouldn't be assigned to Italy. I'd probably be assigned to countries where they speak Spanish."

"You mean like Mexico?"

"Yeah. But hopefully Spain."

After a grimace her father said. "I know my daughter, and I know she wouldn't be happy living in a foreign country."

"Maybe she wouldn't. But shouldn't she have a chance to find out?"

"Why take the risk of making her unhappy?"

"Because she might like it. But if she didn't, then we'd come back home."

"You'd give up your career?"

"Of course I would. I love her, and I'd do anything for her."

"Then why don't you do something for her right away? Why don't you stay here and work for your father?"

The long answer to this question was that his father wanted him to go out into the world and do something adventurous instead of being stuck in St. Paul to run the family business, as he had been. The family business, founded by his grandfather, was the major supplier of dairy products in the city, with a fleet of trucks delivering milk every morning to people's homes. But his father could see that things were changing in ways that would eventually make this business obsolete, so it didn't offer much future. Giving the short answer to the question, Jim said: "My father doesn't want me to work for him. He wants me to do something else."

"Then why don't you work for me?"

"Doing what?" he asked, having been warned by Renata that her father might make him an offer.

"Learning the business. I have no sons," Marchi said as if this was the tragedy of his life, "so I don't have a natural successor. If you do well, you'll have a chance to take over the business when I retire."

"Thanks for the offer," he said sincerely. "But I don't have any experience now, so I wouldn't be very useful to you. If I take this other job and we come back, at least I'll have some experience."

"I don't know what that experience would be worth. You'll be working for the government."

"The government does the same things that businesses do."

Marchi considered. "Well, they do accounting, and they do finance, and they do projects, so maybe it would be worth something."

"Just give us a chance," he said. "If she doesn't like it, we'll come back."

"Is that a promise?" Marchi asked, looking him directly in the eye.

"It's a promise," he said.

"Okay. You have my blessing."

As he left the office he was glad that Marchi hadn't pressed the question of why he wanted to live in a foreign country because it wouldn't have been easy to answer. He could say it was because he wanted to serve his country, but that would be a superficial reason. Deep down, it was because he wanted to live in a place where he wouldn't be known as the grandson of James Wyatt, who had founded a dairy business in St. Paul and made a fortune two generations ago, or as the great-great-grandson of Robert Madigan, who had founded an oil company in Pennsylvania and made a fortune four generations ago. So he understood Renata's yearning to live in a place where she wouldn't be known as the daughter of Joe Marchi, who had founded a construction company in St. Paul and made a fortune during the past thirty years.

When he awoke and heard the birds singing in the garden he didn't remember where he was. He opened his eyes and confronted the unfamiliar ceiling, completely disoriented. Then like a kick in the gut it came back: he was a hostage, and his captors had given the government only a week to ransom him by releasing a man who had been sentenced to ten years in prison.

The realization made him sit up and get out of bed. Though there was nothing he could do but watch for an opportunity, he didn't want to be caught lying in his underwear if one arose, so he got dressed and sat by the window.

As he waited, breaking his resolution not to think about how he had gotten into this predicament, he returned to the critical point in his overtures to Zoraya where he had decided to pose as a CIA agent. If he had posed as a mercenary, war correspondent, or private investigator he wouldn't have had as much value as a hostage, and he might now be in his hotel room, waiting for his breakfast and reading the paper.

Hearing the sound of the door being unlocked, he rose from the chair. At this moment he wanted to be ready for whatever chance he might have of getting away. You never knew what might happen with them.

It was Zoraya, carrying a tray. She was wearing jeans and a tee shirt with the Pepsi logo. She certainly didn't look like a terrorist.

"I've brought your breakfast," she said in Spanish.

"The service here," he remarked wryly, "is as good as it was at the St. Jerome."

"Well, we won't starve you."

"How will you kill me?"

"I hope we won't have to kill you," she told him. "But if we do we'll shoot you."

"Mm." From the way Ramon waved that gun he should have guessed.

She went to set the tray on the table.

As he watched her bend over he still found it hard to believe that a woman who looked so good in jeans could be a killer. "Have you ever killed anyone?"

"No. But I will if I have to."

"You don't have to. You have a choice."

"We don't have a choice. We've told them we're going to kill you, and we have to keep our word. If we don't, we won't have any credibility."

"You'll have more credibility if you don't kill me."

"You don't understand the situation."

"I don't? Explain it to me."

"We're in a war."

"Who do you mean?"

"Muslims and Christians."

"That's nonsense. Where did you get that idea?"

"I got it from observing the world."

"Give me an example."

"All right. Look at what's happening in Bosnia. For three years the Serbs have been killing Muslims. They've been executing men and boys. They've been raping women and girls. And your country has done nothing to stop them."

"That's a good example," he admitted.

"The Serbs are committing genocide, and you just call it ethnic cleansing."

"Yeah. I don't know why we can't see that it's as bad as what the Nazis did to the Jews."

"I can tell you why. It's because they're doing it to Muslims."

"Yeah, you're right. If they were killing and raping Christians, we would have intervened by now."

"You don't care what happens to Muslims. And you know why? You don't consider us as human beings. In fact," she maintained, "you consider us as even lower than animals."

"I think that's going a bit far."

"It is? You have an association to prevent cruelty to animals. But you're doing nothing to prevent cruelty to Muslims. Right now the Serbs have moved into Srebrenica, which was supposed to be a safe haven with UN troops protecting our people. Do you know what's happening there?"

"I know. I was following it on television."

"You were following it. But did you really care?"

"I admit that it wasn't at the top of my mind, but after I saw the news reports on Srebrenica I did get involved."

"What did you do?"

"I called a senator in Washington and told him we should intervene."

"At least you tried," she begrudged. "But your country won't intervene. You won't do anything until the Muslims are driven out of Bosnia or are dead."

"Well, I hope our country does intervene. If I was running our government we would have intervened long ago."

"You're only saying that because your life is in our hands."

"No, I'm not," he argued. "I made that phone call before you kidnapped me."

"But you should have tried to stop it sooner. What were you waiting for?"

"I was concerned with other things."

She nodded. "Yeah. So stopping the genocide in Bosnia wasn't a top priority for you."

"I guess it wasn't. I was blind. But now that you've opened my eyes, I have a different perspective on the situation."

"That sounds good, but after all your bullshit why should I believe you?"

He could think of reasons why she should, but he decided not to pursue the issue for now. He would have an opportunity to work on her every time she brought him a meal, so he only asked: "Did Manuel deliver the tape?"

"Yeah. He delivered it this morning."

"He did? How?"

"He used a messenger."

"Wouldn't that leave a trail?"

"No. He found a person on the street and paid him."

"How does he know the tape was delivered?"

"He followed the messenger and watched him go into the building."

"I assume the messenger didn't know he was being followed."

"He didn't know anything. So if they questioned him," she said, "he wouldn't be able to tell them anything."

He went through the process, looking for a way that the police might find a trail. The only way he could see was for them to catch Manuel in the act of handing the tape to the messenger. But he could do that anywhere in the city, and presumably he would use different locations for successive tapes.

"We're waiting for their response," she said.

"Well, don't hold your breath. It'll take them a while."

"Yeah, I know. Whenever we get it Manuel will record it so we can all watch it."

"That sounds entertaining. You could make popcorn."

She almost smiled. "I'll leave you now. Enjoy your breakfast."

He watched her go, then went to the table and checked the tray. There was a pot of black coffee, a pot of hot milk, and an ample piece of French bread. The bread was fresh, so unless Zoraya had baked it herself—which didn't seem likely—one of his captors had recently gone to a food store. Despite the risk they probably just couldn't break the habit of shopping daily for fresh food, unlike American kidnappers who would have laid in enough processed food to sustain them for weeks.

Sitting at the table, he poured the coffee and added milk until he got the shade he preferred. At least they made good coffee.

He and Renata were married in June. By then he had converted to Catholicism, guided by a priest who served the students at the university, so they had a wedding Mass at St. Luke Church. The reception was held at the Marchi house, which was big enough to accommodate two hundred people, and Joe Marchi spared no expense for this event. People said it was the most lavish wedding reception the city had seen since the union of a railroad family and a lumber family back in the Twenties.

They had a week in Paris for their honeymoon, which Joe Marchi lavishly paid for—it was as if he wanted to be able to say later that he had done everything in his power to make his daughter happy in foreign countries. And then they went to Washington, where Jim began his training.

Renata loved Washington because it wasn't St. Paul and it offered her the chance to take courses in journalism. She even got a job in the office of the Washington bureau of a major newspaper. Though she was a glorified secretary, her work was interesting, and it made her feel that she was on a path toward her goal. So she wasn't happy to leave Washington after a year and go to Caracas, where Jim was assigned.

He had been hoping to be assigned to Spain, but the top priority of the CIA was to stop communism, and at that time Venezuela was on the front line of the Cold War. Its president, Rómulo Betancourt, was a staunch opponent of communism, and he was strongly supported by the U.S. government. The mission of the CIA there was to stop the country from being taken over by communists. Castro was making inroads there, and two guerrilla armies, both of them with roots in communism, were active both in rural and urban areas. Jim was stationed in the embassy with a cover as an economic attaché, and he worked for a man who was fifteen years older and had a degree in international relations from Georgetown University. This man had a lot of skills and experience, but fluency in Spanish wasn't one of them, so he needed an assistant who was fluent in Spanish but was also an American of unquestioned loyalty. So Jim's job was to sit at a desk and sift through communications in Spanish, looking for clues about what the guerrilla armies were planning. It didn't have the romance of what he had imagined, but at least he could feel good about being able to make a contribution.

While Jim didn't mind living in Caracas, Renata hated it. She couldn't continue her courses there because she didn't speak Spanish, even though as Jim's wife she had been given a crash course in the language. And she couldn't work there because she didn't have a permit. To make things worse, there was a problem with the apartment they had rented, so they couldn't move into it for more than three months, during which time she was stuck at the Hotel Tamanaco. It was a nice hotel, with a lot of amenities including a large swimming pool, surrounded by a terrace from which you had a view of the city, but after a week she was tired of the hotel. Lounging around a swimming pool wasn't her idea of life.

He introduced her to the wives of his colleagues at the embassy. They were all older than Renata, and they all had children. They talked about their children, about their maids, and about their husbands. They had no other interests, and they didn't seem to like living in Caracas any more than she did. They were biding time in Caracas, waiting for their husbands to be transferred to another country.

Not that she held her feelings back, but one night after they had been there about four months Renata let them all out. They were sitting on the balcony of their apartment, which like the hotel had a view of the city. They were drinking daiquiris while a servant in the kitchen prepared their dinner.

"I hate it here," she said passionately.

They were on their third drink, having asked the servant not to rush dinner, and Jim could tell that Renata was feeling the influence of the rum.

"I absolutely hate it."

"What do you hate about it?"

"Everything. I hate this city. There's no culture here. All they have is oil money. And I hate my position here."

"What do you mean?"

"I'm the wife of Jim Wyatt, a junior officer at the embassy. I can't study, I can't work, I can't be anything except your wife. And I can't do anything that they might question at the embassy."

"Well, what do the other women do?"

"They have children, and they talk about them. They don't even raise them. Their servants do that. They just have them and talk about them."

He knew better than to suggest that they have a baby.

"I thought it would be different," she said sadly. "I thought I'd have all this freedom. But I don't have any freedom. I'm as much a prisoner here as I was in St. Paul being the daughter of Joe Marchi."

"I'm sorry," he said, feeling bad for her.

"I know you are," she said, "and that makes me feel even worse. I mean, this was your dream, and here I am ruining it."

"You're not ruining it."

"Well, it can't be fun listening to me complain."

"No. It's not fun. I just wish we could find something for you to do."

"I've looked around, and I haven't found anything."

"What about the English newspaper?" He had heard about it from a colleague and suggested that she look into it.

"I interviewed with the managing editor. It didn't go well."

"You didn't tell me about it."

"I didn't want to upset you," she said, grimacing. "The man as much as said I could have a job if I slept with him."

"What? He propositioned you?"

"I guess he figured that I was desperate to get a job. But I'm not that desperate. Not yet," she added ominously.

"God damn him," he said, not missing the implication of her last two words.

"Maybe I should go home early for Christmas," she said after a long silence. "What do you think?"

"Do you want to go home?"

"I never thought I would, but at this point I do. At least it might give me some perspective. I mean, after being with my father for a few weeks I'll probably realize how lucky I am to be here."

"When would you go?"

"A week before we planned. Would that be okay?"

"Yeah," he said. "I couldn't go with you, but I could go the following week."

"Would you mind being here alone?"

"I'll miss you, but I want you to be happy."

"I won't be happy there," she said, "but at least I'll be out of this situation for a while, and then maybe I'll be able to deal with it better."

"That makes sense. And your father will be happy."

"Yeah. He will. In fact, he'll act like he's won a bet. That's almost enough to stop me from going."

"Don't let it. Do what you want."

So she went home the second week of December.

While she was gone he wondered if she would ever be happy in Caracas or in any other foreign city where he would be assigned over the years. He really hadn't thought about what she would do in a foreign country.

In the meantime Jim had picked up clues from a report by a field agent that the FALN was planning to sabotage an oil pipeline. The clues included a location and a date. He immediately told his supervisor, who put it through the system, only to be told that the information was false, so nothing was done about it. A week later a pipeline was sabotaged, precisely where and when Jim had predicted. Needless to say, the incident left him feeling frustrated and wondering what he was doing in Caracas.

He joined Renata in St. Paul a few days before Christmas. They stayed at the Marchi house, but they also saw a lot of his family. Stephen was home on the holiday recess from Princeton, where he was in the middle of his sophomore year, and he talked about dropping out for a year to participate in the civil rights movement. His sister Bitsy was in the middle of her senior year at Summit School and planning to study art in New York. She now wanted people to call her Elizabeth.

He and Renata planned to return to Caracas right after New Year's, but during the last week of the year Renata was feeling nauseous, usually in the morning. He took her to a doctor, who after getting the results of a test confirmed that she was six weeks pregnant. The baby was due in early September.

She didn't feel like flying in her condition, so she waited until she was over the morning sickness before returning to Caracas. By then it was the end of January, and at least she was glad to get away from her father. And now she had something to talk about with the wives of his colleagues, who gave her all kinds of advice on how to get through a pregnancy. Like most of them, she decided not to have her baby in Caracas because she had doubts about the doctors, so in August she flew back to St. Paul, and Jim joined her in time for her delivery.

The baby was a girl, and they named her Carla after Renata's favorite aunt. Her father was happy to be a grandfather but at the same time he didn't conceal his disappointment that Renata hadn't given him a grandson, and he was already waiting for her next baby, hoping that she would end the family curse of girls.

Jim was planning to return to Caracas and have Renata join him when she was ready, but a few days before his departure she told him she wanted to stay in St. Paul. He had seen it coming, so he wasn't surprised. He remembered his promise to her father that if she didn't like living in a foreign country he would bring her home. But more important than the promise was Renata's belief that she could have a self-fulfilling life in St. Paul. As for himself, he had to admit that living in a foreign country wasn't as liberating as he had expected, and working for the CIA wasn't as glamorous as he had imagined. So he agreed to give notice and come home as soon as he could.

Delighted, her father renewed his offer of a job, and Jim accepted it. The two of them drank an expensive bottle of champagne to celebrate. After two glasses Marchi told him: "You made the right decision, son. You're going to live in the best country and work for the best company."

The CIA wasn't happy with his decision, and they made him feel that they had wasted a lot of money on his security clearance and his training. But they agreed to let him go in two weeks and to pay for his return to Minnesota.

When he knew the date of his departure he called Renata. "How are you doing?"

"I'm fine," she said, sounding mellow. "And Carla's fine."

"They gave me a date. I'll be home in two weeks."

"That's wonderful. We both miss you."

"We have a tape for you to watch," Zoraya told him, entering the room.

"You got a response?" He checked his watch: it was only a few minutes after twelve. "That was fast."

"Wait. You'll see."

From her tone as well as the expression on her face he gathered that the response hadn't been satisfactory.

"*Ven*," she said, leading the way.

With a feeling of dread he followed her downstairs to the room where they had watched his tape.

Ramon and Manuel were sitting in chairs that they had brought there the previous evening, staring grimly at scenes of refugees fleeing Srebrenica and of bodies littering the unpaved streets of abandoned villages.

Jim sat at the foot of the bed with Zoraya, who told Manuel to run the tape.

An anchorman with perfect hair appeared on the tube, winding up a story. Then he said: "We've received a tape from a man who identified himself as Jim Wyatt, an agent of the CIA. He said he was being held hostage by the Islamic Human Rights Movement. His captors are demanding the release of a man who was convicted of involvement in the bombing of the World Trade Center. A government spokesman has denied that Mr. Wyatt has any connection with the CIA, either past or present. The spokesperson refused to discuss the government's possible response to the situation but made clear that its policy is not to negotiate with terrorists. We have determined that the man on the tape is actually a prominent state senator from Minnesota, who was visiting New York for a conference and has not been seen at his hotel since Tuesday. We hope to have more information later on this breaking story."

Manuel abruptly stopped the tape as the anchorman yielded to a commercial.

"You see?" Jim said. "I was telling you the truth."

"Your government's denial that you work for them proves absolutely nothing," Ramón said.

"That wasn't the government. It was CNN, and if they've determined that I'm a state senator it must be true."

"Do you believe everything you hear on the news?" Zoraya asked him.

"I don't believe it," Ramón said. "The government could have made them say that."

"The government," he explained to them, "can't tell the media what to say. And even if they could, why would they say I'm a state senator? If we're both lying, how would we both come up with the same story?"

"You could have planned this," Ramón said.

"Oh, I see. I planned to be taken hostage, so I got together with CNN in advance and we both agreed to say I'm a state senator."

"You could have planned," Zoraya said, "that in case you were ever taken hostage, you would say you're a state senator."

"I could have planned that with the CIA, but with CNN?"

"Well, the government could have made them say that."

"So you still believe I'm a CIA agent?"

Zoraya and Ramón looked at each other, reaching a consensus.

"Yes," Zoraya said, speaking for them. "But if we're wrong you're still worth something to them."

"For all we know," Ramón said in Arabic, "a state senator may be worth as much as a CIA agent. What do you think?"

"I think he may be," Zoraya said. Then in Spanish she said: "They said you were a *prominent* state senator. What does that mean?"

"It means I'm well known."

"Then they don't want you to be killed."

"That's right. They don't want anyone to be killed. In our society we believe in the sanctity of human life."

"In our society we do too."

"You don't act like it."

"You don't either," she retorted. "You only believe in the sanctity of human life for white Christians."

"You have a point. We don't always live up to our beliefs."

"You don't. Just look at Bosnia."

"Okay," he said. "But you can't use what's happening in Bosnia to justify what you're doing to me."

"Why not?" Ramón said. "The Jews use what happened to them in Germany to justify what they're doing to the Palestinians."

"It doesn't make what they're doing right."

"Then why doesn't your country stop them?"

"That's a good question. And I don't know the answer."

"Does anyone know?" Zoraya said.

"The Jews know," Ramón said.

"Well, they have nothing to do with what's happening in Bosnia," Jim said.

"Are you sure about that?"

"Yeah. I'm sure. If you want to blame someone besides us, blame the Russians."

"Why the Russians?"

"Because they adopted the Serbs a long time ago," Jim explained, "and they always protect them."

"I wish they had adopted us," Manuel said.

"All right," Zoraya said, interrupting the discussion. "We didn't get the response we wanted, so we have to make another tape."

"Well, what did you expect?" Jim asked.

"I expected your government to release Abdullah."

"Look," he said, appealing to them. "You still have a chance to get out of this. If you let me go, I promise to help you get him released, and I promise not to identify you. I'm on your side."

"They would never believe you don't know what we look like," Zoraya said.

"I can say you wore masks."

"We weren't wearing masks at the hotel."

"I'm not good at remembering faces."

"How could we trust you to keep your word?"

"I always keep my word."

"Infidels never keep their word," Ramón muttered.

"Well, whatever you say," Zoraya told him, "we're not going to let you go unless they let Abdullah go."

"I can help you get Abdullah released," he reiterated. "I have influence. But I can't do anything from here."

"You can use your influence from here."

"How? By making tapes?"

"Do you have a better idea?"

"I could get on the phone and call people."

"We can't let you do that," Ramón said. "You would tell them where you are."

"I won't tell them where we are. I give you my word."

"It keeps coming back to your word," Zoraya said. "That's the whole problem. We don't trust you."

"So the only way we can let you communicate with them," Ramón said, "is by recorded message. That way we can control what you say."

"If you control what I say," he argued, "then I can't use my influence to the full extent."

"Yes, you can," Zoraya said. "You can tell us what you want to say, and we'll make sure you don't betray us."

"Betray you? I couldn't betray you unless I was one of you."

"You can always join us," Manuel said.

"We don't want him," Ramón said.

"So what's your plan?" he asked, hoping to take advantage of their confusion.

"We'll continue operating on the assumption that you're a CIA agent," Zoraya said, addressing her team.

"Why would you do that?"

"Because it won't look as bad if we kill a CIA agent."

"I thought you didn't care about your image."

"I'm learning from you," Zoraya said.

"But my constituents have seen my face, and they know I'm a state senator."

"You could still be using that as a cover."

"Even if that was true," he told her, "they'd never believe it. And if they believe I'm a state senator, that's what I am as far as they're concerned. So you can't get away with pretending that I'm a CIA agent."

"Well, let's see what happens after they see the next tape."

"Okay. I have some ideas of what to say."

"We need to talk without you," Ramón said.

"You're wasting time."

"We have plenty of time," Ramón told him, waving the gun. "You're the one who doesn't have time."

FIVE

WHEN HE RETURNED to St. Paul he joined Renata and the baby in the Marchi house, where they lived until they could move into a house of their own. After looking far and wide around the city for a house they liked, they ended up buying a house in the Crocus Hill area, just three blocks from his parents and seven blocks from hers. It took them until the end of November to close on the house and move in, and during that time Jim had the experience of living in the same house as Renata's father. Though the house was enormous they felt his presence in every room, even when they knew he was out, and at night in their own bedroom on the third floor, far removed from her parents' bedroom, their ardent love-making was still constrained by an awareness of him.

Meanwhile, he started working for Joe Marchi. So that he could learn the business from the bottom up, Marchi assigned him to a construction crew at an office building project in Minneapolis. He had to join the union, which he didn't object to, and he had to work for a tough foreman who had evidently been told not to treat him as the boss's son-in-law. But according to the foreman he proved himself on the job, as Marchi eventually told him. He stayed with the crew for almost a year until the office building was completed, coming home through the back door and shedding his dusty clothes in the kitchen before going upstairs for a shower.

Renata was occupied with being a mother, a role that involved her more with their parents than they had expected. Being the first grandchild, Carla was an object of constant attention by their mothers as well as their fathers. Renata's mother gave her a lot of useful advice on caring for a baby, and even her father seemed to have quickly forgiven Carla for being a girl. Jim's father loved the baby, and his mother took an immediate interest in her, no doubt envisioning another generation of Wyatt girls at Summit School and Smith College.

From that point on their parents saw each other more frequently. His father and Marchi developed a strong relationship based on their mutual love of sports, and his father even got Marchi admitted to an elite group of men who went hunting together every fall for duck, grouse, and pheasant. His mother invited Renata's mother, a quiet woman whom Jim never got to know very well, into her closed circle of friends. By then the two families were spending the holidays together: Thanksgiving, Christmas, Easter, Memorial Day, Fourth of July, and Labor Day. But on the religious holidays Jim always went to St. Luke's with the Marchis, while his family went to St. John's, the Episcopal church that served the Crocus Hill area.

Two weeks after Carla had her second birthday Renata delivered another baby, whom they named Gina after a grandmother. Unlike Carla, who looked like a Wyatt with her fair hair and blue eyes, Gina was definitely a Marchi, which gave Renata's father at least something to be happy about, though he was obviously disappointed with her for again failing to give him a grandson.

At that point Jim and Renata had a discussion about whether they wanted to have more children. Jim was happy with the two girls, and she was too, so they decided to stop there. A birth control pill had become available, and assured by her gynecologist that it was safe and reliable, Renata began taking it. They both knew how her father would react if he knew about it, so they kept it a secret. As she had asserted, it was none of her father's business what she did with her body. Of course the birth control pill was against the doctrine of the Catholic Church, which allowed only the rhythm method, so they were sinners—a state they thought they could somehow live with.

By then Jim was no longer on a construction crew but working as a foreman on a new project. He had learned a lot, not only on the job but also from courses he had taken in the university's continuing education program. He liked his job, but he couldn't see himself working for Marchi all his life. He still wanted to achieve his own identity, and even if he took over the business it would still be what Marchi had created. It would never be his. But he didn't yet have another career in mind, and he had a family to support, so he didn't think about leaving Marchi.

When Gina was about six months old Renata started going to the university with the goal of completing a degree in journalism. It took her two and a half years, using the credits she had earned at St. Catherine. They had a party at their house to celebrate her achievement, which both families attended. His family was represented only by his parents because Stephen was in Vietnam and Elizabeth was in Italy, but Renata's sisters were both there—Angela, who had graduated from St. Catherine and was working in her father's office, and Bianca, a junior at St. Catherine majoring in music.

It was a good party until the end. Around eleven Jim's parents went home, followed by Renata's sisters and her mother, leaving only her father behind. It was obvious that there was something he wanted to talk about.

"Would you like another brandy?" Jim offered, wishing her father had left with the others.

"Sure. Thanks," her father said.

"I'll have another glass of wine," Renata said tensely.

Jim brought the drinks and sat down next to Renata on the sofa, while her father remained in one of the big, comfortable chairs.

"What are you going to do with this degree?" her father asked.

"I'm going to get a job. A part-time job," Renata added.

"How would you have time for that?"

"I'll find the time. And don't worry, I won't ignore the children. They'll always have my full attention."

"How can they have your full attention if you're writing stories for a newspaper?"

"They will. I can manage it."

There was a long silence, then her father said: "I notice you're not having another baby. Is that because you want a career in journalism?"

"It's because I don't want another baby."

"Why don't you?"

"I'm happy with the two I have."

"And so am I," Jim said, supporting her.

Her father ignored him. "Well, I'm not happy. I want a grandson."

"You have two other daughters who can give you a grandson."

"I want one from you."

"Well, you're not going to get one from me."

"How do you know? The rhythm method isn't infallible."

"I'm not using the rhythm method."

"What method are you using?"

"It's none of your business," she said, glaring at him.

He leaned toward her. "You better not be taking that new birth control pill."

She didn't respond, but she didn't blink.

"Are you?" he demanded to know.

"As I said, it's none of your business."

"That means you are," he said, enraged. "Do you know what you're doing, young lady? You're committing a mortal sin."

"If I am," she said, "then God will forgive me."

"Why should God forgive you?"

"He forgives all our sins."

"He doesn't forgive the sins that people knowingly commit over and over, which is what you're doing when you take a birth control pill."

"That's not what the nuns taught me."

"Yeah, they did. You just didn't learn it."

Jim intervened, saying: "I object to the way you're talking to her. She's not a child, she's a grownup woman."

"She's still my daughter."

"That doesn't give you the right to talk to her that way. And it doesn't give you the right to tell her what to do."

Her father looked at him as if he couldn't believe this display of insubordination. "Do you remember who you work for?"

"I work for you. But I can always quit."

"You can't quit. You need the job. You have a family to support."

"I can get a job anywhere."

After failing to outstare him her father said: "I thought you converted to our faith, but I can see you don't take it seriously."

"I do take it seriously."

"No, you don't. If you did you wouldn't encourage her to commit this sin."

"I'm doing it without his encouragement," Renata said.

"Do you support what she's doing?"

"Yes. I support it," Jim said. "We were blessed with two children, and we decided that two is enough."

"How do you know that God doesn't want you to have more?"

"If he did, he'd tell us somehow."

"Well, I'm telling you."

"You're not God," Renata said, "though you think you are."

"That's disrespectful. And it's also blasphemous."

"It's not blasphemous. Only someone who thinks he's God would say that."

Marchi glared at her with fury, and then he turned to Jim and asked: "Are you going along with her?"

"I'm going along with her all the way."

"Then you're fired."

"Fine," Jim said.

"And you're disowned."

"Fine," she said. "I'm finally free of you."

Marchi got up and stormed out, slamming the door.

They hugged each other as if they had won a major victory, but their feelings were mixed because neither of them wanted to break with her father, and they were relieved when he called an hour later, insisting they both get on the phone and then telling them that he didn't mean it, Jim wasn't fired and Renata wasn't disowned. But even those feelings were mixed because it was unsettling to have Joe Marchi capitulate.

He was sitting at the window when he heard the door being unlocked.

Zoraya came in, looking annoyed. It had been more than an hour since she left him to discuss with her colleagues what they wanted him to say on the next tape.

"Have you made any decisions?" he asked, as usual in Spanish.

"No," she said glumly. "There's been a new development."

"Really?" he said, encouraged. "What happened?"

"I'll show you. *Ven.*"

He followed her down to the bedroom where they watched television. Again, he joined her at the foot of the bed while Ramón and Manuel sat in the chairs. They had fallen into a routine.

Ramón and Manuel were watching the news, which showed a column of refugees from Srebrenica trudging along a dusty road. They were mostly women and children who looked as if they were ready to drop from hunger and exhaustion. The camera then showed a curve in the road where the column had been ambushed by Serbian forces. The road was littered with the dead and wounded. The only two moving creatures were a wide-eyed little girl and a skeletal dog.

"The murdering assholes," Ramón said in Arabic.

"I thought it was against the Christian religion to kill innocent people like that," Manuel said in Spanish.

"It is," Jim said. "The men who did that aren't Christians."

"Well, they're not Muslims."

"So why doesn't your government stop them?" Ramón asked.

"They should stop them."

"They should bomb them," Manuel said.

"I agree with you," Jim said. "The only thing they respect is force, so that's what we need to apply. It's too late for words."

"The Serbian soldiers haven't fought a battle," Ramón said. "All they've done is kill unarmed civilians."

"They're fucking cowards," Manuel muttered.

"All right," Zoraya said, taking charge. "Let's watch the tape."

Manuel, the official operator, switched channels and started the player.

"Since our earlier report," the same anchorman said, "we've received hundreds of phone calls from constituents of Senator Wyatt. Overwhelmingly, they're asking the government to do whatever is necessary to get him released."

"You see?" he said, feeling gratified. "Do you believe me now?"

"Wait," Zoraya said, "There's more."

After a break the tape showed a reporter on a street that looked like downtown St. Paul. The reporter, an earnest-looking young man, stopped a woman and asked: "Have you heard about the kidnapping of Senator Wyatt?"

"Oh, ya," the woman said. "I heard about it on the news."

"What do you think of it?"

"I think it's awful. They say they're going to kill him if we don't release some Ayrab priest."

"What would you say to his captors?"

Looking at the camera and talking directly to them, the woman said: "Whoever you are, Senator Wyatt is a wonderful man. He does so many good things for the people of this state. Please don't kill him."

"What do you think the government should do?"

"They should release the Ayrab priest."

"Are you going to pray for Senator Wyatt?"

"You betcha," the woman said.

The tube went blank.

"I told you," he said, loving the woman.

"Okay. You *are* a state senator," Zoraya said grudgingly.

"So you can no longer operate on the assumption that I'm a CIA agent."

"I know. I'm not stupid."

"Of course you're not. You're smart enough to let me help you."

"We're not going to release you," Ramón said.

"If you don't let me help you," he argued, "you won't get Abdullah released.'

"If we don't get Abdullah released, we'll kill you."

"But that's stupid."

"Let me think," Zoraya said. "Since you're a *prominent* state senator, maybe we can use that somehow."

"Of course you can use it—by letting me talk with people in the government."

"We're not going to let you do that," she told him, not yielding. "But maybe we can find another way."

"Well, instead of appealing to the government," he suggested, "I could appeal directly to my constituents. There are more than twenty thousand of them."

"What would you do?"

"I'd ask them to tell the government to release Abdullah."

"That's not a bad idea," she said to her partners.

"How would you do that?" Ramón asked.

"I'd send a tape to the local stations in Minnesota and ask them to broadcast it." He knew the station owners, which would help.

"Could we send the tape by messenger?" Zoraya asked.

"We would have to fly the messenger to Minnesota," Manuel replied, looking skeptical. "And that would be risky."

"We could send the tape by FedEx," Jim said. "They'd get it tomorrow."

"We don't have an account with FedEx," Manuel said.

"We could use my account."

"Would that work?" Zoraya asked.

"I guess it would," Manuel said, "but someone would have to take the package to a FedEx office."

"Could we use a messenger to do that?"

"Yeah, we could. I could find someone on the street and ask him to take a package to the nearest FedEx office."

"All right," Ramón said. "What are you going to say to your constituents?"

"I'll write it," Jim said. "And you can review it."

"It's quarter of three," Zoraya said. "What time do we have to drop off the tape so they'll get it tomorrow?"

"I don't know," Manuel said. "I guess we'll have to drop it off by five o'clock today."

"So you better start writing your speech."

They had a party for Gina's third birthday, inviting their immediate families plus about a dozen girls from the neighborhood who were between the ages of two and four. They had ice cream and cake, which ended up on faces, clothes, chairs, sofas, carpets, curtains, and almost everywhere else they looked while cleaning up. But they saw the mess as evidence of a good party, and Gina went to bed very happy.

She woke up in the middle of the night with a high fever. She was drenched with sweat, and as she wailed she kept saying: "It hurts, it hurts! Oh, Mommy, it hurts."

Jim called the children's doctor, who answered his phone and advised them to take Gina to the emergency room of the hospital that he was affiliated with. He would go directly to the hospital.

After waking up Carla and asking her to get dressed in a hurry, Jim called his mother, woke her up, explained the situation, and asked her if they could drop Carla off with her. His mother said yes, of course, was there anything else she could do for them? Which doctor did they call? Which hospital were they going to?

Renata asked him not to call her father.

Jim drove while Renata held Gina in her lap, praying and trying to soothe her.

"She's burning up," Renata said.

"I wonder what the hell it is."

"The doctor didn't have any idea?"

"He said they'd have to do some tests."

They got to the hospital about ten minutes after dropping Carla off with his mother. The doctor, who was a friend of the Marchis, was already at the hospital. They stayed with Gina while the nurse took her vital signs and got a sample of her blood. They watched while the doctor probed her, peered into her eyes, listened to her breathing, and checked her heart.

"It could be meningitis," the doctor said. "We won't know until we get the results of the tests, but I'll start treating her in the meantime."

They spent the rest of the night in the hospital and most of the next day. It was a Catholic hospital, and Renata found the chapel.

She would wait for the doctor to return to the room and check Gina, she would get his opinion, and then she would go to the chapel and pray, then wait again, get his opinion, and then go and pray again.

By the next evening the doctor told them he believed that the danger had passed and that Gina would recover without any permanent damage. After hugging and kissing Gina, with tears of gratitude in her eyes, Renata went off and thanked God for saving their daughter.

They spent another night in the hospital, and the next day they all went home, picking up Carla on the way and thanking his mother.

That evening, as they were lying in bed, Renata said: "That's the worst thing that ever happened to me."

"I feel the same way," he said, taking her hand.

After a long silence she said: "What if we'd lost her?"

"I don't even want to think about it."

"I don't either, but I can't help it. The whole time we were at the hospital I kept asking why did this happen?"

"She might have caught something from one of the kids at the birthday party."

"That's not what I meant. I meant *why* did it happen?"

"You think it had some meaning?"

"Yes. It didn't just happen for no reason."

"Well, then why did it happen?"

"It happened because God wanted to give us a warning."

"You don't believe that."

"I do," she said. "I believe he did it to warn us that if we use the pill to avoid having more children, we might lose the children we have."

"Oh, come on," he said. "You believe in a God who would do that?"

"I didn't before, but I do now."

"This is coming from your father."

"My father has nothing to do with it. He doesn't even know Gina was sick."

"But he's in your head."

"Well, I don't want to take a chance. If this was a warning," she said definitely, "we'd be stupid to ignore it."

"So what are we going to do about it?"

"I'm going to stop taking the pill. If God wants me to have another baby, I'm not going to stop him."

"What about you?"

"If I'm blessed with another baby, I'll be happy."

"Then I'll be happy too."

"You're so good to me," she said, nuzzling him. "Our girls are lucky to have you as their father."

Renata told her father she was off the pill, and they were at peace for a while. She didn't get a job, but she got some assignments to write stories for a liberal weekly newspaper. It promoted women's liberation, civil rights, unions, concern for the environment, peace, and generally everything that her father opposed. But he didn't complain, evidently hoping that she would deliver him a grandson and make up for all this nonsense.

More than a year passed without her getting pregnant.

On Thanksgiving the two families gathered at the Marchi house for the traditional feast. The conversation at dinner ranged far, but there were no problems until they were having dessert when Renata and her father got into a heated argument over the war in Vietnam. She had just written an article for her paper that criticized the war and called for the withdrawal of troops.

"I read your article," Marchi said. "You don't know what you're talking about."

"I know enough," Renata said, "to realize that the war is wrong."

"So you think we should just hand that country over to the communists."

"It's not about the communists. It's a civil war between the north and the south. Like our own civil war. How would you like it if the British had sent a million troops to our country to support the south?"

"It's not the same. They would have been supporting slavery."

"Well, we're supporting a corrupt dictatorship."

Marchi ignored this and appealed to Jim, asking: "What do you think about it?"

"I think it's a stupid war," Jim said. "I think Lyndon Johnson let those guys from Harvard talk him into something that went against his instincts."

"I hope you don't agree with that idiot McCarthy." Marchi was referring to Eugene McCarthy, the Minnesota senator whose strong position against the war had led to Johnson's decision not to run for another term.

"I agree with his position against the war."

"How can you? Your own brother's in Vietnam."

"From what he's told me," Jim said, "my brother thinks the war is wrong."

"No wonder we're not winning," Marchi said. "Our troops don't believe in what they're doing."

"Our troops are doing all they can," Renata said. "But we never should have sent them there."

"We should have sent more troops. We should have used our nuclear weapons against those bastards."

"And destroyed their country?"

"That would have been better than letting it go communist."

"You sound like the other McCarthy," Renata said. She was referring to Joe McCarthy, the Wisconsin senator who had led the witch hunts against people suspected of being communist.

"That's disrespectful," Marchi said.

Instead of replying, Renata got up from the table and picked up her plate with its unfinished slice of pumpkin pie as well as the empty plate next to her. Before going into the kitchen she asked: "Can I get coffee for anyone?"

"No, thanks," Jim said.

"We should be going," his mother said.

"Stay and have a brandy," Marchi urged them.

"I'd love to," his father said politely, "but I need to take a nap."

"Everything was excellent," his mother said.

When they had left and the girls had gone off to play in a room that was always stocked with toys, Jim went into the kitchen and found Renata scraping plates. The cook had evidently been given the rest of the day off.

"Are you all right?" he asked.

"No. I feel like shit." There were tears in her eyes and her hands were shaking. "He always makes me feel like shit."

"Well, you did the right thing to walk away from him."

"I had to or it would have gotten worse."

"I know," he said, putting his hand on her delicate shoulder. "Try to remember, it's not your problem, it's *his* problem."

"But I can't get away from him. Wherever I go, he pursues me."

"You mean you felt his presence in Caracas?"

"Yes. It didn't help at all to go there."

"You should have told me."

"It would have sounded so stupid," she said, her tears running more freely now. "Like I was still a child."

"Well, you were only twenty."

"What am I going to do about him?" she cried, coming into his arms.

"Nothing," he said, holding her. "You don't have to do anything about him. Just live your own life."

"I'm trying to, but he won't let me."

"He can't stop you. He has no power over you now."

After a long silence she said: "Maybe we should have stayed in Caracas."

"No. We did the right thing."

"Are you sure?"

"Yes." He kissed her forehead tenderly.

At that moment her father came into the kitchen, saying: "I wondered where you were."

"We're cleaning up," Jim said.

"You don't look like you're cleaning up."

"We were just taking a short break," Jim said lightly.

"I don't like the way you talked to me," her father said to Renata, "especially in front of Jim's parents."

"They didn't mind," Jim said. "You should hear us at the dinner table."

"Well, I hope you show more respect for your father."

"She was showing respect for you. She just wasn't agreeing with you. There's a big difference."

"There is, uh? Since when do you know anything about it?"

"I know enough," he said, repeating what Renata had said to him earlier.

"You know nothing. You've never been in a war."

Jim had been excused from the draft because of an arrhythmic condition in his heart, which he had only learned about during the medical examination. Marchi knew this, so Jim didn't need to explain why he hadn't done military service. He said nothing, hoping Marchi would go away.

"And you, young lady. You lied to me."

"What do you mean?" Renata said, tensing.

Jim continued to hold her, trying to shield her from her father.

"I mean about the pill," her father said. "You didn't go off it. You're still on it."

"No, I'm not. Why do you say that?"

"Because it's a year, and you haven't gotten pregnant."

"Well, that's by chance," she insisted. "I'm not doing anything to avoid getting pregnant. Not that it's any of your business."

"Don't talk to me that way," her father warned her.

"I'll talk to you any way I want," Renata cried, untangling herself from Jim's arms. "You have no right to interfere with my life."

"I do have a right. I'm your father."

"You don't own me."

"You don't," Jim said, supporting her.

"You think *you* own her?" Marchi said to him scornfully.

"No one owns her."

"I can't take any more of him," Renata said, heading for the door.

"Where are you going?" her father demanded.

"To get a breath of fresh air."

She left the kitchen, leaving them in a sudden vacuum.

"You have a problem," Jim said.

"I have a problem?" Marchi said with indignation. "Who do you think you're talking to?"

"I'm talking to a man who won't let his daughter have her own life."

"Her own life?" Marchi said as if this was an alien concept. "What kind of life could she have without me?"

"A full life, a happy life."

"You're telling me I make my daughter unhappy?"

"You make her feel like shit," Jim said.

"I don't believe you. What the hell do you know about her?"

"Not a lot, but more than you do."

Marchi scowled, then said: "Well, the whole problem is, she should have been a boy. She should have been my son, not my daughter."

"That's *your* problem, not hers."

"But she could at least try to be a good daughter."

"She is a good daughter. She loves you, she came home from Caracas, and she gave you two grandchildren. What more do you want?"

"I want a grandson," Marchi said stubbornly.

"Well, if you're patient she might give you one."

"She won't if she's taking the pill."

"She's not taking it. She went off it more than a year ago."

"Then she wasn't lying?" Marchi said after a silence.

"She never lies. If you knew your daughter, you would know that."

"Oh, God," Marchi said, striking his forehead as if he had done something stupid. "Where is she?"

"She's probably outside. She was going to get a breath of fresh air."

They left the kitchen and went to look for her.

Outside, standing on the portico, they noticed that Jim's car was missing.

"She must have gone for a drive," Jim said, trying not to be alarmed. In her state of mind she would have wanted to drive as far away from her father as possible.

"Where could she have gone?" Marchi asked, visibly upset.

"She could have gone out to the river." She liked the river. They had driven out there many times, parking the car on the bluff that overlooked it. When they were dating it was their favorite place to make out.

"Well, we should go after her."

He imagined how Renata would feel if she looked into her rearview mirror and saw her father coming after her. "No. We shouldn't. We should let her alone, we should give her space."

"Damn women," Marchi muttered.

They went inside and waited for her to come back.

An hour later, when she hadn't come back, Marchi wanted to call the police. Jim objected, imagining how Renata would feel if she was pulled over by a trooper sent by her father to bring her home.

A half hour later a police officer appeared at the door with a look on his face that immediately told them he had bad news. Without coming into the house he informed them that Renata had been found dead in her car, which had skidded off the road on the River Boulevard and smashed into a tree.

Marchi grabbed the police officer by the lapels of his leather jacket, yelling: "You're a goddam liar!"

The police officer, who must have been used to the reactions of people to whom he had to deliver such news, gently removed Marchi's hands from his jacket and said: "I'm sorry, but it's true."

Jim didn't want to believe the news any more than Marchi did, but he knew the police officer wouldn't have made it up. His body reverberated with interior cries of anguish, which finally came out: "Oh, no. Oh, no."

"Liar!" Marchi roared.

"Where is she?" Jim finally asked.

"We have her at the morgue. Someone will have to identify her."

"I will," Jim said, feeling sick.

"I'm going with you," Marchi said as if he wanted to make sure that this wasn't an elaborate ruse to get Renata away from him.

When he saw the body Marchi believed it. He crumbled to his knees and banged his head repeatedly against the table on which Renata lay, wailing: "I'm sorry, I'm sorry, I'm sorry, I'm sorry."

Jim tried to ignore him as he leaned over and kissed the cold lips of the woman he would always love.

Carla was six, and Gina was four. They both believed their mother was in heaven watching over them, but they didn't understand why she had left them, and they missed her every minute of every day. At night they came into his bed and snuggled against him, one on each side, seeking comfort and security.

Jim took a month off work to be with them. Marchi would have let him take a year off, but sooner or later he would have to resume working, and then who would take care of the girls?

Marchi offered to let them stay in his house during the day, but that was the last place Jim wanted them. He was afraid that Marchi would do to them what he had done to Renata, not having learned a lesson from what had happened to her. So he declined Marchi's offers to help with the girls.

His mother, who had been assisted by a series of young women in raising her own children, suggested that he get an au pair girl to help him. She did the research for him, and within a few months they had a girl from Argentina living with them. She was a pretty, warm-hearted girl who loved children and had experience taking care of her younger brothers and sisters. She was also Italian, which pleased Marchi because he could depend on her to instill the right values in his granddaughters.

Her name was Leonora, and she was just twenty but she was a fully mature young woman, and even in his state of mourning Jim was conscious of her as a female. Leonora was completely proper and would never have welcomed an advance from him, while he would never have made an advance, so they were completely safe with each other.

The girls adored her. Of course there was no way she could ever replace their mother, but she helped them through a difficult period of their lives, and for this Jim would always be grateful to her.

It took Marchi almost a year to come out of the depths he had fallen into when they lost Renata. By then he had elevated Jim to a higher level in his business, and in fact Jim had virtually been running the business during Marchi's mental absence. Marchi was treating him almost as an equal, so it seemed natural when Marchi wanted to share with him the things in life you could buy with money.

One of those things was going to New York, where Marchi went several times a year. He would spend three or four days there, always staying in the same hotel, where they knew him, and always eating in the best restaurants. The other thing he did, as Jim later found out, was buy himself a woman for one night—not a common prostitute but a high-class woman who did this sort of thing for a lark. So on the last night of their first trip to New York, Jim was on his own.

Not knowing what to do with himself, he went to the hotel bar, where he met a young woman with curly black hair and striking blue eyes. She made the first move by asking if the place at the bar next to him was taken.

After ordering a mixed drink whose name he didn't recognize, she introduced herself, saying: "Hi. I'm Eileen."

"I'm Jim," he said, noticing that she had a Midwestern accent. "Are you here on business?"

"Oh, ya. But I'm also here for a good time."

"Me too. Where are you from?"

"Des Moines," she said as if it was the most boring place in the world.

"What do you do?"

"I'm a claims adjuster."

"That sounds interesting."

"It's not," she said definitely. "What do you do?"

He paused, not wanting to admit he worked for his father-in-

105

law's construction company. Realizing that in this situation he could be anyone he wanted, he said: "I work for the government."

"The government? What area?"

"International," he said, implying that he worked for the CIA. To make sure she understood, he added: "Covert operations."

She perked up. "Really?"

"I'm involved in plots to overthrow dictators."

"Wow. So you're out of the country most of the time?"

"Yes. I could be working in Buenos Aires, Nairobi, Manila, Warsaw— It depends on my assignment."

"Now, that sounds interesting," she said, moving closer to him. "Can you tell me what you're doing in New York?"

"I really can't," he said apologetically. "All I can tell you is that I'm involved in a plot to overthrow a dictator in Latin America."

"Can you tell me which country?"

"No. I'm sorry. You'll read about it in the papers."

"So how do you overthrow a dictator?"

"I organize people who want to get rid of him, people who have the opportunity and the means."

"Do you give them the plot?"

"I work with them to develop it. I want them to succeed. If they try and fail, they'll be tortured and killed."

"What if *you* get caught?" she asked, her eyes dilating with excitement.

"The same thing will happen to me."

"Have you ever come close to being caught?"

He nodded. "Yes. More than once. The last time was in Cuba. I was involved in a plot to kill Castro."

"What happened?"

"The secret police infiltrated our group and found out what we were doing."

"How did you escape?"

"In a small boat. Two of us rowed to Jamaica."

"Wow." She finished her drink and ordered another. "I wish I could do things like that. Men have all the fun."

He took her to dinner at La Grenouille, where Marchi had taken him the night before. She hadn't ever been there, and she was impressed not only by the luxury of the restaurant but also by the fact that the waiter remembered him.

Over dinner he regaled her with more stories about his exploits, and by the time they returned to the hotel he didn't have to ask her if she wanted to come to his room. It was taken for granted.

The way she gave herself to him without reservation filled an emptiness inside of him and validated his identity as someone other than Jim Wyatt, assistant to Joe Marchi. As for her, in the physical union she was evidently trying to come as close as possible to a life that wasn't open to her. In her euphoric cries of release she sounded as if she had cut the bonds that tied her to the earth and was rising into the endless sky, leaving the claims adjuster from Des Moines far below her.

Zoraya actually knocked on the door before unlocking it. Maybe she felt that a state senator deserved more respect than a CIA agent.

He had drafted a speech for the next tape, but he had some questions.

"Are you ready?" she asked, coming into the room.

"Almost. Have you got a minute?"

"Yes. Of course." She sat down in the chair on the other side of the table.

"Can you tell me more about Abdullah?"

She frowned suspiciously. "What do you want to know about him?"

"I want to know why you're willing to risk your lives for him."

"I told you. He's a holy man."

"What does he do?"

"He's an imam at a mosque in New Jersey."

"Is that how you met him?"

"We go to his mosque."

"What makes him holy?"

"The same things that made Jesus holy."

He knew that Islam revered Jesus as a prophet, though not as the Son of God. "Could you be more specific?"

"He preaches that we should love God and love our fellow human beings, and he sets an example with his own life."

"What does he say about *jihad?*"

"There's a misunderstanding about the meaning of *jihad*. You think it means holy war, but that's not what it means. It means an internal struggle for the soul."

"It also means an external struggle."

"How do you know?"

"I read the Quran." In Arabic, he could have added, but he didn't want to show that card. "It was assigned in one of my courses at college."

"Well, the external struggle—the holy war—can only be against oppression and persecution."

"You mean a defensive war."

"That's right. We're not supposed to use violence unless we've been attacked."

"We believe that too, though we don't always practice it."

"We don't either," she admitted. "It's not easy to practice a religion."

"I assume you're religious."

"Yes, I am," she said seriously. "A friend of mine in college, an Irish girl, said that if I had been Catholic I probably would have become a nun."

"Well, I'm glad you didn't become a nun."

"Why? If I had, you wouldn't be in this situation."

"That's true. But I wouldn't have known you."

She lowered her eyes, not replying.

"What did they convict Abdullah of doing?"

"I told you. They convicted him of inciting violence."

"Is there any truth in that?"

"None at all," she assured him. "He preaches internal *jihad*, and he's against all forms of violence."

"Even in self-defense?"

"Even then. In that respect," she added, "he's what you call heretical."

"You mean he doesn't completely accept the established doctrine?"

"That's what I meant about his being like Jesus."

"How do you know what Jesus was like?"

"I read the Bible. It was assigned in one of my courses."

"So it's a good thing we both went to college," he said, smiling. "At least we each have some idea of the other's religion."

"But it doesn't seem to help."

"It helps us understand each other."

"Maybe it does. But what does it have to do with the tape?"

"Before I say what I plan to say, I need to know that Abdullah was innocent and wrongfully convicted. I need your assurance that he never said anything in favor of violence, that he never preached a holy war."

"I swear by Allah," she said solemnly, "that Abdullah never did those things."

"That's good enough for me. Now, what about you?"

"What about me?"

"Do you believe in a holy war?"

"No. I don't. But we were attacked, so we have to fight back."

"How were you attacked?"

"They arrested our religious leader and sent him to prison. That's how."

"Okay. I understand. So if that hadn't happened, you wouldn't be involved in kidnapping people."

"Of course I wouldn't."

"What would you be doing?"

"I don't know." She stared longingly into the distance as if she could imagine the possibilities. Then, snapping out of it, she said: "We have a tape to make. You better finish writing your speech."

He reviewed his speech and made some changes. "Okay. I'm ready."

They left his room and walked down the hall to what he now called the production room. Ramón and Manuel were waiting for them.

"What took you so long?" Ramón asked his sister in Arabic.

"We were working on his speech," she said.

"Are you ready?"

"I'm ready." He sat down in front of the camera and joked: "If we want to do this professionally we should have a makeup person."

"We want you to look pale and haggard," Zoraya said.

"You have a point," he agreed. He set the piece of paper on the table and faced the camera. "Any time."

Manuel, who had gotten up, turned on the light and the camera.

"Hi," Jim said, addressing his constituents. "This is Jim Wyatt, your state senator. As you all know, I'm being held hostage. The people who are holding me have asked our government to release their religious leader, Abdullah ibn Hasim al-Qahtani, who was wrongfully convicted of inciting violence. They have assured me that this holy man never said a word in favor of violence. They say he preaches the gospel of peace, just as your priests, ministers, and rabbis do. And I believe them. They're serious young people, religious people, who have been driven to this extreme by injustice in our society. I think it's significant that they call themselves the Islamic Human Rights Movement. All they want is fair treatment of Muslims. You know the positions I've always taken on human rights—for African-Americans, women, the elderly, and other groups that haven't been treated fairly. Well, here's another group that's not being treated fairly. So I'm asking you to call your elected representatives and tell them to use their influence to get this man released from prison. You have the power to get him released, you have the power to change the world."

"That was good," Zoraya said admiringly.

"It was all right," Ramón said. "Let's see if it works."

This kind of speech had worked for him before. It had worked because he always meant what he said, and in that respect this situation wasn't any different. After his conversation with Zoraya he believed in their cause, and he was willing to fight for it. But in one respect this situation *was* different. It wasn't an election, which he knew how to win. It was a contest for his life.

SIX

THAT WINTER HE went to Spain with Marchi, who fell in love with the country, having rejected Italy a long time ago because it had been on the wrong side of the war. He didn't know which side Spain had been on during the war, so since he had nothing against the country he was open to its charms.

They went to Madrid, where they rented a car, and they drove to Córdoba, Sevilla, Granada, and finally Málaga. There they saw a building being constructed right across the road from the beach, and Marchi of course had to see if they were doing a good job. Wherever they went, while Jim wanted to see old buildings in historic quarters, Marchi wanted to see new construction.

Marchi liked the job they were doing, so much so that he decided to buy four condominium units in the building—one for himself, one for Angela and Bianca, one for Jim, and one for good measure. It was agreed that Jim would pay for his unit out of his salary over twenty years.

When he got home Stephen was visiting their parents. Stephen had completed his military service and was planning to interview with some international banks in New York, hoping to get an overseas assignment. Elizabeth was still in Italy, living with a sculptor whose gender she avoided revealing in letters to her parents, though her mother had correctly guessed that it was a man. Over drinks in a bar on Selby Avenue the two brothers tried to figure out why all three children in their family wanted to live in foreign countries, wondering if they were afflicted by a genetic condition. But they were unable to come up with a satisfactory explanation.

The next day Jim got a phone call from Bianca, who had finished college at St. Catherine and was teaching music at the elementary level at Visitation, one of the increasing number of lay

111

teachers. At a local conference Bianca had met a woman who taught music at a public school and was performing that weekend as a folk singer at a bar near the university. Bianca, who was still living at home, had to report to her father what she did in the evening, and her father disapproved of her going to bars for whatever reason. So Bianca wanted to know if Jim and Stephen would accompany her and Angela to the bar on Saturday. He checked with Stephen, who was available, so the two brothers took the two sisters to hear the folk singer after assuring Marchi that his daughters would be well chaperoned.

The singer, whose name was Inga Torvald, was the warm-up act for a successful male singer who the girls said was being promoted as the next Bob Dylan, so few of the people in the bar were there to hear Inga, but they quieted down and showed respect after she started singing. She looked like she was in her early twenties, about the same age as Bianca, and she had a high lovely voice in the style of Joan Baez. She accompanied herself on the guitar, which she played very well. She had long straight blond hair and wide eyes, which glistened in the spotlights.

Her first song was about lost love, and it moved the audience to a point where no one moved, no one spoke, no one even lifted a glass. When she finished the song they exploded in applause.

The young woman sincerely thanked them, speaking into the microphone with a soft voice.

"That was a nice song," Jim said to Bianca.

"She wrote it," Bianca said. "She writes all her songs."

"I really like her," Angela said.

"She sings beautifully," Stephen said.

Jim was smitten by the young woman. He could have listened to her all night, and he was disappointed when she left to make way for the male singer.

He lay awake that night thinking about her. He realized that he couldn't tell what she was like from the way she sang because she was performing, but he believed that the feelings she had conveyed in her music were genuine.

The next day he wanted to call her, but there were several Torvalds in the phone book. So he called Bianca and found out the school where Inga taught. When he called the school on Monday they wouldn't give him any information about her, but they agreed to take a message, and late that afternoon she returned his call.

"Do I know you?" she asked warily.

"No," he said. "I heard you sing on Saturday, and I wanted to tell you how much I enjoyed it."

"Thank you," she said as if she didn't get compliments very often.

"Will you be performing again this weekend?"

"No, that was it. I'm not a regular there."

"Where else can I hear you sing?"

"Well— I don't have anything else booked."

"So are you free to have dinner with me?"

"I don't think so. I don't know you."

"We could meet for a drink."

"Where?" she asked.

"How about Frost's on Selby Avenue?"

"I've heard of it, but I've never been there. I don't go to bars except to perform."

"Where do you go?"

"I don't go anywhere. I stay at home and practice."

"Then why don't you let me come to your house and hear you sing?"

There was a pause. "You really want to hear me sing?"

"I really do."

Another pause. "Well, maybe I could meet you after school."

"What time are you done there?"

"Around three."

"We're talking about tomorrow, right?"

"I thought we were."

"Okay." He could leave his office early without any problem. "I'll meet you at the main entrance."

"Fine," she said dubiously.

It was cold waiting outside the entrance of the school, and as he watched the children run, skip, and hop by, escaping to freedom, he wondered what he was doing there.

When she finally emerged he almost didn't recognize her because her hair was braided and coiled at the back of her head while her eyes were shielded by heavy horn-rimmed glasses. It was as if she had put on a disguise so he wouldn't recognize her, just to teach him a lesson.

But when he called her name she smiled the way she had on Saturday when the people applauded.

"I'm Jim," he said, extending his gloveless hand.

She shook it politely without removing the mitten from her own hand. Peering through the glasses, she examined him. "I think I remember you. Weren't you with two girls and another guy?"

"Yeah," he said, pleased.

"It's hard to see with those spotlights," she said. "I'm not used to them. I don't perform very often."

"You should be performing all the time."

"Thank you," she said modestly.

"Where do you live?"

"On River Boulevard."

That was at least two miles away. "How do you usually get home?"

"By bus," she said.

"That must take a while."

"I'm in no hurry to get home."

"You don't have a car?"

"I don't drive."

"Why not?"

"My father believes that women shouldn't drive."

"Where's he from?"

"Sweden."

That didn't explain it. As far as he knew, women were very liberated in Sweden. "Well, I can give you a ride home."

"If you do, then you'll know my address."

"So? Are you afraid of me?"

114

"I should be. You're a strange man."

"I'm not strange. I'm pretty normal," he assured her.

"I meant that I don't know you."

"How are you going to get to know me unless you trust me?"

"Maybe I don't want to get to know you."

"That's your choice."

They were at an impasse.

Breaking it, she said: "I think I do want to get to know you. I mean, you look like a nice man. How old are you?"

"I'm thirty," he said.

"That's not too old. I'm twenty-three."

"So can I give you a ride?"

"Well, this is exactly what I've been told all my life not to do—get into a car with a strange man." She smiled as if she had suddenly decided to ignore these warnings. "Okay. Why not?"

On the way he learned that she was wearing glasses today because her eyes were bothering her. It was probably her brother's latest cat. She normally wore contact lenses, as she had for her performance. Without the lenses or the glasses she was as blind as a bat. She couldn't even see the eye chart.

When they got to her house, a mansion overlooking the Mississippi, she showed him the way to the basement while she went upstairs to freshen up. The basement was finished, with all kinds of specialized rooms. He easily found the music room, where there was a Steinway grand piano, a cello, a violin, and a guitar. He wondered if she played all these instruments.

She joined him after about ten minutes, having removed the glasses and unbound her hair. She now looked the way he remembered her, and without the spotlights on her face she was even more beautiful, with clean features, pure blue eyes, and perfect skin. Her beauty was enhanced by the vulnerability that he had sensed during her performance and that he could feel more strongly now, being closer to her. Then it had been like a faint perfume, and now it was like a rich vapor

"I feel better now," she said, picking up her guitar.

"You look better," he said lightly.

"You don't like the glasses and the braids?"

"I don't mind them. I still recognized you with them."

"You almost didn't."

"How do you know?"

"I could tell." She sat down and started tuning the guitar. "My father likes me better with the glasses and the braids."

"I wonder why."

"I'll tell you why. He doesn't want men to be attracted to me."

"You mean he wants to keep you all to himself?"

She nodded seriously.

It crossed his mind that there might be something sick going on between her and her father, but she looked so innocent that he couldn't believe it.

"What would you like to hear me play?"

"Anything," he said.

"Well, this is something I just wrote." She strummed a few chords and then began to sing. Her high, quavering voice was as lovely as he remembered. The song had a haunting melody as well as truthful lyrics. It swept him away into a realm of undefiled emotion, where he could imagine all being forgiven.

He stayed there for more than two hours, and she kept playing as if he was the ideal audience. She was about to start another song when they heard someone tromping down the stairs into the basement.

"That's my father," she said, alarmed.

He felt as if she expected him to hide, but even if he had gone along with this ridiculous idea it would have been too late.

Her father, a giant with cropped blond hair and cold blue eyes, lumbered into the music room and seeing him asked: "Who is this man?"

He had an accent that sounded Swedish.

"He heard my performance on Saturday," she mumbled, looking down, "and he wanted to hear me play some more."

"So you brought him home with you?"

"I thought it would be a safe place."

"And you've been here alone with him?"

"I've been playing songs, and he's been listening."

Jim got up and introduced himself, extending his hand.

Her father refused to take it. "I don't want to meet you. I want you out of here."

"You're not being very hospitable," Jim said, beginning to get angry.

"I don't have to be hospitable to people who come to my house uninvited."

"Daddy, please," she said, embarrassed.

"Did you look at his hand? Can't you see he's wearing a ring? Don't you understand that he's cheating on his wife?"

"I'm not cheating on my wife," Jim said indignantly. "My wife is dead."

"A likely story. He'd tell you anything to get into your pants."

Furious, he clenched his hands into fists and said: "If you weren't her father, I'd beat the shit out of you for saying that."

"Forget I'm her father. Go ahead."

"Don't," Inga begged him. "Please don't. Just leave."

He looked at her, knowing that if he did anything to her father it would only make things worse for her, so he said: "Okay. I enjoyed the music. I think you have a lot of talent, and I hope you go far."

"Thank you," she said with the same modesty as before. There were tears in her eyes, but there was also a faint light.

Zoraya brought him dinner, tagine with lamb, and instead of standing while he tried it she sat down and waited for his comments.

"This is really good," he said after taking a bite.

"Thank you," she said as if she appreciated the compliment.

"Have you already eaten?"

"Oh, yes. So don't worry about eating in front of me."

"Okay," he said, taking another bite. He sensed that she wanted to talk with him.

"You know," she said, "when you made that speech for the tape you sounded like you really meant it."

"I did mean it."

"Then you're on our side."

"I'm on your side as far as wanting our government to release Abdullah."

"Well, that's all we want. We don't want revenge."

"A lot of people on both sides do."

"I know. They kill one of our people, so we kill two of their people, and they kill four of our people, and so on without end."

"God is merciful and forgiving," he quoted from the Quran.

"You *have* read it," she said, impressed.

"From what I remember," he said, "that statement occurs more often than any other. God is merciful and forgiving."

"Your God also forgives your sins."

"We have no fundamental differences."

"So we're not really fighting about religion."

"We're fighting about the same thing that kids fight about. You have a toy that I don't have, I take it or break it, you take or break one of my toys, I hit you, you hit me back, and we end up with black eyes and bloody noses."

She smiled sympathetically. "You sound like you have experience with children."

"I have seven of them," he told her, cutting a piece of lamb on his plate. "Four boys and three girls. They're all grown up except the youngest boy."

"Tell me about the girls," she said.

"Carla is the oldest. She's thirty-two. She lives in Boston, and she's a lawyer. She was married, but she got divorced a year ago. She caught her husband cheating on her. She has a daughter who just turned four."

"So you're a grandfather?"

"Yes," he said, still not used to the idea.

"You don't look like a grandfather."

"Thank you," he said. "Gina is the next one. She's thirty. She lives in St. Paul, and she's what we call a stay-at-home mom. She has three children, two boys and one girl. Her husband runs a construction company that was started by her grandfather, who lived to see her produce two great-grandsons for him."

"It sounds like that was important to him."

"It was," he said. "He never forgave his wife for not having a boy, and he never forgave his daughters for not having a boy."

She looked puzzled. "You said you have four boys."

"They're from later wives," he explained. "My first wife, his daughter, was the mother of Carla and Gina."

"What happened to her?"

"She died in a car accident."

"I'm sorry," she said compassionately.

He still couldn't think about what had happened without feeling a stab of remorse. "She drove off in a car after having an argument with her father. It was winter, and the streets were icy. She lost control going around a corner."

"What was the argument about?"

"The fact that she hadn't produced a grandson."

Zoraya frowned. "I don't understand why fathers are so destructive to their daughters. Is it because they wanted us to be boys?"

"I can't tell you. I wasn't like that. I loved having daughters."

"Maybe because you love women."

"Maybe. I mean, I love my sons. But I didn't need to have one. I would have been happy with my two daughters."

"So how did your wife deal with her father?"

"She tried to get away from him."

"I understand. I tried to get away from my father. I came here and got a degree, but I still didn't get away from him."

"Even though he's dead?"

"Yes, even though he's dead."

"Well, you'll never get away from him completely," he told her, "but you should be able to rise above whatever he did to you and find yourself."

"I'm trying to find myself through commitment to a cause."

"You are? What cause?"

"Justice," she said without hesitation.

"What about mercy? God is merciful and forgiving."

"God is strong. He's in a position to be merciful."

"So are you. You just have to realize it."

He tried to forget about Inga, but he kept remembering that faint light in her eyes behind the tears, and he was distressed by the thought of its being snuffed out, so a few weeks later he went to the school and waited for her at the entrance.

Her hair was braided, but she wasn't wearing glasses, and when she saw him the light turned up to its full intensity—it flooded her face and rolled toward him in a welcoming smile.

"I thought I'd never see you again," she said candidly.

"I'm sorry it took me so long," he said.

"I guess you don't want to go to my house."

"I'd rather have a coffee somewhere. There's a place on Grand Avenue."

"That sounds fine."

She got into his car as if it was something she did every day.

As they drove toward Grand she said: "Believe it or not, my father apologized for his behavior."

"He did?"

"Ya. I think he felt bad about saying you were cheating on your wife when he found out she was really dead."

"Well, I shouldn't have gotten so angry."

"I'm glad you did. I think he respects you for standing up to him."

"Then maybe we didn't get off to such a bad start after all."

The coffee shop was in an area of Grand where a number of trendy shops had sprung up within the past few years. The coffee was good, and the ambience was conducive to conversation.

She had a cappuccino, and he had a double espresso.

"Where did you study music?" he asked as they sipped their coffee.

"I had private lessons. I also took music courses at college."

"Where did you go to college?"

"Gustavus Adolphus."

He knew that it was a highly regarded Lutheran college in St. Peter, Minnesota, but he didn't know anyone who had gone there. "Did you major in music?"

"Oh, ya. But the program was oriented toward teaching, not performing."

"Do you play other instruments?" he asked, remembering what he had seen in the music room.

"I play the violin. I can also play the piano."

He wondered who played the cello, but he didn't want to go off on a tangent. "Did you want to be a teacher?"

"No. I wanted to be a performer."

"And your father doesn't want you to pursue that career."

"No. He doesn't," she said with a sigh.

"Well, it's a tough life. I know a concert pianist who travels all the time. One night in Cleveland, another night in Chicago, and another night in Dallas."

"Is he happy?"

"Yeah. He's doing what he loves."

"So I wouldn't mind traveling all the time."

"How does your mother feel about it?"

"She wouldn't stop me."

"Then why do you let your father stop you?"

"I don't know," she said dolefully.

"You went away to college. You didn't have to come home after you graduated."

"I almost didn't. I had a friend who went to New York, where she got a great job in advertising. She loves it there."

"Have you ever been to New York?"

"No. My friend keeps asking me to come and visit."

After a long pause he said: "Tell me more about your father. I noticed he has an accent."

"He was born in Stockholm, and he came here when he was eighteen to study engineering at the university. He met my mother, so he decided to stay here. When the war came along he joined the army. He was in the corps of engineers, and when he got out he had an idea to start a business."

"What does he do?"

"He makes components that have a high level of tolerance. I'm not sure what that means, but that's how he explains it."

"Do you have any brothers and sisters?"

"I have a younger sister and a younger brother. My sister plays the cello, and my brother plays the clarinet."

"It sounds like music runs in your family."

"My mother played first violin in the Minneapolis Symphony Orchestra."

"She must have been good."

"She was. She gave up her career to raise a family."

"Does she still play?"

"She plays with friends."

"What do they play?"

"String quartets. They play on Friday evenings, and when the other violinist can't make it, I play with them."

"So you were trained on the violin."

She nodded. "Ya. But I prefer the guitar now."

"Well, it doesn't make sense that your parents would train you as a musician and not want you to perform."

"My mother didn't want to push her children to pursue a career that she gave up. And my father believed that music was part of a good education. So training us to play musical instruments wasn't supposed to lead to careers."

"Do you still want to be a performer?"

"Ya," she said. "At least I want to try it."

He called his friend the concert pianist, who gave him the name and phone number of his agent, who gave him the name of an agent who handled the kind of music that Inga played, and this agent offered to represent Inga, subject to an audition. Jim gave her the information so she could talk directly with the agent.

The audition went well, and over the next six months Inga had regular gigs at places in the Twin Cities. He attended almost all of her performances, missing them only when some event involving his children took priority.

She received favorable reviews from the local newspapers, which her agent said would help her get booked in other cities.

Meanwhile, he had met her mother and started over with her father. He took them to see one of her performances, which they both enjoyed, though her father did comment that this wasn't the kind of music she had been trained to play. No doubt he would have been happier to hear her playing Lutheran hymns on a church organ, properly clad in a black robe.

He introduced Inga to his children, and they both liked her. Carla, a step ahead of him, asked him if he was going to marry her. Put on the spot, he asked Carla how she would feel if he did marry Inga, and Carla replied that she didn't know Inga well enough to answer that question. So over the next several months he gave Carla and Gina plenty of opportunities to get to know Inga better. Observing her with them, he could see how well she got along with them, and he imagined the stability that she would offer them, unlike the au pair girls who changed every year.

By the time he introduced her to his parents he had already decided to ask Inga to marry him, and since he expected a positive response he wanted to have his parents on board. Remembering his mother's reservations about Renata being Italian and Catholic, he wasn't surprised when his mother had the same kind of reservations about Inga being Swedish and Lutheran.

"She's very sweet," his mother told him, "but we don't know anything about her family. We don't even know any Lutherans."

"How could you live in Minnesota all your life and not know any Lutherans?"

"We don't move in the same circle."

"Have you ever thought of widening your circle?"

"Why should we? We know more people than we could possibly keep up with."

"Okay," he said, granting her point. "But you like her, don't you?"

"Of course I like her. She's a lovely girl. And from what I hear, your children both like her."

"They told you?"

"Yes. They tell me everything."

"So you wouldn't have a problem if I married her?"

"No. I wouldn't have a problem. But I wish she was a girl from a family we know."

"If I was ever going to fall in love with a girl from a family you know, I would have by now."

"I understand," his mother said.

Last but not least, he introduced Inga to Joe Marchi, who had a strong interest in any woman who might become the stepmother of his granddaughters. Marchi took them out to dinner at a new French restaurant in Minneapolis that had received great reviews, and things went well. He liked Inga, and his only reservation—which he expressed to Jim the next day at the office—was that she was Lutheran, so she wouldn't be committed to raising his granddaughters as Catholics. Jim assured Marchi that he had discussed this issue with Inga, and it wouldn't be a problem.

They were married in early June at a Lutheran church near Macalester College where Inga's father, Halvar, was an important member of the congregation, having given a lot of money to the church for building and maintenance. When the time came for the father of the bride to hand his daughter over to the groom after escorting her up the aisle, Jim thought he detected some hesitation on the part of Halvar, though he could have just imagined it, and from then on everything went according to ritual. Afterward his mother, applying her scale for evaluating events, declared that the wedding had been perfect, and even Marchi was pleasantly surprised to discover that the Lutheran service had many elements in common with the Catholic service. In fact, the only difference he commented on was that unlike the pews in his church the pews in the Lutheran church had cushions.

For their honeymoon they went to Spain, leaving Carla and Gina for the first week with the Marchis and for the second week with his parents. The girls, who had enjoyed participating in the wedding, were very excited about staying with their grandparents, who always spoiled them, though Gina cried when Jim kissed her goodbye, evidently afraid that he might not return, remembering what had happened to her mother. Jim told her not to worry, he would be back in two weeks, and they would pass quickly because she would be having such a good time with her grandparents.

They flew to New York, where they connected with an overnight flight to Madrid. By the time they got to their hotel it was almost noon, and they were exhausted. They collapsed in the bed and slept until the early evening. They went out and walked to the Plaza Santa Ana area, where he and Marchi on previous trips had found some good *tapas* bars. They hopped from one bar to another, drinking wine and eating olives, cheese, shrimp, mussels, and eggplant. Then they returned to the hotel and made love for the first time. For Inga it was the first time ever, and in the days that followed it was as if she wanted to make up for lost time. They adopted the Spanish custom of taking a *siesta* in the early afternoon, except that they didn't sleep or rest until several hours after they had jumped into bed, and when they awoke in the early evening they were both famished. So they went out in search of *tapas*, roaming the city from Plaza Santa Ana to Plaza Mayor to Plaza de la Puerta de Moros.

One night, as they were walking back to their hotel they found a flamenco place on Mesonero Romanos just off Gran Vía. The first show of the evening was about to begin, and Inga had never been exposed to flamenco, so he took her into the place and they watched the show. By the time it was over Inga had fallen in love with flamenco, and they went to a show every night for the rest of their week in Madrid. Later, if someone other than her father had asked her what she liked best about Spain she probably would have said sex and flamenco.

At the end of the week they rented a car and drove to Córdoba, Sevilla, and Granada, where they stayed in a hotel inside the walls of the Alhambra. After dinner they had the Alhambra to themselves without a mob of tourists, and they strolled in the moonlight among the gardens, the pools, and the fountains. Aroused, they made love in a dark corner under a tree, gambling that no one would wander by, and no one did. If anyone had been out there listening, their cries of pleasure would have been masked by the sound of water plashing in the pools and fountains.

They spent the last four days of the trip at his condominium in Málaga, where they went to the beach. Inga had brought a conservative one-piece bathing suit, which after seeing the other women she replaced with a bikini she bought in a store. She looked good in a bikini, better than all the other women, and it inevitably made Jim suggest that they go back to the apartment for a *siesta*.

At such times she would smile at him, warmly welcoming the suggestion.

Meanwhile, along the way from Madrid they had gone to flamenco shows, and when they returned to Madrid for their last night they went to a shop they had seen on Mesonero Romanos, across from the flamenco place, and he bought Inga a dress like the ones the dancers wore as well as the accessories, including three pairs of castanets. At a music shop he bought her a guitar and several records.

Being a trained musician, Inga didn't take long to learn how to play flamenco. One evening about three weeks after they returned from Spain she gave a concert in their living room, accompanied by Carla and Gina on the castanets.

"I'll have to learn to dance," he told them, "so we can go on the road as a family doing a flamenco show."

"That would be fun," Gina said.

"Can you imagine Dad as a flamenco dancer?" Carla said, smiling.

"I have Spanish blood," he reminded his daughter.

"We'll need a singer," Inga pointed out.

"We could ask Grampa," Gina suggested, meaning Marchi.

They all laughed hysterically.

A few weeks later Inga confirmed that she was pregnant. She seemed happy about this development, but Jim wondered how she felt about her career being interrupted just as it was getting started.

"It's okay," she assured him. "I can always pick up where I left off, and anyway, I want to play a different kind of music."

"You mean flamenco?"

"Why not?"

"Well, you need a group to play flamenco."

"I could do solos."

"Yeah. I guess. But people expect dancers and a singer—a whole show."

"Then you'll have to learn how to dance flamenco."

"Okay. And your father will have to learn how to sing it."

She laughed even harder than she had at the idea of Marchi singing flamenco. "Can you imagine? Deep song with a Swedish accent."

When Zoraya brought his breakfast the next morning there hadn't been any response to their second tape, but an hour later she returned and led him downstairs to what he now called the screening room.

Ramón and Manuel were waiting for them, watching the news, which showed a scene at a river where the bodies of Bosniak men had been found. They had evidently been executed by the Serbian troops. With their hands tied behind their backs, they had been mown down by automatic weapons. The attempt to hide them in a mass grave had been interrupted by the arrival of Bosniak troops.

"How can your government stand by and do nothing?" Ramón asked.

"I don't know," Jim said. "They can see what's happening. We can all see it on television."

"What we're seeing," Zoraya said grimly, "is only a small part of it. Thousands of people are being killed where the cameras aren't recording it. Thousands of women are being raped. Thousands of children are being mutilated. We won't know all of it for a long time, if ever."

They saw a scene of a village where virtually all the houses had been destroyed. There were bodies in the streets, apparently unnoticed by everyone except the person behind the camera. They must have been a common sight.

"All right," Zoraya said when the commercial interrupted. "Let's watch the tape."

Manuel started the video player.

"We have the latest developments on the kidnapping of Senator Wyatt," the anchorman said ponderously. "Yesterday some TV stations in Minnesota received a tape in which Senator Wyatt talked about a Muslim religious leader who's serving a ten-year prison sentence for inciting violence. He said he believes that this man was wrongfully convicted. He referred to positions he has taken for human rights on behalf of various minorities who had not been treated fairly, and he said that Muslims are not being treated fairly. He appealed to his constituents to call their elected representatives and tell them to use their influence to get this man released from prison."

They cut to the last few sentences of Jim's appeal.

"Based on the information we have," the anchorman said, "we estimate that more than a hundred thousand people have called their representatives and told them to get the prisoner released."

They showed a congressman from Minnesota, a good friend of Jim's, who said his phone lines were jammed with calls.

"Since the government has no way to respond to Senator Wyatt's captors," the anchorman continued, "it has asked us to deliver the following message. Quote. Our policy is not to negotiate with terrorists. But if you release Senator Wyatt unharmed by no later than noon on Saturday, July 15, we will give you safe passage to a country of your choice. End quote."

Manuel stopped the tape.

"Your government," Ramón said disdainfully, "is offering us something we can already do at any time."

"He's right," Zoraya said. "They don't know who we are, so we could leave you and get on a plane without any problem."

"After we killed you," Manuel said.

"Where would you go?"

"Back to Spain," Zoraya replied. "We're Spanish citizens."

"No one would know what we did," Ramón said. "But if we accepted this offer, then everyone would know, and the Spanish government might arrest us."

"I agree," Jim said. "It's not a great offer. I think the best thing you could do is leave now without killing me."

"We won't do that. You can identify us."

"I promise not to identify you."

"You would promise anything to save your life," Manuel said.

"We've had this conversation before," Zoraya said. "Yes, we could leave and go back to Spain. But what would be the point?

Abdullah would still be in prison, and we would have to start all over again."

"We could kidnap someone more important," Ramón said in Arabic.

"A state senator should be important enough. If they won't exchange a prisoner for him, they won't do it for anyone."

"They would if we had a hundred hostages," Manuel said.

"We would have to take over a building to get that many hostages," Zoraya said. "And even then they might not do it."

"How can we get them to release Abdullah?" Ramón asked Jim in Spanish.

"By political pressure," he said. "It's the only way to get things done."

"You already tried that," Zoraya said, "and it didn't work."

"They made an offer, didn't they?"

"A lousy offer," Ramón said.

"It was still an offer. They say they don't negotiate with terrorists, but they've begun to negotiate with you."

"If they have, why didn't they make a better offer?"

"In negotiations you always start with an offer you know the other party won't accept. That's how you feel them out."

"They're feeling us out?" Manuel asked.

"Of course they are. They have nothing to lose by making such an offer. If you did accept it, then they'd win at almost no cost. If you don't accept it, they can always make you a better offer."

After a moment Zoraya said: "So how can we get them to make a better offer?"

"By political pressure," he repeated. "I'll make another tape, and I'll tell my constituents that the government hasn't listened to them. I'll ask more people to call, and I'll ask the people who already called to call again."

"And that will persuade the government to make a better offer?"

"I believe it will. There are millions of voters following this story," he reminded them.

"Well, the only offer we'll accept is the release of Abdullah," Ramón said.

"I know. And you might not get that on the next round, but if we keep putting pressure on them you *will* get it."

"What makes you so confident?" Zoraya asked.

"Next year is an election year," Jim said. "The party in power won't want to alienate the voters from Minnesota. Not to mention the voters from other states who are watching this whole thing on television."

"We have to talk about it," Ramón said, meaning without him.

Zoraya took him back to his room, but instead of leaving him she lingered and asked: "What does it feel like to have more than a hundred thousand people respond to your speech?"

"It feels like an election campaign."

"No, seriously. They're making phone calls to save your life."

"They're making phone calls because I asked them to do the right thing."

"You mean they would call if you weren't in danger of being killed?"

"They would if they felt it was the right thing to do."

"Are you sure they're not doing it for you?"

"They're doing it because I appealed to what's good in them. So they're really doing it for themselves."

"You make it sound like they want to treat us fairly."

"They do," he assured her. "And they will if you give them a chance."

"They had a chance with Abdullah."

"Okay. They made a mistake. But you know what they say about Americans—"

"No. What do they say?"

"They say we're the best people in the world at correcting mistakes because we make so many of them."

She almost laughed. "Do you believe that?"

"Well, having made a lot of mistakes, I can speak from personal experience. And I have to admit that I haven't corrected all of them, and some of them I can never correct, but I have corrected some of them."

"You haven't corrected the mistake you made with me."

"You mean believing that you were a princess from Granada?"

She nodded. "Yes. And that I was in New York to talk with the Rockefellers about historic preservation."

"That wasn't a mistake. It could all be true."

"What do you mean?"

"You have your whole life ahead of you," he told her, "and you could still be anything you want."

"I couldn't be white."

"Well, almost anything."

"Do you think I could be a princess?"

"Yeah. If that's what you want."

"I felt like a princess once," she said wistfully.

"When was that?"

"In Granada."

He waited for her to continue.

"You asked me what happened there, and now I'll tell you." She wandered over to the window and gazed out into the summer night. "I went there when I was fourteen. I didn't know it, but my father had sold me into slavery. I think you call it white slavery, but in my case it was brown slavery."

"You said you were a maid."

"I was. But my other job was to have sex with my employer whenever he wanted it, however he wanted it."

"How long did this go on?"

"Almost two years. I had one night a week off from it. He needed a rest for the next onslaught," she said bitterly. "I was out one night walking around, and I met an American, a college student. I was sixteen, and he was about twenty."

Jim listened, imagining a boy like himself at that age.

"He took me up to the Alhambra, and there in the garden near a fountain he put his arms around me and kissed me. He made me feel like I was a princess. And you know what? He kissed me for hours, but he didn't try to go any further."

"I understand. He must have thought that you were as pure as the freshly fallen snow on the Sierra Nevada."

"You sound just like him."

"I could have been him."

"When I got home I felt different. I guess I was seeing myself through his eyes. I wasn't a maid or a concubine, I was a princess. And the next night when my employer came to my room for his nightly pleasure I refused him."

"What did he do?"

"He beat me."

"Didn't people hear?"

"Oh, yes. And they came to see what was the matter. He said that he had caught me with a man, and that I had brought disgrace to their house. He said that he should have known better than to hire a Muslim."

"And they believed him?"

"Of course they believed him. He threw me out in the middle of the night. I had no money, and I had no clothes except what I was wearing. I wandered the streets like a homeless gypsy."

"Did you try to find the American?"

"I went to his hotel, but they turned me away. So I went looking for a place to sleep. I ended up in the doorway of a bank." She paused and took a deep breath. "The next morning I went back to his hotel and stood on the other side of the street, waiting for him. He finally came out. He was with another boy his age. He looked different in the daylight. But I had no one else to turn to, so I crossed the street and approached him. He was talking with his friend, and when he saw me he must have thought I was a beggar because before I could say anything he said he was sorry, he had no money. And then he turned and walked away without another word."

He could easily imagine the scene, having rejected countless beggars.

"I stood there for a long time staring after him, remembering how he had made me feel the night before. I didn't understand how someone who had treated me with such consideration the night before could treat me with such disdain now. But I finally did understand. It was later that morning when I saw myself in a mirror at the bus station, where I had gone to use the bathroom. I looked different in the daylight. I had brown skin, which hadn't been so apparent at night. Or else it had fit his image of a Moorish princess. But by day it fit his image of a beggar."

"He was blind," Jim said.

"You mean he couldn't see who I was?"

"He could only see a beggar instead of a princess disguised as a beggar."

She made the face of nausea that Carla used to make as a teenager in response to his efforts to get her to feel positive about life. "When you said things like that to your children, did they believe you?"

"Not always, but sometimes they did."

"Well, I don't believe you."

"You don't believe I can see you as a princess?"

"Why should I believe you?" she asked. "You lied to me when you told me you were a CIA agent."

"Well, I shouldn't have done that. I'm sorry."

"You're only sorry because it got you into trouble."

"I *am* sorry because it got me into trouble," he admitted. "But I'm also sorry because I didn't start out right with you."

"What do you mean?"

"I mean in a relationship with you."

She puffed out air. "Oh, don't tell me you wanted to have a relationship with me. You wanted sex."

"Yeah, I wanted sex. But that's not all I wanted."

"What else did you want?"

"It's hard to explain. I wanted validation of an alter ego. And that was for me. But after being with you the past few days, I want something for you."

She didn't ask what. Instead, she said: "I probably shouldn't tell you, but it wasn't in the plan for me to have sex with you. I was only supposed to lure you here so we could kidnap you."

"I wondered about that."

"Do you know why I changed the plan?"

"No. Why did you?"

"I wanted to find out how you would treat me."

"And how did I treat you?"

"With consideration," she told him softly. "You weren't at all like that pig who fucked me in Granada."

"So now you know."

"What do I know?"

"You know it's possible," he said, "for a man to treat you with consideration."

"I have to go," she said as if she had stayed too long with him. "I have to talk with Ramón and Manuel about what to do next."

"Well, remember what I said. They *have* begun to negotiate, and I believe you can get what you want."

"I thought you would try to talk us into accepting their offer. Why didn't you?"

"As Ramón said, it's a lousy offer. I mean, it would be great for me, but it would be a disaster for you. Of course, the best thing for all of us would be if you just leave me here—alive—and go away."

"If we did that, then you could identify us."

"By now I think you know I wouldn't."

"Maybe you wouldn't," she allowed, "but Abdullah would still be in prison."

"I could help you get him out."

She searched his face as if she wanted to believe him, and then she said: "I have to go."

Feeling that he had influenced her as much as possible for now, he didn't try to detain her any longer.

SEVEN

INGA HAD A baby boy. They named him Erik after her paternal grandfather, which made Halvar happy, even made him smile. Erik took after her side of the family, looking like a baby Viking. The girls, who by now were nine and seven, were delighted to have a baby brother—for them it was like having a live doll—and they competed to help Inga take care of him.

Meanwhile, impressed by his grasp of public issues, people were urging Jim to run for office, and he was interested, seeing an opportunity for service. The race for state senator was expected to be wide open in his district because the man who had filled the position for the past twelve years was retiring for health reasons.

His first decision, whether to embark on a political career, was much easier than deciding which party he should represent. His father and Marchi were staunch Republicans, as was Halvar, though he didn't talk much about politics, so there was strong family pressure to run as a Republican, but his values were more aligned with the other party, which in Minnesota was known as the Democratic-Farmer-Labor Party. The DFL was the party of Hubert Humphrey, Eugene McCarthy, and Walter Mondale, who were regarded as firebrands by the established families of St. Paul and as dangerous liberals by newly successful people like Marchi, so in their houses DFL was a term of opprobrium as FDR had been a generation ago.

Inga supported the idea of his running for office and also encouraged him to represent the DFL in spite of the likely opposition from their families. His father, after listening to his reasons for choosing the DFL, presented some reasons for not choosing that party but in the end agreed to support him whatever he decided. Halvar, instead of trying to talk him out of it, tried to get him to think about changing the DFL's position on taxing businesses, which was driving them to friendlier states.

The main obstacle was Marchi, who not only opposed his representing the DFL but also opposed the whole idea because it would interfere with his job.

"You can't do your job and be a politician at the same time," Marchi told him. They were at the office, with Marchi seated behind his desk and Jim in front of it. "You can't do both."

"It's a part-time job," Jim argued. "The legislature meets only twice a year, and even then it'll take only about ten hours a week."

"That's ten hours less you'll be working for me."

"I'll work a longer week. You won't know the difference."

"I *will* know the difference, and so will you. Are you forgetting that you have a wife, three children, and another on the way?"

"I have Inga's support on this."

"Well, she doesn't know what you're getting into."

"Look," Jim said, trying to reason with him. "It's a four-year term. If it doesn't work, then I won't run for another term."

"How will you know if it's not working?"

"You'll tell me if it's not."

"I can tell you now it's not going to work, so why waste your time?"

"I want to try it. There are a lot of things that need to be done."

"Yeah. Things like raising taxes and spending more money on welfare. If you had to do this, why the hell couldn't you run as a Republican?"

"I don't believe in their values."

"Your family's position was built on those values. Why are you turning against your family?"

"I'm not turning against my family."

Marchi glowered. "I remember those articles Renata wrote for that lefty newspaper. I wondered where she got her ideas, and now I know."

"Those were her ideas."

"She wouldn't have had them on her own."

"Are you saying that your daughter wasn't capable of having her own ideas?"

"I'm saying she wouldn't have had them if someone hadn't planted them in her."

"So every idea that Renata had was planted in her."

"Well, how else could she have ideas?"

"She went to college, where presumably she learned to think for herself."

"She didn't get those ideas at St. Catherine."

"She didn't get them from me," Jim said. "In this area, and in many other areas, she was way ahead of me."

"Then where did she get them?"

"Maybe she developed them in opposition to you."

"Why would she do that?"

"To free herself from you and become her own person."

Marchi shook his head. "She had no reason for wanting to do that. We had our differences, but we agreed on the main things."

"What were they?"

"Family and religion."

"Okay. But her ideas about improving the lives of the poor were not against her religion. In fact, the church supports those ideas."

"You mean she got them from the church?"

"That's where she got her basic values, and her ideas came from those values, so yes, you could say she got them from the church, though I still say you have to give her credit for developing her own ideas."

With his elbows on the desk, Marchi pressed his forehead against his fists as if he was thinking hard. He remained in that position for a long time, and finally raising his head, he said: "If I understand you correctly, you're running for office because you want to implement the ideas that Renata got from the church. Is that it?"

Feeling that this was as close as they were ever going to get on the issue, Jim replied: "Yes. That's it."

"Then you have my blessing."

Jim was elected with a solid majority. The party strategists were delighted. They introduced him to Hubert Humphrey, who had just made a comeback by getting elected again to the U.S. Senate, and they began to talk about him as a possible heir to Humphrey and a future leader of the DFL.

While the job of state senator didn't require more than an average of ten hours a week, the time was extended by new projects that Jim sponsored. After a year he was spending almost twenty hours a week on his new career, and he didn't spend less time on his family, so he had significantly less time to spend on the company. At that point Marchi could have told him that it wasn't working, but the company was doing better than ever. Revenues were up, costs were under control, and profits were soaring. Of course it helped that the economy was booming.

During his second year in office Inga had another baby, another boy, whom they named Lukas after a Swedish ancestor, but unlike Erik he didn't look Swedish. He had the dark hair, dark eyes, and tan skin that had been transmitted through Jim's mother from a presumed Spanish ancestor. In one version of the family history this ancestor was a sailor from the Spanish Armada whose ship was sunk in a battle with the British, who had swum ashore to Ireland and mated with a local girl. In another version the ancestor had come to Ireland with migrants from Spain during the time when that country was occupied by the Moors. There were other versions, but there was no evidence for any of them other than the fact that Jim's mother had dark hair, dark eyes, and skin that wasn't tan from lying in the sun.

Carla and Gina were glad to have another baby brother, though the novelty had worn off. By now they were eleven and nine, with interests outside the family. Since first grade they had gone to Visitation, which they could walk to from their house, and they had networks of friends from school at whose houses they played and did the occasional sleepover. Since Inga was occupied with a baby and a two-year-old, the girls were relatively free of direct supervision at home. At school they were kept in line by the nuns, but after school there were times when they didn't come home and Inga didn't know where they were.

"Where are they?" Jim asked when he got home one evening after six and didn't find the girls there.

"I don't know," Inga said, worried. "I thought they were playing at a friend's house, but they weren't there."

"Did you call around the neighborhood?"

"I called everyone I could think of, but no one had seen them."

"Well, I'll go out and look for them."

He took the car and started driving around the neighborhood. On a hunch he headed toward Linwood Park, which was on a bluff overlooking the valley that had been carved by the Mississippi. It was only a block from where they lived, and he guessed they might have gone there because he and his brother and sister had played there when they were the same age as the girls. Among the trees and gorges of the park you could pretend that you were anywhere in the world.

As he entered the park he spotted them on the edge of the bluff with two boys who looked older. He could see the four of them only as silhouettes because the sun was setting behind them over Minneapolis, so he wouldn't have recognized the boys even if he had known them.

When he stopped the car and opened the door the boys bolted over the edge and out of sight, presumably down the steep incline.

"Who were those boys?" he asked.

The girls looked at each other, then shrugged as if they didn't know.

"You were with them, weren't you?"

"Yeah. We talked with them," Carla admitted.

"Do you know them?"

"No. They live down there," Carla said, indicating the valley.

"You shouldn't be hanging around here with boys you don't know."

"Why not?" Gina asked innocently.

"Because you could get into trouble with them."

"What kind of trouble?"

He wondered if Inga had explained to them what boys and girls could do together. "If they're not nice, they could hurt you."

"They seemed nice," Carla said.

"Maybe they are, but this isn't a good place for you to find out."

"Because there aren't any parents around?"

"That's right. If you want to play with boys, you should bring them home."

"Well, Inga wouldn't know what we were doing. All she does is pay attention to Erik and Lukas."

"She has her hands full," Jim agreed.

"So how could she keep us out of trouble?"

"You have to keep yourselves out of trouble by using your heads. Your parents can't do everything for you."

"I wish she paid more attention to us," Gina said.

"She will if you help her more with the boys. You were so good with Erik."

"He was the first baby," Carla said.

"Will she have more babies?" Gina asked.

"She probably won't have any more," he said, knowing that Inga had gone on the pill. "She's happy with two."

"Well, maybe we could help her more," Carla conceded. "We just don't want to be stuck at home."

"You don't have to be stuck at home. But if you want to play with your friends after school, you have to tell Inga where you are. And I don't want you to come to the park without a parent. Do you understand?"

They nodded.

"Good. Now, let's go home and have dinner."

After almost two years of serving in the senate Jim finally admitted that he couldn't do both jobs, and since he was more interested in his political career he had started to neglect his job at the company. By then the economy had gone into recession following the spike in oil prices, and the company wasn't doing so well. Marchi could have blamed him for the company's lackluster performance, but instead he waited for Jim to come to his own decision.

On a Friday afternoon as things were slowing down for the weekend he went into Marchi's office, sat down in front of the desk, and said: "It's not working."

"I know," Marchi said unhappily. "I told you it wasn't going to work."

"I have to give up one of my jobs."

"It better not be this one."

"It is. I'm sorry."

"You're going to walk out on me after all I've done for you?"

"This isn't what I want to do with my life. It never was."

"Then why the hell did you take the job?"

"Renata wanted to come home. Remember?"

"You could have worked somewhere else."

"You offered me this job," he said. "You promised me all kinds of things."

"I've kept my promises, haven't I?"

"Yes. And I've done a good job for you."

"You have," Marchi admitted, "until recently."

"Well, that's my point. I can't keep trying to do both jobs."

Marchi leaned toward him. "You know, I'm going to be sixty this year. I was counting on you to take over when I retire."

"How soon do you plan to retire?"

"I don't know. What difference does it make?"

"If you don't plan to retire within the next ten years, and I'm sure you don't, then you have time to develop someone else."

"What if I dropped dead tomorrow?"

"You're not going to drop dead tomorrow."

"How do you know? And don't you care what happens to the girls?"

"What does this have to do with them?"

"If there's no company, they won't have anything."

"They won't have money, but they'll have everything else."

Marchi sighed, dropping his hands onto the desk. "So that's it? That's the end of our relationship?"

"You know it's not. We still have the girls."

"That's all I ever have—girls, girls." He was referring to the fact that Angela's two children were both girls, and Bianca's first baby was a girl. "Do you think I'm being punished for something I did?"

"No," Jim laughed. "You're being rewarded."

Marchi shook his head as if he didn't believe this. "What good are they? They can't help me run the company."

"What about their husbands?"

"Angela's husband couldn't do it. He's a lawyer."

"Bianca's husband is an engineer."

"Yeah. He is," Marchi said, considering. "He has the right background. I just don't know if he has what it takes."

"You'll never know unless you give him a chance."

"Well, I guess he's a more likely candidate than you were. When you started working for me you didn't know shit."

"I didn't," he agreed, remembering how little he knew.

"So what if you don't keep getting reelected?"

"I don't know. I haven't thought about it."

"You expect me to take you back?"

"No. I've burned my bridge."

"You're crazy," Marchi said with grudging admiration. "You could have been the top dog in this city."

Zoraya brought his lunch, a tuna sandwich, and told him what the group had decided. "We're going to do what you suggested. We're going to use political pressure to get them to make a better offer."

"Good," he said because this approach was the next best thing to abandoning the venture and leaving him alive. "You understand that their next offer probably won't be what you want."

"It's Thursday," she reminded him grimly, "and the deadline is Tuesday, so we don't have much more time."

"You could extend the deadline."

"No, we couldn't. If we did, they would stop negotiating."

"Not necessarily," he said, though he knew she was right. "They might just think you were willing to compromise."

"But we're not willing to compromise. We want them to release Abdullah, and we won't accept anything less."

"What if they offered a new trial?"

"We wouldn't accept that. We know they would find him guilty again."

142

"You believe they would, but you don't know."

"Why would the outcome be any different?"

"For one thing, you've gotten a lot of publicity, and that would influence people, even though it's not supposed to. Also, some time has passed since the bombing, and people's heads are clearer now."

Zoraya looked doubtful. "Well, I don't think it would be any different. People are still prejudiced against Muslims. They think we're all terrorists."

"So how will you ever change their minds?"

"We're not trying to change their minds. We're trying to get justice."

"But if you use violence to get your way, you'll never have justice. You'll only have war."

"Maybe we will, but we didn't start it."

"Who started it?"

"You started it—by establishing Israel and driving millions of Palestinians out of their homeland. As you say in your religion, that's the original sin."

"It's a bad situation," he admitted. "But it's a good example of what I was talking about. Both sides go back and forth killing people from the other side, trying to get justice—or revenge. It makes you wonder if they know the difference."

"Between what?"

"Justice and revenge."

"I don't know. What do you think?"

"I think people in those situations don't see any difference. They want revenge, and they call it justice."

"We don't want revenge."

"I know you don't. But if you kill me, will that be justice?"

"I don't know," she said uncomfortably. "I don't want to kill you. I really don't. But if we have to, we will."

"Why would you have to?"

"We would if they don't release Abdullah."

"If you did kill me, what do you think would happen to him?"

"They would kill him," she said without hesitation.

"Would that be justice?"

143

She turned away from him, facing the window.

"You went to college here," he said, "so you should know more about our system. You should know they wouldn't kill Abdullah."

"Why wouldn't they?"

"Because our system isn't based on revenge. It's based on justice."

"Then what would they do to him?"

"They'd leave him in prison until he served his sentence."

"Well, that would be as bad as killing him."

"No, it wouldn't."

She didn't argue. She stood there with her back to him, and after a long silence she asked: "You said I could be anything. Did you mean it?"

"Yes. I did mean it."

"What do you see in me?"

"I see a lot of things. Intelligence, passion, integrity, empathy, generosity—the things that make a leader."

"Oh, I can't see myself as a leader."

"But you *are* a leader. You're running this show."

She turned from the window and faced him as if she was seeing him for the first time. "How old are you?"

"Fifty-six."

"You could be my father."

"I know," he said.

"Do you feel like a father with me now?"

"Yes." He could have been talking with one of his daughters.

"I wish my father had been like you."

"What happened to him? You said he was in hell."

"He died of a heart attack when I was eighteen. He left us some money. All his life he hoarded money, but he never got to use it."

"Maybe he just wanted to hoard it."

"Well, that's what he did. And he would have died again if he had known that I used his money to go to college."

"So that's how you and Ramón paid for it? I was wondering. The last I knew you were living on the streets in Granada."

"I went back to Ceuta."

144

"I assume your father didn't welcome you back."

"He didn't, but he couldn't get rid of me. I wasn't a girl of fourteen any more. And luckily he died within a year."

"What made you go to college in New York?"

"It was the only city I knew in America."

"Why America? Did you think you might run into that boy again?"

"Not consciously, but I must have hoped I would. I must have hoped he would see me as a college girl."

"Maybe he would have. College girls all dress like beggars."

"You're right," she laughed. "The cool thing was to have holes in your jeans."

They had reached a point where if he pushed the conversation further he might have spoiled the feeling of rapprochement, so he stopped it there.

After a long silence she said: "I hope the political pressure works."

"It will," he assured her.

"Then you better write your speech so we can make the tape."

"It'll be ready in a half hour."

In the spring of 1975 Elizabeth returned from Italy after ten years accompanied by Patrick, the man she had lived with for most of that time and had married just before leaving Florence. Except for her sporadic visits home Jim hadn't seen her during this period, and he had never met Patrick, who was twenty years older than Elizabeth. Actually, she was no longer Elizabeth, she was Anna now, the Italian form of her middle name. She had dropped her first name, probably because of the nickname that had been derived from it and given to her when she was a baby, sticking with her through high school. His sister now winced when their mother slipped and called her Bitsy.

Since Patrick was a sculptor and Anna was still painting in oil they bought an old commercial building on Grand Avenue in which they created a working studio as well as space in front for a gallery. The zoning allowed them to live upstairs. Their timing was good. The blocks on Grand between Dale and Lexington were becoming a vibrant retail area, with coffee shops, antique stores, specialty shops, and ethnic restaurants. So their location was ideal for selling their work. But from the beginning they didn't like being "shopkeepers," as Patrick put it, and until they finally hired a girl to mind the gallery you could walk in and not find anyone to help you. Nor would they respond from the studio in back, where they were working, if you called and asked: "Is anyone here?"

It wasn't long before Patrick, who labeled himself as a communist, began getting involved in politics. Like many radicals that Jim had observed, instead of targeting the opposition he attacked the people whose positions were closest to his, presumably because he had a better chance of aligning their positions with his, and Jim often found himself on the receiving end of his brother-in-law's diatribes. But Patrick was intelligent, articulate, and well informed, so their debates helped to clarify Jim's thinking on issues and to improve the resulting legislation.

They were involved in such a debate a year later when his brother Stephen visited from Argentina, where he had been working in a bank for five years. Stephen brought with him the young woman he intended to marry. He had been married before to a woman named Leila who came from the Virginia horse country. Their marriage hadn't lasted long, and Stephen had been living alone in Buenos Aires since his divorce. At the time Argentina was at war with itself, and the situation was so bad that most American managers had been evacuated from the country. Stephen had volunteered to stay and keep an eye on things for head office, which didn't completely trust the local people to run their branches there.

Jim hadn't seen his brother for two years, and he was glad that Stephen had found a woman who shared his values. Her name was Cathy, and though she had a cover story about being the daughter of an American oil engineer and a Venezuelan flight attendant, as Jim later learned she was actually from a poor family in Colombia with at least some African ancestry. She was going to the University of Buenos Aires, taking a program that would qualify her as a teacher.

On Saturday his parents had a family party at their summer house at White Bear Lake. The house was in a family compound that his grandfather on his father's side had established on the Peninsula before World War I. His parents' house, at the edge of the woods, had screen porches all around it. They entertained on the front porch, which overlooked a wide lawn and had a view of the lake between two of the other houses.

They were all there: Jim, Anna and Patrick, Stephen and Cathy, Carla, Gina, and Inga with Erik and Lukas, who were five and three. It was unusual for his parents to have their three children all together at the same time, so it was a special occasion. At one point the three of them walked across the lawn to the lake and out to the end of the dock, where they stood and talked.

On the lake the sailboats were winding up a race, heading for the Yacht Club, attended by inboard motorboats. In an abstract way the white sails were like sheep and the brown launches were like sheepdogs herding them home.

"It's a long time since I saw a sailboat race," Anna said.

"I can't remember when I last saw one," Stephen said.

"Why did we all go overseas?" Jim asked.

"To free ourselves of our old identities," Anna said. "It was liberating to live in a place where no one knew me as Bitsy Wyatt."

"I agree," Stephen said. "I wasn't rejecting who I was, or where I came from, but I wanted to see what I could do where no one knew a thing about me."

"They knew you were an American," Jim said.

"Yeah, they knew that, but they don't know where I was coming from."

"Well, I was looking for the same thing, but I sure didn't find it living overseas."

"You found something here. I mean, who would ever have imagined a Wyatt in the DFL?"

"Grampa must be turning over in his grave."

"I can just hear him," Anna said. "Remember how he used to rant about FDR?"

"He should see us now," Jim said. "A liberal, a socialist, and a communist."

"So we did achieve new identities," Stephen said.

"I even got a new name," Anna said.

"Did it take ten years in Italy to change your name?" Jim asked her jokingly.

"No. It took about ten days. I might have come back years ago, but then came the flood in Florence. I got involved in cleaning up the mess."

"That's why I stay in Argentina. I don't want to leave it in such a mess."

"So where did we all get it from—this urge to fix things?" Jim asked. "We don't come from a broken family."

"We live in a broken world," Stephen said. "Someone has to fix it."

"I agree," Anna said. "If we don't fix it, who will?"

Jim was reelected in 1976 for another four-year term with almost seventy percent of the vote. His family joined him at the victory celebration, which he held at the St. Paul Hotel, and a picture of him, Inga, and the four children appeared on the front page of the next day's paper. The girls, who were thirteen and eleven, thought the celebration was long and boring, but they liked having their pictures in the paper. The boys, who were five and three, enjoyed the attention.

Hubert Humphrey, who was reelected to the U.S. Senate, called him personally to congratulate him. They talked about the victory of Jimmy Carter and Walter Mondale, their fellow member of the DFL, agreeing that it was a great day for the party. Looking ahead, they envisioned Mondale succeeding Carter as President and Jim succeeding Humphrey as U.S. Senator.

Shortly after the election Inga began to practice her guitar more intensively, playing flamenco, listening to the masters, and emulating them. A few months later she played in public, at the bar where Jim had first heard her play, and a young man in the audience came up to her after the performance and complimented her. He told her that he was looking for someone to play lead guitar in a band he was putting together. He played bass guitar, and he already had people on the drums and the keyboard, so all that was missing was a lead guitarist. He had some ideas on the kind of music they would play, but he was open to suggestions.

Inga suggested that they play *nuevo flamenco*, and the young man loved the idea, so they went with it. At first this new venture didn't cause any major disruptions because they had to compose and arrange music before they could perform, and Inga could do this at home with the young man, whose name was Danny. They worked in the family room where she could keep an eye on the boys. When they brought in the keyboard player she could still work at home, but when the time came to involve the drummer they needed more room and had to go elsewhere. The obvious place was her parents' house, where they could work in the music room and her mother could keep an eye on the boys. So she was there working with the band three or four days a week.

When Jim first heard them perform in the music room he was impressed. The music was derived from flamenco, but it was transformed by elements of Latin and rock into a whole new sound. It had a beat that you could dance to in the multicultural style that people had adopted, neither rock nor Latin but some amalgam. In most of the numbers you felt like stomping your feet and clapping your hands.

The band, which they named New Granada, made its debut at the bar where Inga had met Danny, and it was a hit. Within a few weeks they were solidly booked in the Twin Cities, and within a few months they were booked in Chicago. By then they had made their first tape, which sold well.

Since they performed on weekends the boys could be left with her parents and the girls with his parents, so Jim didn't miss any local performances. But he couldn't accompany them to Chicago or the other cities where they played, and on those weekends he kept all four children at home. By then he had begun to worry about the kind of family life they would have with Inga's and his expanding careers, which inevitably would leave them with less and less time not only for the children but also for each other.

What he had set in motion seemed to be going out of control.

When Inga returned from her third trip to Chicago he could sense right away that something was wrong. She waited until the children were in bed before she told him. They were in the kitchen sitting at the table, drinking wine. "I don't know how to say this," she said, staring into her glass.

He waited, fearing what she was going to say.

"I'm in love with Danny. I don't know how it happened, but it did. I'm sorry."

"You're in love with him? What does that mean?"

"It means I'm going to leave you and live with him."

"Have you really thought about it?"

"Oh, ya. I've been thinking about it for the past six months."

That surprised him because he hadn't noticed anything until tonight. "You mean all this time you've been—seeing him?"

She shook her head. "We didn't do anything until this trip. But I fell in love with him the first time we played together."

"I don't understand."

"If you were a musician you'd understand. We communicated through the music. We discovered that we were soul mates."

"Well, that might explain why your music is so good."

"I still love you," she said, facing him with tears in her eyes, "but I love Danny in a different way. And since music is my life I want to be with him."

"I still love you," he said, "so I want what's best for you. But we have to think about the boys."

"I know. We can share custody of them."

"You're a few steps ahead of me."

"I've been thinking about it longer than you have."

"So give me some time to catch up."

"Okay. I'm sorry."

He wondered if there was any way he could talk her out of it, or if he should even try to. He could already feel the damage that had been done, and he doubted if it could ever be repaired. And yet the thought of parting with her was so much worse than the damage that he didn't want to let her go. "Maybe we should try living with it for a while and see what happens."

"I already have been living with it."

"But I haven't, so it's different now."

"It's worse now."

"Maybe it is."

"I feel awful," she said after a silence. "You're the one who encouraged me to pursue a career. If it weren't for you, I'd still be teaching music."

"With horn-rimmed glasses and braided hair."

"You introduced me to flamenco."

"Remember Granada?"

"I'll never forget it."

He sighed. "Okay. Where are you going to live?"

"Oh, not far from here," she said. "There's a house for sale over on Fairmont."

"You really *have* been thinking about it."

"I wanted to know what I was doing before I told you."

"So when is this going to happen?"

"By the end of the month."

"Okay. You just have to give me some time to get used to it. This is a shock, as you can imagine."

"I'm sorry."

"Don't be. You have a great career ahead of you."

"Whatever I have, I owe it to you."

Jim and the girls stayed in the house where they had been living, while Inga and the boys moved into the house on Fairmont. By now the girls, who were fourteen and twelve, could almost take care of themselves, but he still didn't want them coming home from school to an empty house, so he arranged for them to go directly from school to his parents' house, where he could pick them up after work. If they went to a friend's house after school, they had to let his mother know.

The boys, who were six and four, were only a few blocks away, so he saw them frequently, and they stayed with him every weekend, sleeping in their old rooms. There were no obvious problems with them. But as time passed, there were problems with the girls, especially Carla.

One afternoon she didn't show up at his parents' house after school, and she didn't call his mother to let her know where she was. He was in a meeting about a tax relief proposal for senior citizens when he got the phone call from his mother, who told him she hadn't heard from Carla. He left the meeting and drove to his parents' house. He grilled Gina, who either didn't know anything or didn't want to betray her sister, so he got nothing out of her. Remembering how he had found them in Linwood Park, he drove there and looked around. He didn't see her, and he was about to leave when he stopped at the edge of the bluff and gazed down into the valley.

At the bottom of the bluff, following the valley that the river had carved, was a railroad line that connected St. Paul and Minneapolis, running west and east respectively from the two cities. Going west there was a steep grade, which slowed the long freight trains almost to walking speed, making it an ideal place to hop a train, as Jim knew from his own experience as a boy. As he looked down he spotted two girls in blue jumpers and white blouses, standing on the track bed, waiting for a train. Though they were far away from him, he could tell that one of them was Carla.

At that moment he heard the train approaching from the east, climbing the grade. He shouted to the girls, but they evidently couldn't hear him, so he headed down the bluff, grabbing branches of stunted trees to stop himself from falling and bringing a lot of dirt with him. From time to time he glanced down at the girls, who were poised and ready for the train. It was almost upon them.

Carla was hanging onto a freight car by the time he reached the bottom of the bluff, but he managed to stop the other girl from following her, and he yelled after Carla to get off the train. Surprised to see him, Carla released her grip and fell off onto the track bed, clear of the freight car. She rolled a few times, then got to her feet and brushed the gravel off her jumper as if she wanted to destroy the evidence of what she had done. When she looked up she was defiant. "What are you doing here?"

"I came here looking for you. What the hell are you doing?"

"Hopping a freight train," she said as if it was something she did every day.

"Well, that's not allowed. Do you understand?"

"I'll bet you did it when you were my age."

He almost pointed out that he was a boy, so it was different. Instead, he said: "I did, but it was stupid. I could have been killed."

"No way. The train's barely moving."

"You could slip and fall. It happens all the time."

"I know how to do it."

"I don't care. You're not going to do it ever again. You hear?"

"I hear," she said impudently.

"Whose idea was this?" he asked, suddenly conscious of the other girl.

"It was my idea," Carla admitted.

"So you got a friend of yours into trouble."

"My name is Megan," the girl said, joining them. She had red hair and freckles. "You won't tell my parents, will you?"

"Of course I'll tell them," he growled at her. "They should know what you're doing."

"Come on, Dad. Don't be mean."

"Mean? How is that mean? It's for her own good."

"What good will it do her?"

"If her parents know what she's doing, they can stop her."

"What if I promise not to do it again?" Megan asked, looking scared.

"I don't know you. I don't know if you keep your promises."

"I do. It's a sin to break a promise."

"Well, at least you learned something from the nuns. What would they say if they knew you were hopping freight trains?"

The two girls exchanged a look of consultation.

"They wouldn't like it," Carla said.

"They'd tell our parents," Megan said.

"One of your parents already knows, so what are we going to do about this?"

"You know me," Carla said. "You know I keep my promises. So if I promise not to do it again, along with Megan, then you don't have to tell her parents."

"You said it was your idea," he said, considering.

"It was," Carla said. "I talked her into it."

Megan, whose eyes were on the ground, said nothing.

"And she didn't ever get on the train," Carla pointed out.

"She would have if I hadn't stopped her."

"But she didn't," Carla said. "So all you could tell her parents truthfully is that she looked like she was going to hop a train."

He smiled in spite of himself, imagining what a good lawyer Carla would make. "Okay, guys. I won't tell Megan's parents. But you have to promise, both of you, that you'll never pull this stunt again."

"I promise," Carla said, raising her hand solemnly.

"I promise," Megan said, looking relieved.

"Okay. Now, what's the best way to go back up the bluff?"

"This way," they said almost in unison, heading toward a well-worn path.

Later that year he was invited to speak at a conference on healthcare in New York. The timing was perfect. He needed to get away from Minnesota, and at this point he didn't feel like going to Spain because it would evoke memories of his honeymoon with Inga. So he accepted the invitation and booked a room at the St. Jerome.

His speech was a success, and he left the conference with invitations to speak at other events. He should have felt good, but as he left his room that evening he was aware of an empty space inside of him, which almost never went away.

He had no plans for the evening, having politely declined several invitations to dinner from people at the conference, so he headed for the hotel bar with nothing in mind other than the clear memory of the woman he had met there several years ago, the claims adjuster from Des Moines who had briefly escaped from her dull life, cutting loose from the bonds that tied her down.

He found a place at the bar and ordered a vodka martini, which he would never have ordered at home. He sipped the drink, idly listening to the conversation around him and waiting for an opportunity to engage with someone.

"Is this seat taken?" a woman with a Southern accent asked.

"No," he said, glancing at her. She looked as if she was dressed up for a party. "It's all yours."

"Thank you," she said melodically.

Without looking at her directly he watched her maneuver her prim bottom onto the seat and summon the bartender with her index finger. When the bartender sauntered over she asked: "Do y'all have Wild Turkey?"

"Yes, ma'am," the bartender said, falling in with her accent.

"Are you from the south?"

"I'm from Baltimore, ma'am."

"Well, that's almost south. I'll have a Wild Turkey on the rocks."

While she waited for her drink the woman consecutively drummed the fingers of her left hand on the bar as if she was playing arpeggios. "Did anything happen in the world today?"

"Probably," Jim said, "but I can't tell you what."

"For all we know, a war could have started."

"Wars are starting all the time."

"Not where I live. The last war we had in our area was with you Yankees."

"Where are you from?"

"Montgomery, Alabama."

"I've never been there. What's it like?"

"Boring," she said. "Nothing ever happens there. A cat could make headlines by getting stuck up in a tree."

At that point the bartender brought her drink, which she accepted graciously, thanking him. She took a sip, closing her eyes. "That's just what I needed."

"Are you here on business?"

"Yes," she replied. "Are you?"

"No. I'm here to relax."

"Well, that's what I fully intend to do now. I'm Jolene."

"I'm Jim. What do you do?"

"I'm a buyer for a department store."

"That sounds interesting."

"It's not. What do you do?"

Prompted by their talk about wars, he said: "I'm a mercenary."

"Really?" she said, turning to him. Her brown eyes were wide with interest. "You're one of those men who fight wars for money?"

"Yeah," he said as if it was nothing.

"My goodness. I'll bet you have an interesting life."

"It's never dull," he admitted.

"What was the last war you fought in?"

"I just came back from Angola."

"Really? What was it like?"

"It was brutal," he said. "They've killed hundreds of thousands of people, and the war's still going."

"Have you ever been wounded?"

"Yeah. A few times. But nothing serious."

"Where else have you fought in wars?"

"A lot of countries in Africa. They have wars all over the continent. But also in Lebanon, Argentina—"

"Argentina? Which side did you fight on?"

"The right side," he said. "I always fight on the right side."

"You mean the side that wins?"

"No. The right side doesn't always win."

"Well, how do you tell which side is right?"

"You can tell by what they're fighting for. If they're fighting for power or money," he told her, "it's not the right side."

"I thought all wars were for power or money."

"They always are for one side."

"So what's the right side fighting for?"

"Justice," he said. "The right side is always fighting for justice."

He took her to dinner at La Grenouille, and when they returned to the hotel she got off at his floor and went to his room.

Though he had sensed her need, he was surprised by the force of her passion, which ignited in their first kiss and exploded in their coupling. For a woman with such a delicate body, she amazed him with her muscular strength and raw energy. As she climbed successive peaks, like someone traversing a range of mountains, she cried and sighed, pinning him between her thighs and then releasing him for another round. Transported, she had left behind the buyer from Montgomery and become a soldier of fortune in darkest Africa.

"Are you ready?" Zoraya asked, entering his room.

"Yeah. I'm ready." He made a small change in the wording of his speech, and then he got up and followed her to the production room.

"Let's hear it," Ramón said.

He sat down and laid the paper on the table. He spoke with minimal prompting from his written speech. "Hi. This is Jim Wyatt again. I spoke with you yesterday about Abdullah, the Muslim religious leader who was wrongfully convicted of inciting violence. As I said then, I believe he never preaches a word in favor of violence but always preaches the gospel of peace, just as your priests, ministers, and rabbis do. I asked you then to call your elected representatives and tell them to use their influence to get this innocent man released from prison. Many of you responded to my appeal, but our government didn't listen to you. So I'm asking you again to call your representatives and tell them to use their influence to get him released. Remind them that there's an election next year, and tell them that if they don't listen, then you'll vote for people who do listen. Remind them that you have the power to change the world, including the government."

"That sounds good," Zoraya said.

"It's all right," Ramón said.

"No changes?" Manuel asked.

"I don't have any," Zoraya said.

"I don't either," Ramón said.

"So let's tape it," Manuel said.

"Let me read it over one more time," Jim said.

He went over his speech, reading to himself and wondering if he had gone far enough. He didn't want to expend all of his ammunition now because he believed that the government would improve its offer but wouldn't agree to release Abdullah on this round, so he had to save something for the next round.

When they had finished taping his speech Ramón said: "I hope you know what you're doing. You don't have much time."

"I've never been in this position before," he admitted, "but I do know how to run a campaign."

"Well, I don't understand why you haven't mentioned in your last two speeches that we're going to kill you if they don't release Abdullah."

"I don't want to remind people that the government is dealing with terrorists. That'll only make it harder for them to negotiate with us."

"You mean," Zoraya said, "that your government would rather negotiate under political pressure from you than under a threat from terrorists."

"You got it," he said, feeling proud of her. "So we don't want to keep reminding people that you'll kill me if the government doesn't release Abdullah."

"But we *will* kill you," Ramón said.

"You don't need to keep reminding me of that," Jim said testily.

"At times you act like you forget it," Manuel said.

"I don't forget it. How could I?"

"So what do you think your government will offer this time?" Ramón asked.

"I think they'll offer to review his trial."

"Is that all? It's not enough."

"I know it's not enough," Jim said, "but rather than speculate, let's see what they offer, and then we can talk about it."

Zoraya took him back to his room and lingered there with him, wandering again over to the window. "You know," she said, still speaking in Spanish, "I'm beginning to see that there might be another way of getting justice."

"You mean without resorting to violence."

"Yes. I mean, I'm not convinced that your way works, but I can see how it might work. And if it does—"

He waited for her to complete the thought. "If it does, what?"

"If it does, then I'll adopt it."

"Well, let's assume that it does work. You have to get away, so no one will ever know you were involved in this."

"That shouldn't be a problem."

"So you believe I won't identify you?"

"Yes. I believe it."

"And you can convince Ramón and Manuel that I won't identify you?"

"I can," she said. "But I don't have to. I'm the leader."

"An effective leader doesn't tell people what to do. She convinces them that it's the right thing."

"Then I'll convince them."

"If you do, then you don't have to kill me no matter what happens."

"If they don't release Abdullah, we still have to kill you."

"Why? You agreed that it wouldn't be justice."

"If they don't release Abdullah," she said, "then it will prove that your way doesn't work, and if we don't kill you we won't have any credibility the next time."

"You mean the next time you kidnap someone."

"Yes. We're not going to stop until we get justice."

"Then we have two lives riding on this."

"Two lives?" she asked, not understanding.

"Yours and mine."

For a long moment she gazed at him as if she was almost tempted to believe that he cared what happened to her. Then she said: "I have to go."

EIGHT

IT WAS LATE afternoon, and Jim was sitting in his office, thinking about what had happened at lunch with the governor and a party strategist. Humphrey had died, and someone had to be appointed to finish his term, which ended in 1982. The party would have appointed Jim to the position, but evidently Humphrey had asked that his wife Muriel be appointed until a special election, and during lunch both the governor and the party strategist tried to convince Jim that it would be better anyway for him to wait because he wasn't ready for the position despite his having served six years as a state senator. They told him that four years from now, with his experience and his ability to garner votes from a broad range of the political spectrum, the party would back his candidacy for U.S. Senate.

Actually, he agreed with them, though not for the reasons they stated. He felt he was ready for the position professionally but not personally because he had two teenage girls, fifteen and thirteen, who without a mother depended to a great extent on their grandparents. If he went to Washington now, in the middle of the school year, he would have to leave them with his mother at least until June, and then he would have to find a school for them in Washington, a Catholic school. But they would be unhappy to leave their friends, especially at this stage of their lives, and they would be removed from their grandparents. In fact, they would have no support system. Even if he was able to find a competent professional caretaker to help him, which didn't seem likely, it would be virtually impossible for him to do a good job both as a Senator and as a parent. But five years from now when he would take office if elected, Carla would be in college and Gina would be in the last semester of her senior year in high school. So that would be a better time. Still, he had mixed feelings because he had come close to being appointed as a U.S. Senator, and a lot of things could happen between now and the next election, including the emergence of a serious rival.

His ruminations were interrupted by the voice of a woman who had soundlessly appeared in his doorway. "Senator Wyatt?"

"Yes," he said, startled. The secretary, who left at five, had closed the outer door, and though that door wasn't locked, its being closed was supposed to discourage people from walking in.

"Do you have a minute?" the woman asked, advancing into his office.

"A minute?" he said doubtfully. That usually meant at least a half hour. But his resistance was softened by the tight curls of dark hair that spilled over the woman's forehead, the worshipful gaze of her dark eyes, and the readiness of her full lips, which looked as if they had just been moistened by her tongue.

"Well, a few minutes. I'm Thea," she said, extending her hand.

"I'm Jim," he said, taking her hand. It was soft and warm but also firm. "You can sit down, but I have to leave in ten minutes."

"Okay. It won't take more than that, I promise." She sat down in one of the chairs that were available for visitors, crossing a leg over the other and in the process flashing the underside of a thigh.

While he waited for her to explain the purpose of her visit he suppressed the desire aroused by the glimpse of flesh.

"I want you to know how much I admire the things you're doing to improve our health insurance system."

"Thank you," he said, wondering what she wanted.

"Your program does a fantastic job of covering physical health problems, but it doesn't do enough for mental health problems."

Inferring that the woman was a lobbyist, Jim said: "I thought about it, but I concluded that we can't afford to use taxpayers' money to pay for psychoanalysis."

"I'm not talking about psychoanalysis," Thea said, with a hint of passion in her voice. "I'm talking about preventing and treating mental health problems, which cost the economy billions of dollars every year in lost time and low productivity."

"Can you give me an example?"

"Sure I can. Suppose you have an office worker who suffers from depression. She takes a lot of sick days, and when she's at work she doesn't do a good job because she has low motivation. There are doctors who can help her."

"By having her lie down on a couch and talk about her mother?"

"Where have you been? That's not what happens any more. The doctor who treats her is a psychiatrist, not a psychologist, and he gives her medication to treat her depression."

"He gives her a pill that makes her happy?"

"It doesn't make her happy, but it makes her functional."

"I guess I haven't kept up in this area," he admitted, trying not to look as she changed legs and crossed them again.

"I can give you literature if you want to learn."

"I always want to learn."

"Then I can help you," she said eagerly. "I can help you understand that there's no difference between physical health and mental health. They both have a physiological basis, and they're interrelated. So a good health insurance program should cover them both. It should integrate them."

"What about visits to psychologists?"

"They should be covered. Psychologists still play an important role in mental health."

"Then mental health problems aren't entirely physiological?"

"They can be caused by environmental as well as physiological factors. If you have a predisposition, which is physiological, and it's triggered by something your father does to you, which is environmental, then you have a problem."

He thought of his mother, who had suffered from postpartum depression after her second child was born dead, a depression that continued to afflict her even after she had another son and a daughter. If there had been medication back then like what Thea was talking about, it might have helped his mother.

"I know you have to go," Thea said, checking her watch. "So I'll give you my card, and I'll drop by tomorrow and leave the literature with your secretary."

"That sounds fine," he said, suddenly wishing he had more than ten minutes to talk with her. But it was almost six, and his mother would be expecting him to pick up the girls and take them home.

He took her card and glanced at it while he got up. She had a last name that sounded Greek, and as he had guessed, she represented an association that lobbied on behalf of the pharmaceutical companies.

She walked out with him, waiting for him to lock his office and the outer door, and as they parted on the sidewalk, shaking hands, she told him: "You have a chance to help a lot of people who are suffering from mental health problems. If you know people in that situation, think of them, and imagine what the right treatment could do for them. And then imagine them not having money for the treatment."

He got the message, not only hearing it but also seeing the words being formed by her full lips, which still looked as if they had just been moistened by her tongue.

That weekend he read the literature that Thea had left at his office, and he was convinced that the health insurance program should include specific treatments for mental health. Over the next several months he worked with Thea and some experts who were not lobbyists to draft the necessary legislation. It was fiercely debated, and it cost him support from the right of center, but it finally passed in a form that both parties could live with and that satisfied Thea.

Though he saw her frequently during this period it was always business, and they never met in the evening, which was reserved for the girls. Still, his concentration on the project was occasionally disturbed by an unpredictable gust of desire for her, which passed but always threatened to return. Of course, there were a lot of obstacles to his ever consummating this desire, starting with the lack of opportunity and ending with the knowledge that an affair with her, a lobbyist with whom he had worked on legislation for mental health, would be terminal for his career. But the biggest deterrent was the effect that an affair with Thea would have on his efforts to make sure that the girls emerged from the perilous teens without any permanent damage.

When the legislation passed he had no reason to keep seeing Thea, and at that point she disappeared from his life as if her mission had been accomplished. He stopped thinking about her, though at random moments, especially at night when he was lying alone in bed, a gust of desire for her would return, aroused by the image of the exposed underside of her thigh or her moist lips.

One afternoon about a year after he met Thea a colleague offered him tickets to a rock concert by a group that the girls both liked. The concert was that evening, and the colleague had planned to take his children but something had come up at the last minute, so the tickets were available.

He called his mother, expecting the girls to be at her house. Gina was there, but Carla had gone to a friend's house, where she had been going regularly, so he called the number that his mother gave him in order to tell Carla about the concert and arrange to pick her up at the friend's house, with the idea of taking the girls out to dinner before the concert. The friend's mother told him that Carla wasn't there, and that she hadn't come home with her daughter after school. In response to a further question the mother told him that Carla had never come home with her daughter.

Upset, and at the same time angry with Carla for lying to his mother and by extension lying to him, he tried to imagine what she was up to. She was almost sixteen now, a little old to be hopping trains, and in any case it was the middle of January and too cold to be doing anything outside. If she was inside, she wasn't likely to be at another friend's house because in that case there wouldn't have been any reason to lie. Which raised the possibility that she had gone home.

Imagining the worst, he got into his car and drove to his house. As soon as he opened the door he heard them. The sounds were coming from upstairs, presumably from Carla's bedroom, and the female sounds—which reminded him of the sounds she had made while plummeting in a scary ride at the state fair—were unmistakably coming from Carla, while the male sounds were unrecognizable.

They were probably so immersed in what they were doing that he could have gone upstairs and caught them in the act, but as angry as he was, he didn't want to do that to his daughter. Instead, he stamped his feet heavily on the hall carpet as if he was ridding them of snow.

The sounds stopped, and after a long absolute silence he heard her queasy voice call down to him: "Dad, is that you?"

"Yes," he called up heartily. "I'm home."

There was an unspoken: "What are you doing here?"

He waited, hearing a scramble of feet as they frantically got out of bed and put their clothes on.

"We'll be right down," Carla said in a voice that almost sounded normal.

"Okay," he said, unbuttoning his overcoat. Don't kill the guy, he told himself, just get his name and scare the living shit out of him.

When they finally came down the stairs they tried to look innocent but they were still flushed from their exertion. The guy's fly was only half zipped, and a piece of his shirttail was hanging out.

"Hi," Jim said. "I'm Carla's father."

"I'm Greg," the guy said. He was very tall, but he probably wasn't a basketball player or he would have been in practice now.

"What were you doing?" Jim asked as if he didn't know.

"We were studying," Carla said, not looking directly at him.

"What were you studying?"

"Math," she told him unconvincingly. "Greg's having trouble with geometry, and I was helping him."

"Are you sure it wasn't anatomy?"

"What do you mean?"

"I heard you," he said, finally letting loose his anger, "and I know what fucking sounds like."

"I better go," Greg said.

"You're not going anywhere."

Greg didn't move.

165

"Okay," Carla said defiantly. "So we were fucking. What's it to you?"

"You're not supposed to be doing that. You're fifteen."

"I'm almost sixteen. And all the girls my age are doing it."

"I don't believe that. But even if it's true, I don't want you doing it."

"You can't stop me."

"I can stop *him*," he said, indicating Greg. "I can have him convicted of statutory rape and sent to prison for ten years."

"You can't," Carla argued. "I consented."

"You're not old enough to consent."

"Yes, I am. I'm sixteen."

"You're not sixteen. You won't be sixteen for another three months, so you're still under the age of consent." He turned to Greg and asked: "How old are you?"

"I'm eighteen," Greg admitted.

"So you're old enough to be tried as an adult."

"Tried for what? I didn't rape her."

"The law says you did. But don't worry, when you get out of prison in ten years she'll be old enough to consent."

"You're not being fair," Carla protested.

"I'm being perfectly fair. I'm giving him the benefit of a fair trial. What I really should do is kill him on the spot."

"You wouldn't do that."

"I would if you give me the slightest provocation."

Carla looked as if she believed him, and Greg took his cue from her. He edged toward the front door.

"You're provoking me," Jim warned him.

Greg stopped moving.

"Now, I want to know your last name, and where you live, and where you go to school. I want your father's name and his phone number."

"You're going to talk to my father?" Greg said, looking even more frightened than he had been by the prospect of prison.

"Of course I'm going to talk to your father."

"He'll beat the shit out of me."

"Good. Then I won't have to." He got all the information he wanted, and then he invited Greg to leave, saying: "If I ever see you near my daughter, or if I hear that you've been near her, I'll call the police and charge you with rape. Is that clear?"

Greg nodded. "Yes. That's clear."

"So get the hell out of here," Jim said, giving the boy a swift kick in the butt as he grabbed his coat and headed for the door.

When he had gone Carla said: "It was really my fault."

"I know it was. I'm not stupid."

"But it's no big deal."

"It is to me."

"Well, that's because you're hung up on sex."

"I'm hung up on your getting pregnant."

"I won't get pregnant. I'm on the pill."

"You're on the pill?" He was as shocked by this announcement as he had been by her having sex. "Where did you get it?"

She shrugged. "Oh, it's available everywhere."

"It's not available at the convent."

"The girls all have it."

"Then at least you won't get pregnant," he said, trying to assimilate everything. "But you could still get a disease."

"You don't get diseases if you have sex with people you know."

"Who told you that?"

"Someone who knows."

"Well, whoever it is, she doesn't know. You can get a disease from anyone who has it. And people you know can have diseases."

"You mean like syphilis?"

"That and others. In fact, they've discovered a new disease that could become an epidemic."

"If you mean herpes, it's not new."

"I mean something they don't yet have a name for."

"What does it do?"

"It destroys your immune system and you die."

"That doesn't sound good," Carla said respectfully.

"Look," he said, trying to reach her. "I'm not trying to scare you out of having sex. I'm not against sex. I happen to like it. But

167

you're too young to be having sex, especially with dumb guys like that."

"He's not as dumb as he looks."

"Yeah?" He had to laugh. "If he's only half as dumb as he looks, he's not smart enough to have a meaningful relationship with you. So save yourself for a better guy, and don't take risks for nothing."

She started to cry. "Well, I'm sorry for lying to Gram, but if I'd told her what I was doing she would have had a fit."

"She would have had a heart attack."

"And what if I'd told you?"

"I would have come running."

"So I had no choice."

"Yeah, you did. You could have waited."

"Okay," she said, thinking. "So am I supposed to tell you the next time I want to have sex with a guy?"

"If I remember correctly what it's like at your age, you'd be telling me that every five minutes. How about telling me the next time you *decide* to have sex with a guy? And how about letting me meet him first?"

"Is that what Mom did with her father?"

"Oh, no," he said, trying to imagine Renata going to her father and telling him she wanted to have sex with a guy. "She could never have done that. She couldn't have had sex before she was married."

"So you were the only guy she had sex with?"

"Yeah," he said, remembering their wedding night.

"Well, I hope you were worth saving herself for," Carla said with a faint smile.

"I hope I was," he said, putting his arm around her. "Please don't do anything that would break her heart."

"I won't," Carla promised.

It was Friday, the fourth day that he had been held captive in this room. He had four more days, including today, to get Abdullah released from prison. Sometime today they would have a response to his third tape. He had already warned his captors not to expect to get what they wanted on this round, so as long as the government improved its offer he would probably be able to get them to keep using his approach. If it didn't, they would have to revert to the threat of violence.

Zoraya had brought him breakfast, which he had finished more than an hour ago, and he was pacing back and forth like an animal in its cage trying to get some exercise when she returned to get him.

"Any news?" he asked her, unable to read her face. She had the ability to remove any expression from it, including from her mouth and her eyes, if she didn't want people to know what she was thinking or feeling. She must have learned how to do this at an early age, no doubt to avoid giving satisfaction to the man who abused her.

"Come and see," she told him impassively.

He followed her downstairs to the screening room, where he took his assigned place at the foot of the bed. Ramón and Manuel were completely engrossed in what they were watching—like his children in front of the television when they were younger, they seemed to have tuned out the world.

"We're seeing a tremendous response to Senator Wyatt's latest appeal," a blond anchorwoman was saying. "Based on our surveys, we estimate that more than one million people have already called their representatives and told them to get the Muslim cleric released from prison. And this number is steadily rising."

They cut to a scene on a street corner where a reporter was interviewing a man in a khaki suit and a bright red tie.

"Did you watch Senator Wyatt's appeal?" the reporter asked.

"You bet I did," the man said, nodding.

"What do you think of it?"

"I think Senator Wyatt is right. I think we should treat these people fairly. Just because they're Moslims, that doesn't make them terrorists."

"Do you think our government should release this cleric?"

"You bet I do," the man said without hesitation. "If Senator Wyatt says he was wrongfully convicted, that's good enough for me."

"Did you call your representative?"

"I called him after hearing the first appeal, and I called him again after hearing the second one. I'll keep calling him until he does something."

"What if he doesn't?"

"Then I won't vote for him in the next election."

Jim smiled, feeling that the man's performance couldn't have been better if he had been scripted. The next scene showed the reporter interviewing two young women in pretty summer dresses.

"Did you hear Senator Wyatt's appeal?"

"Ya, ya," the women said together.

"What did you think of it?"

"Oh, we just love Senator Wyatt," the taller one said.

The shorter one giggled.

The reporter, seeing an opportunity, asked: "Why do you love him?"

"Because he's done so much for the people."

"He's also attractive," the shorter one said, rolling her eyes.

"So what do you think? Should the government release this cleric from prison?"

"Oh, ya. We know he's innocent," the taller one said.

"I feel sorry for the poor man," the shorter one said. "I mean, how would you like to be in prison for something you never did?"

"How do you know he's innocent?"

"Senator Wyatt says he is," the taller one said.

"We trust Senator Wyatt," the shorter one said.

"Have you called your representatives?"

"Ya. We call them every hour."

"What if they don't release this man?"

"We'll change the government," the taller one said.

"We have the power," the shorter one said.

The reporter passed the story back to the anchorwoman, who said: "Thanks, Bob. That gives you an idea of what's happening.

So far there has been no response from Washington, but we'll keep giving you the latest on this story."

Manuel muted the television.

"Is this what you were hoping would happen?" Ramón asked.

"Yes," Jim said. "It's exactly what I was hoping would happen."

"And you believe the government will respond to this kind of pressure?"

"It has to respond sooner or later."

"Well, it better be sooner," Manuel said.

"Don't worry. We have more than a million people calling their representatives and telling them to get the government to release Abdullah. That's going to have some influence, believe me. I know how politicians think, and right now," Jim stressed, "they're thinking about the next election."

"Let's see what happens," Ramón said, unconvinced.

Manuel turned on the television, and they saw an expert analyzing the situation in Bosnia. He estimated that more than forty thousand people had been displaced by the Serbian takeover of Srebrenica, and based on the difference between the number of people who had evidently fled the area and the number who had either reached a safe destination or were still in flight, he estimated that at least eight thousand had been killed. He warned that the number could go higher every day.

"So what should we do?" the interviewer asked.

"We should intervene," the expert said. "We should stop this calamity."

"You see?" Ramón said. "We have an expert on our side."

"You have a state senator on your side too," Jim said, heading for the door.

Zoraya took him back to his room and closed the door behind them, saying: "It looks like your approach is working."

"So far, so good," Jim said, sitting at the table.

Zoraya sat down across from him. "Those people obviously love you. What does it feel like to be loved by so many people?"

"They don't love me, they love what I've done for them."

"You mean they're like children who love what their parents have done for them."

"They're like that, yes. But children don't really know their parents, so how could they love them?"

"Do you have to know someone in order to love him?"

"I think you do. I'm not talking about sex," he said. "With sex I think it's the opposite. The less you know someone, the more attractive the person is."

"And the more you know him, the less attractive?"

"With pure sex, yes. But when sex is an expression of love, then it's like love."

After a long silence she asked: "So how well do you think you know me?"

"Not too well, but I'm getting to know you."

"Still, there are a lot of things about me that you don't know."

"There are," he agreed. "For one thing, I don't know how old you were when your mother died."

"I was four," she said.

"In that respect, you have something in common with my daughters. They were five and three when their mother died."

"They probably don't remember her."

"Carla does a little. Gina doesn't, though she thinks she does."

"I remember only one thing. I remember falling and hurting myself, and how my mother picked me up and held me in her arms. She smelled of cinnamon."

"Cinnamon?"

"Yes. She must have been using it in something that she was cooking, or maybe putting it into her tea. I don't know. But every time I smell cinnamon," Zoraya said with tears forming in her eyes, "I remember my mother."

"It's hard," he said. "My girls never got over losing their mother."

Zoraya wiped her eyes with the back of a hand. "Well, at least they had you as a father. That saved them."

He shook his head. "All I did was keep them alive until they made it through their teens. They saved themselves."

She gazed pensively into the distance. "You said that children really don't know their parents. But they must get to know them as they grow up."

"They do. My children know me better than they did before. But they're not children any more. Except for the last one."

"How old is the last one?"

"Fifteen."

"When I was that age I was living in Granada." A look of regret filled her eyes. "It's very ironic. I didn't kill a man I should have killed, and now I might have to kill a man I shouldn't kill."

"You think you should have killed your father?"

"Yes. I should have."

"You could have. Why didn't you?"

"I don't know. I often thought about it, but something always stopped me."

"Well, it's a good thing you didn't kill him."

"Luckily he died so I didn't have to."

"How well did you know him?"

"Well enough to hate him."

"From my experience," Jim said, "most daughters hate their fathers at times, but you had a very good reason for hating your father."

"Did your daughters hate you?"

"At times they did. But they got over it."

"I'll never get over it."

"I have to admit, I can't see any way of justifying what your father did to you. So you can't get over it by believing that what he did to you was for your own good. You have to rise above it."

"I do? How?"

"By seeing yourself through your own eyes."

She looked almost hopeful.

About a month after he had caught Carla having sex with that boy Thea appeared in the doorway of his office as soundlessly as she had the first time. It was after five, and the secretary had left for the day.

"Senator Wyatt?" she said, reverting to formality.

Again he was startled, being immersed in the legal language of a proposed bill. Turning and seeing her, he said: "Oh, hi."

"I thought I'd drop by and say hello," she said, advancing into his office.

"Sure," he said, getting up. The sight of her moist, full lips aroused the desire that he had kept under control for more than a year.

She closed the door behind her and unbuttoned her overcoat.

"Have a seat," he said, coming around to the front of his desk and bringing a chair for her. "How have you been?"

"Oh, I've been fine." She tossed the coat over the back of another chair. "But I've missed working with you."

"We were good together."

"Yes. We were."

"Do you have another project in mind?"

"Well, it's not a project. But I do have something in mind."

"What?" he asked, not guessing.

"This," she said, kissing him.

It was as if her mouth was a trapdoor that opened underneath him and he fell through it, into an abyss.

Somehow he had the presence of mind to lock the door and turn out the lights before things went further. As they resumed kissing he felt her hands undoing his belt, unzipping his fly, and pulling down his pants. She maneuvered him to the chair that he had brought for her, sat him down, and then knelt and tugged at his briefs. He clutched the tight curls on her head as she took him into her warm, wet mouth.

After a while she rose from her knees and stepped out of her panties and lifted her dress and straddled him, guiding him into her with an unerring hand. He soon realized that the gusts of desire that had unsettled him from time to time had their counterpart but in her they were storms.

It was after six when he called his mother, telling her that he would be a little late in picking up the girls.

As he and Thea left the office they didn't talk about what had happened and they didn't make a date to see each other again.

They parted with a handshake, acting as if they had been discussing legislation.

Driving away from the capitol, he tried to imagine having a relationship with Thea, but there were the same obstacles, starting with the logistical one. During the week he picked up the girls at his mother's house at six o'clock, and he had dinner with them at home. On Friday evenings Inga or her au pair dropped off the boys to spend the weekend with him. On Sundays on their way to the twelve o'clock Mass he left the boys at Inga's house or at her father's house if she was out of town, and then he took the girls to church. After church they went to the Marchi house for a traditional Sunday dinner, which lasted until late afternoon, and then they went home, where they usually watched television together. So other than lunch there was no time in his schedule for Thea.

By the time he arrived at his mother's house he had decided to call Thea later that evening and arrange to have lunch. At least that way he could get to know her. Though they had worked together for more than six months, he hadn't learned much about her personal life. He knew that her father owned a large distributor of food and liquor, that she had grown up in an affluent suburb informally known as Sunfish Lake, and that she had dropped out of college without completing her bachelor's degree. But that was all because until this evening their relationship had been strictly professional.

Of course he was tempted to repeat what they had just done, but he had to rule that out. If a colleague or an aide had come to talk with him and found the door locked and paused to listen, it would have been all over town that Senator Wyatt was having sex with someone in his office. Lunch would be safe, and if they were seen together in a restaurant or a club, it would look as if they were working together on another project. In fact, the more public they were, the better.

After dinner, while the girls were upstairs doing their homework, he called Thea at her home number, which she had given him months ago so that he could contact her on weekends if necessary. She answered after three or four rings.

"It's Jim," he said. "Are you free for lunch tomorrow or the next day?"

"I have a commitment tomorrow," she told him without the slightest pause. "But the next day would be fine."

"I'll meet you at the University Club at twelve-thirty. Okay?"

"Okay. I'll see you then."

He arrived ahead of her, and he got a table with a view of the city. You could see the bridges over the river and the downtown buildings, including the courthouse and the First National Bank Building. It was February, so except for a channel that they kept open for barge traffic the river was covered with ice and snow.

Thea was on time, and as she approached he rose from the table to pull out a chair that would give her the best view. Despite what they had done in his office he felt like a kid on a blind date.

"This is nice here," she said, looking out the window.

"You've been here before, haven't you?"

"No. I'm a Sunfish Lake girl."

"Well, it's a family tradition with us."

"I'll bet your grandfather was a founder of the club."

"He was," Jim said. "How did you guess?"

"I know a lot about you."

"Yeah, my life is public information."

"Most of it is. But luckily not all of it," she said, smiling.

"Well, I don't know anything about you."

"You don't," she agreed. "And maybe we should keep it that way."

"Maybe we should. But it wouldn't be fair."

"I guess it wouldn't. It would put you at a disadvantage."

"I wouldn't mind that. I'd just like to know more about you."

"Okay," she said, rolling her eyes upward as if she was going to the top of a list.

At that point the waitress came to take their order.

When they had dealt with that she began: "I was born on April 16, 1951, so in two months I'll be twenty-eight. My grandfather didn't found a club. He had a business in Greece, and he was lucky to escape from the war there."

"Is your grandfather still alive?"

"No. He died last year. He was ninety-seven."

"So you have longevity in your family."

"Unfortunately, yes. My father will probably live that long."

"What's your father like?"

She paused as if she was trying to find the right words to describe her father. She finally said: "He's worse than an animal. At least male animals desert their offspring and leave them alone."

"Sometimes they eat them."

"That would have been a mercy."

"What did he do to you?"

"I'd rather not talk about it at lunch."

"Okay," he said warily. "What's your mother like?"

"She's his property. And she enjoys it. She loves belonging to a rich man."

"Do you have any brothers and sisters?"

"I have a younger brother."

"How old is he?"

"He's twenty-five. He works for my father. And he's trying to be just like my father. He'll probably succeed."

"So you're close to your family."

"Very close."

He liked the way she said this with a perfectly straight face. "Well, families can be a challenge."

"Is yours a challenge?"

"At times, yes. But I was thinking of other people's families."

"You mean the families of your wives?"

"Yes. You have something in common with them."

"I must," she said, "or I wouldn't be interested in you."

"I thought you were interested in passing legislation for mental health."

"I still am. We've only just begun. But what happened last evening had nothing to do with mental health."

"Well, it was good for *my* mental health."

177

She smiled. "I'm glad. It was good for mine too."

"So what do you want to do with your life?" he asked after a silence that looked as if it might lead to a repetition of last evening, though he couldn't imagine where—would they have to sneak off to a motel?

"I want to help women like me," she said with some passion. "I mean, women who have low self-esteem because they've been abused by their fathers."

"That sounds like a worthy purpose. But you don't act like a woman who has low self-esteem."

"No. I don't. I act like I have high self-esteem. But it's an act."

"It's a good act. You could have fooled me."

"I've been doing this act all my life."

"Okay," he said, returning to her statement. "You want to help women like you. So why aren't you a psychologist?"

"Psychologists are limited in what they can do. It's better to be a psychiatrist."

"So why aren't you a psychiatrist?"

"I didn't believe I could get into medical school."

"Let me guess why. Because you have low self-esteem?"

"You understand," she told him as if no one ever had.

"But don't you have to help yourself," he asked, "before you can help others?"

"Not necessarily. You can help yourself by helping others. Isn't that what you do all the time?"

"Me? I never thought about it."

"Why are you in politics?"

"To help people."

"That's what you all say," she said. "But you know what's special about you?"

"No," he said, curious.

"You really mean it. The others just say it."

"I guess that's a compliment."

"It is. So you're my inspiration. I figure that if you can do it in politics, I can do it in mental health."

"You mean you're going to try to get into medical school?"

"That's what I came to tell you last evening," she said with brightening eyes. "I've decided to go back to college."

"Well, that's great," he said, happy for her.

"I wanted you to know about my decision because if I hadn't met you and worked with you, I wouldn't have believed that I could do it. But I never got around to telling you. I was too distracted."

"I'm glad you told me now and not then."

She laughed. "Yes. It's better now."

For a while he saw her only for lunch, about once a week, but then in late March came an opportunity to spend more time with her. As usual, Marchi took the girls to Florida for their spring break, which left Jim free in the evenings for a week. They spent the first of these evenings at her apartment, a one-bedroom condo that had been developed in a mansion on Summit Avenue, next to the one where his mother had lived when she was growing up. It began with dinner, which Thea prepared—a pot roast cooked in red wine with roasted potatoes and braised carrots—and it ended in her bed, where he stayed all night.

By the end of June he believed that he knew Thea well enough to introduce her to the girls, which he did by inviting her for dinner at his house on a Saturday night, having previously arranged for the boys to stay with Inga's parents that weekend. They had spaghetti with meatballs, which he cooked, and they ate informally at the kitchen table. The girls seemed more interested in the food than in Thea, but there were no evident problems. The girls had learned to be adaptable.

When Thea had left he talked with the girls one at a time to get their impressions, starting with Gina, who he knew would be easier. At fifteen, Gina was interested in boys, and she obviously grasped the fact that Thea was interested in her father in the same way. She also seemed to understand that her father had needs that as his daughter she couldn't fulfill, and she was evidently willing to give Thea a chance to fulfill them.

Carla was another matter. Instead of answering his questions she raised her own questions, starting with: "Why do you care what I think of her?"

"Because you're my daughter. We live together."

"Only for another year," Carla pointed out. With his strong encouragement she was planning to go away to college.

"I know. But we'll still have a relationship."

"Are you going to marry her?"

"It's a possibility."

"It must be more than a possibility," Carla said, searching his face. "Or you wouldn't have introduced her to us."

"Okay. It's more than a possibility."

"Well, if you want to marry her, go ahead. You don't need my approval."

"You're right. I don't need it, though I'd like to have it."

"I'm sorry, but I don't know enough about her."

"You'll get to know her better."

"Maybe I will, but I still won't know enough to approve your marrying her. How could I ever know enough?"

"That's a good question," he admitted.

"I'm not against your marrying her. I just don't know enough to take a position either way."

"Okay," he told her, "I appreciate your candor."

A few weeks later he introduced Thea to his parents. They had drinks and snacks with his parents on a Sunday afternoon at their summer house.

Jim had beer with his father, while Thea had white wine with his mother. His father questioned him about a tax reform that he had proposed, and his mother interrogated Thea about her background, her family, and her education, among other things. He could tell that his parents weren't crazy about Thea. Even his father had greeted her without the warmth he usually bestowed on females.

At one point Jim left her alone with his father, giving her an opportunity to charm him, and he followed his mother into the kitchen, where she was going to replenish the snacks. As she opened a box of crackers she said: "I assume you had a reason for introducing us to this young woman."

"I want to marry her," he said.

"That's what I thought. How long have you known her?"

"A year and a half. Actually longer."

"Why haven't we heard about her before?"

"For most of that time," Jim explained, "our relationship was professional. We worked together on a mental health program."

"So you knew her professionally."

"That's right. We worked together very well."

His mother shook some crackers out of the box and onto a plate. "I haven't been able to find out much about her background. I understand that her grandfather came here from Greece, and that her father makes a lot of money distributing liquor."

"Food and liquor," Jim corrected her.

"Have you met him?"

"No. I'm going to meet him next weekend." This wasn't quite true because Thea had only agreed to introduce him to her family at the first opportunity but she still hadn't set a definite date.

"Well, I can't make any judgments about her. I don't know her family, and I haven't ever known a Greek."

"It sounds like you *have* made a judgment."

"I haven't made a judgment," his mother insisted, picking up the plate.

They returned to the porch, where Thea didn't seem to be doing any better with his father. She was patiently explaining to him why mental health was so important, and he was struggling to feign interest.

As they drove away on the winding Peninsula Road she said: "You're parents are the worst snobs I've ever met."

"They're exclusive," he admitted.

"You mean they exclude from their world anyone who isn't white, Anglo-Saxon, and Protestant."

"Basically, yes. But they're willing to include people who aren't. As you know, my first wife was Italian and Catholic. And my brother married a woman who was Afro-Latina."

"How did your mother feel about them?"

"She had reservations about them," he said. "She believes that marriage is hard enough when the two people come from the same background."

"Well, just because she had problems with her own marriage that doesn't make her an expert on marriage."

"I don't think she claims to be an expert on marriage."

"You know," Thea told him after a long, strained silence, "you don't need her approval to marry me."

"I know I don't."

"But you want her approval."

"I wouldn't mind having it. We all live in the same town. And the girls spend a lot of time with her."

"I think it's stronger than that," Thea said. "You want her approval of everything you do. You're still her little boy, and she knows how to keep you in that position—by withholding her approval."

Resisting this analysis, he said: "You should wait until you have a license before you start practicing psychology."

"I don't need a license to tell you what I think."

"No. You don't."

"And I think your relationship with your mother explains a lot about you."

"What does it explain?" he asked, going along with her—and trying not to hit a tree that seemed to jump out onto the road.

"It explains why you need a woman to validate your identity."

"You mean I need a woman to tell me who I am?"

"You don't need a woman to tell you who you are. You need a woman to validate who you wish you were."

"And how do they validate it?"

"By having sex with you, or by falling in love with you."

"By either?" he asked, trying to be amused.

"Yes, by either. But sex only gives you a temporary validation. Love gives you a validation that lasts longer."

"So who are you validating?"

"The state senator who does wonderful things."

"I don't need you to validate that," he said, smiling. "I got seventy percent of the vote in the last election."

"That's not enough," she argued. "Even if you got a hundred percent of the vote, it wouldn't be enough."

"Why not?"

"Because you'd still need your mother's approval."

"I get her vote," Jim argued back.

"That's not the same as her approval."

Turning onto the main road that went around the lake, he said: "It's an interesting theory. But I think it's a crock of shit."

She laughed almost graciously. "Of course you do. If you didn't, I wouldn't have any respect for you."

"We got a response from the government," Zoraya said, entering his room.

"What was it?" he asked hopefully, though he could see from her face that it wasn't what they wanted.

"They offered to review Abdullah's sentence."

"Is that all?" he said, trying not to show his disappointment.

"That's all. And they didn't explain what it means."

"Well, it probably means they're willing to consider giving Abdullah a shorter sentence, or maybe even commuting the time he's already served. If they did that, then they could release Abdullah immediately."

"But it's not certain."

"No. It's not."

"What would it depend on?"

"It would depend on a legal process. There would be a hearing, and a judge would render a decision on it."

"A Jewish judge."

"The judge could be anything."

"He couldn't be a Muslim."

"Maybe he could be. I don't know."

"Well, we've discussed this offer," Zoraya said, "and we've decided to turn it down. We don't trust your legal system."

"Why don't you give it a chance?"

"We already did. And look what happened."

"It's a different situation now."

"I don't believe it. Nothing has changed. So you better start thinking about what you're going to say in your next tape."

"I already know," he told her.

"You mean you didn't expect them to give us what we want?"

"Not on this round. You have to understand. This is a process of negotiation."

"They keep saying they don't negotiate with terrorists."

"They have to say that. But look what they're doing. They've already given us a better offer. And their next offer will be even better."

"I hope so, but if it's not what we want, we might not have time for another offer."

"As long as we're making progress toward our goal," he argued, "we should keep negotiating with them."

"The deadline is Tuesday," she reminded him.

"Well, let's see what happens," he said, deciding not to argue this point. If they could get the government to make a better offer, at that time he would have a better chance of convincing her to extend the deadline.

NINE

A FEW WEEKS after meeting his parents Thea introduced him to her father. They met for lunch at the Athletic Club. Her father, Leon, was a big man, almost as tall as Halvar but much heavier. Jim could imagine him playing linebacker for the Vikings and littering the field with the broken bodies of running backs or any blockers who got in his way.

"So what's the purpose of this meeting?" Leon asked after they had sat down and ordered. With folded arms he leaned back in his chair as if he was about to hear an unwelcome business proposal.

"I wanted to meet you," Jim said.

Thea said nothing. She just watched her father warily.

"Why did you want to meet me? Do you want my opinion on how you should reform the tax system in this backward state?"

"If you have an opinion, I'd be happy to hear it."

"Lower the taxes on businesses."

"I've heard that before from other business owners," Jim said, thinking of Halvar, who raised this issue almost every time they saw each other.

"Then why don't you do something about it?"

"I'm working on it."

"Yeah, sure. You don't care about business owners," Leon said disdainfully. "You only care about people on welfare. But where will you get the money to pay people on welfare if you kill all the businesses?"

"A record number of new businesses were started in the state last year."

"And a record number failed—or moved to another state."

"Actually, the net increased."

"You can make up all the numbers you want, but you can't hide what's going on. If I had a business that I could relocate, I'd do it tomorrow."

185

"Why don't you sell it and move to Florida?" Thea suggested.

"Why don't you mind your own business?" Leon growled at her. "The senator and I are trying to have a conversation."

She glared at him but didn't respond.

"The reason I wanted to meet you," Jim said, redirecting, "is that Thea and I want to get married."

Leon laughed unpleasantly. "You want to marry *her?*"

"Yes. I want to marry her."

"Well, you don't need my permission."

"I know. I'm not asking for your permission."

"Then why did you want to have lunch with me?"

"I wanted to meet you." Jim added: "It's customary to meet the parents of the person you intend to marry."

"Then meet her mother," Leon told him. "I have nothing to do with this girl."

"She's your daughter."

"So her mother claims, but I don't believe it."

"Oh, here we go again," Thea said, "with the justification."

"Watch your mouth," Leon warned her.

"He justifies what he did to me by pretending that I'm not his daughter."

"I don't have to listen to this crap," Leon said, rising.

"He's in denial," Thea said.

"She has a sick imagination," Leon said.

"It was very nice meeting you," Jim said, rising and extending his hand.

Leon shook it, almost breaking his bones. "Good luck to you."

When he had left, Thea said: "I told you."

"Yeah. You didn't exaggerate."

After a long silence she said: "I haven't told you what he did to me. Would you like to know?"

"Yeah, tell me," he said, believing that he had to know.

It was what he had imagined. Her father had violated her, starting when she was twelve. He had threatened to kill her if she told anyone, and she had believed him. She had also believed that it was her fault. Her mother hadn't noticed, or she had pretended not to notice. Finally, at the age of fifteen Thea decided that she would rather have him kill her than let him continue abusing her, and she told him that if he laid another finger on her she would go to the police. So he stopped, but whenever it came up he justified what he had done by pretending that Thea wasn't his daughter but the offspring from a love affair that her mother had with a real estate agent.

"So I'm not only a slut," she said, "I'm also a bastard."

"Terms of endearment," Jim said, appalled by the image of that three hundred pound gorilla lying on top of a twelve-year-old girl. Of course he had known from their first conversation at the University Club that her father had done something terrible to her, so only the details were new information. But they made him want even more to help Thea rise above what her father had done to her.

In early August they were married in a private ceremony at the courthouse. The legislature was in recess at that time, so he could get away, and they went for a week to a resort in Mexico that only ten years ago had been a fishing village. Thea obviously didn't want to go to Spain, where he had honeymooned with Inga, and since neither of them had been to Mexico it had no past associations for them. The girls stayed with his parents at the lake, and the boys stayed with Inga's parents at their place on the St. Croix River because Inga was traveling frequently, with trips to Europe, Latin America, and Asia. If he hadn't been famous himself, people might have referred to him as Inga Torvald's ex-husband.

When they returned from their honeymoon Thea moved into the house with him and the girls. Carla was about to start her senior year in high school, and her mind was focused on getting good grades so she would be accepted by Boston College. Gina was about to start her sophomore year, and her mind was focused on boys, but either she wasn't having sex with them yet or she was lucky enough not to get caught. By then he had adopted a policy of warning them about the risks of having unprotected sex but not trying to stop them from doing what they were going to do no matter what he said or did because their peers were doing it. His warnings were supported by the rapid spread of the new disease that he had told Carla about, which now had a name, AIDS, and which even the nuns had warned the girls about, implying that it was a new form of punishment for committing a mortal sin.

About six weeks later he was surprised to learn from Thea that she was pregnant, presumably having conceived on their honeymoon.

"I thought you were on the pill," he said, wondering if he should have extended his parental lectures to include Thea. They were in the kitchen, where he was preparing dinner. The girls were upstairs doing their homework.

"I was," Thea said, "but I went off it."

"You decided to have a baby?"

"Yes. I've always wanted one."

"Well, you could have shared this decision with me."

"You're not having the baby, I am."

"We're both having it," he said. "And since we're going to share the responsibility, we should have shared the decision."

"You act like you don't want me to have a baby."

"I want you to have a hundred babies if that's what you want. But I thought you wanted to go to medical school."

"I still do."

"Well, won't your having a baby now get in the way?"

"Not unless I let it. I can do both."

"You've never had a baby. You don't know what it's like."

"So you're an expert on having babies?"

"I have some experience at raising children."

"Your mother's raising the girls," she said as if this was a bad thing.

"No, she isn't. They go to her house after school for a few hours every day, but they spend most of their time with me."

"I'll bet they spend more time with her."

"I'm not going to argue about it. You haven't been with us long enough to know how the girls spend their time. So let's talk about this baby."

"What's there to talk about? Do you want me to have an abortion?"

"Of course I don't," he said. "I'm against abortion."

"I'm not talking about your political position."

"My political position is based on my personal position. There's no difference. Not on this issue or on any issue."

"So you don't want me to have an abortion," Thea said, "because it's against your personal belief."

"That's not it," he said, shaking his head. "I want you to have a baby if you want to have one. I just didn't know you wanted to have one."

"Every woman wants to have a baby."

"But why now when you're trying to finish college and get into medical school?"

"Well, as they say, there's no time like the present."

"Fine. But if you wanted to have a baby, you could have at least let me know."

"If I had, you might have withheld your sperm from me."

"Oh, sure. I might have trained them all to swim the other way. But why would I have done that?"

"To stop me from having a baby."

"Why would I have wanted to stop you from having a baby?"

"Because you already have four children."

"And four's the limit?"

"It's beyond the limit for most people."

"Well, I'm not most people."

Her dark eyes filled with tears. "You're right. I should have trusted you. But it's hard for me to trust men."

"I understand."

"From what you said, it sounds like you don't believe I can both have a baby and finish college."

"I believe you can do both. A lot of women do. I was just saying that it'll be harder when you have a baby to take care of."

"I know it will. But I don't know how long it'll take me to get through medical school, and if I wait until then it could be too late for me to have a baby."

"I understand," he repeated. "My only point is that we should have made this decision together."

"We should have," she agreed, wiping her eyes.

"Then I have no issue."

"Are you happy?"

"Yes. I *am* happy." He took her in his arms and hugged her. "What would you like? A girl or a boy?"

"A girl," Thea said. "So she can have you as her father."

The baby, a boy, was born in May. They named him Matthew, which they chose because it had no history in either of their families. Thea was adamant about his not being James IV, and of course she didn't want to name him after her father.

The girls welcomed him, but Carla was accepted by Boston College and by the end of the summer she was gone, so she didn't get too involved with the baby. On the other hand, Gina got very involved with the baby. Thea had completed her spring courses before the delivery, and she resumed classes in September, so at that point Gina assumed a major role in taking care of the baby.

Jim had two concerns about this. One was that a sixteen-year-old girl might not be an adequate substitute for a mother, and the other was that the responsibility would interfere with Gina's schoolwork. Since he wasn't sure if these concerns were valid, he consulted with his mother before raising them with Thea and Gina.

"I had girls Gina's age helping me," his mother reminded him. They were in her living room, having a drink. "And they were fine."

"Yeah, I remember some of them. Breda, in particular."

"Breda was the best. She taught you how to ride a bike, which I couldn't have done." His mother had always shunned physical activities other than swimming and walking, which kept her in satisfactory shape.

"Did they help you when we were babies?"

"Of course. A mother needs a rest now and then."

"Well, Thea's not resting, she's going to class and doing homework."

"That still gives her a rest from the baby, so she'll feel more positive during the time she spends with him."

"Then you don't see a problem?"

"No, I don't. I'm assuming," his mother added, "that when Thea's not going to class or doing homework she's with the baby."

"Oh, yes. She's with him until three every day when Gina gets home, and she's with him at night after she gets home."

"When does she get home?"

"Around eight."

"So Gina has him for five hours?"

"Well, I relieve Gina at six when I get home."

His mother smiled. "Did you ever learn to change diapers?"

"I finally did. It's not as bad as I thought it would be."

"That's something your father would never do."

"I don't blame him. You had employees to do that. But I don't take advantage of Gina and call her every time a diaper needs changing."

"Good for you," his mother said.

It was surprising how this made him feel. After all, he was forty-one, the father of five children and a widely admired state senator, so her praise shouldn't have mattered a lot to him. But it made him glow.

When he got home he talked with Gina. The baby was sleeping, so Gina was in her room doing her homework. Unlike her sister Gina wasn't a star student, though with application she could perform at the B level. But she was easily distracted by her interest in what Carla disparaged as "girlie-girl" things such as hair, clothes, shoes, and accessories, and more recently by her interest in boys.

"How are you doing?" he asked, going into her room.

"Fine," she said, looking up from a book.

"What are you studying?"

"History," she said as if it was broccoli, which she absolutely refused to eat.

"American?"

"Yeah."

"What period?"

"The colonial period."

"A lot of things happened then."

"I know. But it's boring."

"How's your teacher?"

"She's all right. At least she's not a nun."

"What's wrong with nuns?"

Gina sighed. "They talk about religion and about the things you shouldn't do."

"They don't want you to get into trouble."

"You mean they don't want us to get pregnant."

"Well, that's one kind of trouble."

"That's the kind they always worry about. I guess if you're not allowed to have sex, you think about it all the time."

"What about you?"

"I'm allowed to have sex," Gina said frankly, "so I don't think about it. At least not all the time."

"What do you think about?"

"I think about the baby. I think about having my own babies someday."

"That's fine." He could easily imagine Gina as a mother, especially after seeing how good she was with Matthew.

"You know, you don't have to worry about me."

"What do you mean?"

"I mean about me getting pregnant."

"I don't worry about that," he told her.

"Well, you don't have to. I'm saving myself for my husband."

He didn't think girls did that any more, and at first he didn't know what to say. Then he said: "Your mother would be proud of you."

From the look of beatitude on her face he knew he had said the right thing.

"What I came to ask you," he said after a moment, "is whether the time you spend on the baby is interfering with your homework."

"It's not a problem," she assured him. "He sleeps a lot, and while he's sleeping I can do my homework. When he wakes up, it gives me a rest from this boring stuff."

"You mean the baby's more interesting than your homework?"

"Of course he is. Even *you* are more interesting than my homework."

"It must be awfully dull," he said, laughing. He laid his hand on her shoulder and tenderly kissed the top her head. "I love you."

"I love you too."

Zoraya brought him chicken couscous for lunch and waited for him to try it.

"It's good," he told her.

"Can you taste anything different?"

"Mm." He took another bite. "I taste cinnamon."

She smiled. "That's right."

"Did you think about your mother when you smelled it?"

"Yes. You remember what I told you."

"Of course I remember."

"You listen to people."

"I do," he said, "but I don't always understand what they're saying."

"Do you understand your daughters?"

"Better than I used to. Carla was a challenge. Gina was easy. Kelly was—" He couldn't find the right word for her.

"Kelly? You haven't mentioned her before."

"She came later. I adopted her."

"What about your wives?"

"They were all a challenge."

"So why did you keep getting married?"

"I kept meeting women I wanted to marry."

"But why marry them? Why not just have sex with them?"

"Because sex was only a part of it."

"I thought that for men it was the only thing."

"You haven't met the right kind of man."

"If you were younger, would you have been the right kind of man for me?"

He paused, considering. "Maybe I would have."

"Could you have helped me rise above what my father did to me?"

193

"I don't know. At least I could have tried."

"Do you want to help me rise about it?"

"Yes, I do," he told her, conscious of having tried all his life to help women rise above what their fathers had done to them.

"I wish I could believe you."

"You *can* believe me. But you have to make a leap of faith."

"A leap of faith?" She frowned. "That sounds Christian."

"It applies to any religion," he said. "You can't know for sure if God exists, so you have to leap beyond the knowable."

"Well, I guess that could apply to Islam. But we're not talking about God, we're talking about men."

"I know we are. What I'm saying is, you have to make a leap to rise above what your father did to you."

"I tried with that boy in Granada."

"That boy was blind. And he hurt you. But that's no reason to stop trying."

"I haven't stopped trying. I'm trying with you."

"So keep trying. And I'll do what I can to help you."

She searched his face. "You know, I almost believe you."

"Then we're making progress," he said hopefully. "Just as we're making progress with the government."

"What will you say in your next tape?"

"I'll ask people to demonstrate."

"You mean on the streets?"

"On the streets, and in front of their state capitols. Wherever they can be shown on television."

"You really believe it will work?"

"Yeah. It worked for other minority groups."

"I know. But we're different."

"What do you mean?"

"We're the enemy."

"You're not the enemy. Only a few extremists see Muslims that way, and they see all minorities as the enemy."

"Whatever you say, I still believe we're different."

"Then you have to make another leap."

"Well, I can only make one leap at a time," she said, almost smiling. "But if you can get people into the streets, then maybe I'll believe what you say."

In the fall of 1981 the party strategist for the DFL came to his office and gave him the bad news: "We've decided not to back you for the U.S. Senate."

"What?" He was shocked. "Why the hell not?"

"We think you have too many liabilities."

"Liabilities? What do you mean? I won my last election with seventy percent of the vote."

"But this will be a state-wide election, and you'll have trouble with the more conservative districts upstate."

"What kind of trouble? Are they pro-choice?"

"No. They like your position on abortion."

"Are they against extending healthcare insurance?"

"No. They like your position on that."

"Then which of my positions are they against?"

The strategist, a cerebral man with rimless glasses, finally admitted: "They're not against any of your positions. It's your personal life."

"What about my personal life?"

"You've been married three times."

"Are they against marriage?"

"They're against divorce."

"I've only had one divorce."

"I know, but you're on your third wife."

"I have five children. Are they against children?"

"They love children. It's your being married three times that bothers them."

"How do you know?"

"We've been polling up there."

"Well, if I get seventy percent of the votes in the Twin Cities, it doesn't matter how I do up there."

"If you don't win really big here, you'll need those votes."

"So I'll win really big."

"Not if the other party succeeds in tarring your reputation. And they've already started," the strategist said, reaching into his briefcase.

Jim waited while the man pulled out some newspaper clippings.

One was a column by a right-wing bigot who had attacked him from the very beginning of his career. Referring to him as a "serial bigamist," the columnist said it was no surprise that his ex-wife, Inga Torvald, traveled the world playing degenerate music that promoted drugs and kinky sex.

"That's ridiculous," Jim said. "Inga should sue him."

"You better hope she doesn't. That would only pour gasoline onto the fire."

"Someone has to hold this guy accountable."

"Not you. If you get into a pissing match with him, then you won't even have a career as a state senator."

He read the other articles, which were almost as bad. "This is garbage. It's pure garbage. People aren't stupid enough to believe this."

"It sounds like you've forgotten the first maxim of politics," the strategist said. "Never overestimate the intelligence of voters."

"That's cynical."

"It's true."

"I don't believe it."

"Well, the party has made its decision. You can always run as an independent, but that would hand the election to the Republicans."

"Then maybe I'll run as a Republican."

The strategist laughed. "For them you'd have even more liabilities than you have for us. You want my advice?"

"No. Not really."

"I'll give it to you anyway. You're a terrific state senator, so be content with this position, which you can keep as long as you want."

"Thanks for your support," he said sarcastically.

After the man had left his office he made some phone calls, but he got the same answer from everyone he talked to. They all believed that his being married three times was a major liability, and they weren't willing to take a risk on him.

For a while he seriously considered running for U.S. Senator as an independent, but after talking with his campaign manager he realized that it would be almost impossible to raise the kind of money he would need without the backing of either party. But maybe if he ran for state senator as an independent, it would be possible to raise the money for that campaign without the backing of a party. As an independent he might even get bipartisan support for the things he wanted to do.

The decision by his party not to support him left him in a state of depression that he had never experienced before. He had been laid low by the death of Renata and the defection of Inga, but these events hadn't affected his professional life, whereas now his personal life was being used by others to affect and limit his professional life, and after an initial surge of anger he lapsed into a despondency in which he had trouble finding a reason to get up in the morning and go to work.

He shared his feelings with Thea, who said that they were a normal response to what had happened, but she recommended that he see a psychologist whom she had heard good things about. He resisted the idea because it went against his upbringing and his view of himself as someone who helped others, rather than as someone others helped, but after Thea assured him that the man wasn't a Freudian but a Jungian and a practicing Catholic who specialized in adult development, he agreed to have one meeting with him if for no other reason than to show respect for the profession.

The psychologist, whose first name was Andrew, had an office near the university, where they met late one afternoon in early November. Andrew, who had wavy gray hair and a deeply lined face, was evidently older than he was, which helped because he preferred not to talk about his problem with a younger man. They sat in chairs that were at right angles and not directly facing each other, with a coffee table in front of them, on which Andrew put a mug with his green tea.

After the preliminaries Andrew said: "So tell me what's happening with you."

"I don't know. I don't feel like doing anything."

"How long have you felt this way?"

"For about two months."

"Have you ever felt this way before?"

"I've never felt anything like it."

"Did something happen to you two months ago?"

"Yes. My party decided not to support me for the U.S. Senate."

"Did they explain why?"

"They said it was because I've been married three times."

"Do you believe that's the reason?"

"Oh, yes. I believe it."

"So your party has expressed its disapproval of your personal life," Andrew said after a moment. "Why do you care?"

"Because it stopped me from running for the U.S. Senate."

"What if they had decided not to support you because of your positions? Would you have felt the same way?"

He considered. "No. I don't think so."

Andrew said nothing, just looked at him expectantly.

Responding to this silent prompt, he finally said: "Are you suggesting that I feel this way because the party disapproves of my personal life?"

"It's possible. What do you think?"

"I guess it makes sense. I mean, I care about their approval."

"Do you know why?"

"Because they're my party. I depend on them."

"In what way do you depend on them?"

"I depend on them," he said, "to support me in elections."

"So your party," Andrew recapitulated, "disapproves of your personal life. You care about their approval because you depend on them to support you in elections. Which puts you in a tough position. Is there any way out?"

"Yeah. I could stop caring about their approval."

"Could you? Could you stop caring as long as you depend on them?"

"I guess not. The only way out is to leave the party."

Andrew nodded. "Yes. To separate yourself from them."

"Well, maybe I could run as an independent in the next election for state senator. Maybe I don't need a party to raise money for my campaign. Maybe I could do that on my own."

"So why don't you run as an independent?"

"I don't know. I guess I have doubts about whether I could win without the party."

"But why do you have doubts? In your last election you won seventy percent of the vote."

"You've done your homework," Jim said, impressed.

"You're a public figure. It's easy to get information about you. Most of my patients are under the radar."

"Okay. I shouldn't have doubts about whether I could win without the party. But I guess I still have them."

"Maybe you need to understand why you're a politician."

"Oh, I know why. I want to help people."

"What do you get by helping them?"

"It makes me feel good about myself."

"Do you want their approval?"

"I want their votes."

"Is that the same thing?"

"It might be. But it might be different," Jim said, groping in the dark of his mind. "I mean, getting their votes enables me to do things for them, whereas getting their approval would do something for me."

"What would it do?"

"It would validate my identity."

Andrew smiled. "It sounds like you've been reading a book on psychology."

"My wife's a psychologist."

"Did you get that idea from her?"

"Yeah. But I'm not just repeating it."

Andrew reached for the mug and took a sip of tea. "The great thing about elections is that you can get votes and approval at the same time, so we don't need to sort that out for now. But we do need to deal with your fear of separating yourself from your party, which isn't justified by your record—unless you believe you got all those votes because of the party."

"No. I don't believe that."

"Then you know what you have to do."

Three days later he met with the party leaders and told them he was leaving the party and becoming an independent. They tried to talk him out of it, which made him feel they needed him more than he needed them, and he left the meeting in a state of euphoria, which lasted quite a while.

The following week he saw Andrew again. He reported with pride what he had done and how it had made him feel. As he talked it occurred to him that he was seeking Andrew's approval, and when he mentioned it Andrew said: "We have to watch out. We don't want you to transfer your need for approval to me."

"I guess it happens a lot with your patients."

"It does, but I try to head it off."

"So why am I doing this?"

"Why do you think?"

He paused to reflect. "I must have a need for approval that I transferred to the party from somewhere else."

"Do you know where?"

"I don't know. It could be my mother."

"Are you just saying that because you read it in a psychology book?"

"No. But my wife suggested it."

"Well, don't listen to her on this subject."

"Okay. I won't. But it's a possibility."

"Then you need to deal with it. If you still need your mother's approval for what you do in your life, then you'll keep transferring this need."

"So what can I do? I can't leave her the way I left the party."

"No, but you can separate yourself from her."

"I can? How?"

"Well, before you can figure out how, you have to understand your situation with her. So that's what you need to work on."

He worked on it, and he concluded that he still needed his mother's approval for what he did in his life, and that he was still dependent on her. As evidence he cited the fact that he had sought her approval for his three wives, which went beyond the formality of introducing them to his parents. Even when he had sought her advice on the care of his children, he had wanted her approval.

But it wasn't easy to figure out how to separate himself from her. It wasn't enough to resolve not to need her approval in the future. He needed to take some kind of action, as he had with the party.

He finally decided to make a separation agreement with her. Andrew wasn't crazy about the idea but didn't try to stop him because within limits he believed that his patients should find their own ways of dealing with their problems. He helped Jim to edit the agreement, which finally read as follows:

SEPARATION AGREEMENT

WHEREAS there exists a relationship between Abigail Wyatt as mother and James M. Wyatt as son; and whereas James believes that he needs Abigail's approval for what he does in his life; and whereas Abigail may or may not use this need to control his life, the parties agree to the following:

James will recognize that his roles and actions have their own validity, and that they do not need the approval of Abigail or of any other person or institution whatsoever in order to be validated.

Abigail will recognize that James is an independent adult individual, and she will refrain from consciously using any of his needs to control his life.

IN WITNESS WHEREOF we have set our hands this 25th day of January, 1982.

When he showed this agreement to his mother she asked: "Is this a will?"

"No, it's an agreement between you and me," he said, hoping it wasn't a big mistake. "Please read it."

She read it, then said: "There's nothing objectionable in this. But why do you call it a separation agreement?"

"Because I want to stop being dependent on you."

"I didn't know you *were* dependent on me."

"You must have noticed."

"Frankly, I didn't," his mother said. "But if you think you are, then I guess you are."

"I am. Believe me."

"All right. But why do we need a written agreement?"

"Because I need to take some action."

"And this is your action?"

"That's right."

"Well, I don't have a problem in signing it," his mother said. "But your father won't like it. Maybe we shouldn't tell him about it."

"We have to tell him. We can't have secrets in this family."

"We've always had secrets."

"That's not good."

"It may not be good, but at times it's necessary. There are things people don't need to know. Would you like the world to know everything about you?"

"They do," he said.

"They don't know everything. They won't know about this, will they?"

"No. This is in the family."

After a silence his mother asked: "You really believe you need my approval?"

"Yes. I do. I needed it for my wives."

"You didn't get it for this one, and you married her anyway. So you must not have needed it."

His mother had a point. "Well, I wanted it."

"That's not the same as needing it. People want a lot of things that they don't need, and they survive."

"Okay. You're right."

"If you wanted to declare independence from me, you already did it by marrying Thea. You did that on your own. In fact, if you think about it," his mother continued, "you've done almost everything on your own. Do you think we approved of your going into politics? Do you think we approved of your joining the DFL?"

"You voted for me, didn't you?"

"Of course. I would have voted for you if you'd run as a communist. But it wouldn't have meant that I approved of your being a communist."

"Okay," he admitted, remembering his conversation with Andrew about votes and approval not being the same thing. "I did those things on my own."

"Then why do we need to sign this agreement?"

"Are you unwilling to sign it?"

"No. I'm just asking why you need it."

"Because I need to show my shrink that I've done something about my problem."

"All right," his mother said unflappably. "That's a good reason."

That spring Thea completed her bachelor's degree. She had taken the MCAT, the admission exam for medical school, but she hadn't done very well on it, and she was disheartened when she wasn't accepted by any of the medical schools that she had applied to. Jim encouraged her to prepare intensively for the MCAT, take it again, and apply to other medical schools. Meanwhile, she got a job with a psychiatric institute that was located in a suburb of Minneapolis, where she worked as an assistant to a doctor who was doing research on depression.

About six months after she started the job at the institute she started getting home late from work. At first it was eight, and then it was nine, and then it was later. By then he no longer believed that she was staying late to help the doctor analyze data.

"What's going on?" he asked after she had come home at midnight. They were in the living room, where he had been waiting up for her.

"I'm sleeping with Dr. Abramson," she admitted, sinking down into an armchair and looking at the floor.

"Well, that's nice. When were you going to tell me about it?"

"I wasn't going to tell you. I thought it was just a fling, but it's not." She looked up and faced him with teary eyes. "It's serious."

"What does that mean?"

"It means I'm going to leave you and live with him."

He had heard this from Inga in almost the same words, and maybe that was why they didn't hurt as much as they had coming from her. Maybe there was a scar where they had wounded him. "Do you know what you're doing?"

"I never know. But I think I do."

"What about Matthew?"

"He'll be fine. David loves children."

"David? Does he have any children of his own?"

"Yes. He has two children. They live in Ann Arbor with his ex-wife."

"How old is he?"

"Your age."

"Where does he live?"

"Near the institute."

"That's convenient."

"I don't want to go into the details," Thea said, getting up from the chair. "But I do want to tell you how much I appreciate everything you've done for me. If it weren't for you, I wouldn't have finished college."

"Do you still plan to go to medical school?"

"Yes. If I can get into one."

"Well, maybe he can help you."

"I think he can. He has connections."

He felt as if he was passing her along to a man who could help her more at her next stage of development.

They ended up sharing custody of Matthew, who spent the weekdays with Thea and the weekends with him, or with him and Gina, who was happy that she could still play a role in Matthew's life. In other respects Gina became the woman of the house, preparing meals and doing the laundry and cleaning. Though he tried to help her with these tasks, she resolutely took them over, implying by her behavior that men weren't good at such things. When he offered to hire someone to do the cleaning, Gina declined, saying that it would be a waste of money.

In the spring he was invited to speak at a conference in New York, and he gladly accepted, needing a break. After checking into the St. Jerome and hanging up his clothes he walked out into the mild April evening and relished the feeling of being in New York. His keynote speech at the conference the next morning was a big success, though as usual he had the feeling that there was one person in the audience who hadn't applauded. From his therapy sessions, which he had discontinued after showing Andrew the signed separation agreement, he might have concluded that the unidentified person was his mother, but he had doubts about this explanation, especially after his mother had pointed out that her lack of approval hadn't stopped him from doing what he wanted. Recently he had confided in a priest, who had suggested that the holdout might be God—an idea that provoked some serious thinking.

That evening he went to the bar, where he talked with the bartender and watched the Yankees on television in the hope that someone might join him. Finally, a young woman with short blond hair appeared beside him. She was wearing a gray sweatshirt over khaki pants, implying that she had dressed down for the evening.

"What kind of beer do you have?" she asked the bartender. After hearing the list she selected one, placing a foot on the rail at the bottom of the bar. She was wearing sneakers.

He watched as she raised the glass of beer and took a healthy swig and wiped her mouth with the back of her hand.

"Man, that tasted good," she said.

"You must have been thirsty," he said.

"I jogged around the reservoir," she explained, checking him out. "I drank a lot of water, but it wasn't enough."

"Do you live here?"

"No. I'm here on business."

"What do you do?"

"I'm a stringer for a national magazine."

"That sounds interesting."

"It's not," she said. "I live in Boise, Idaho, and nothing ever happens there."

"Do you have a job with a local newspaper?"

"Yeah. But it doesn't pay me enough to live on, so I also work as a gym teacher."

"I imagine that keeps you in shape."

"Yeah. It keeps me in shape for what I really love to do."

"What's that?" he asked, trying to imagine.

"Skiing," she told him.

"What do you love about skiing?"

"I love going downhill," she said with a gleam in her wild blue eyes. "I love a slope that's so steep that you feel like you're falling."

"Well, you live in a good place for skiing."

"Yeah. But it's not a good place for doing anything else."

"What else would you like to do?"

"I'd like to be a real journalist."

"Then why don't you take a shot at it?"

"I just did. I asked the magazine for a regular job.'

"And what did they say?"

"They said I don't have the talent. They're willing to use me as a stringer, but they won't give me a regular job."

"You could try another magazine."

"Yeah. I could. But I don't know." She lifted her glass and took another swig of beer. "What do you do?"

"I'm a war correspondent."

"You're kidding," she said, lighting up. "Who do you work for?"

"I freelance," he said. "You never heard of me because I don't get bylines. But I love what I'm doing."

"Where have you been recently?"

"Sri Lanka, Ethiopia, Mozambique, and other places."

"Wow! That's fabulous. I wish I could cover wars instead of local crimes."

"It's a dangerous life."

"I don't mind danger. In fact, I love it."

After she had finished the beer he asked her if she was hungry, and she said, yes, she felt like eating meat, so he took her to Smith & Wolensky, where she devoured a slab of prime rib. During the meal he found out that her name was Lori.

They walked off the meal, returned to the hotel bar, and had some after dinner drinks, and then they went up to his room.

From the sway of her breasts he had known she wasn't wearing a bra, but he hadn't guessed that she also wasn't wearing panties, so when she pulled her sweatshirt up and off and dropped her pants she was immediately naked and ready for action. Charged with energy, she joined him and was carried away to a battlefield where mortar shells exploded in bursts of orange flame.

"Are you ready?" Zoraya asked, entering his room.

"Yeah," he said. "Let's go."

They went to the production room, where Ramón and Manuel were waiting.

By now Jim was beginning to feel as if the four of them were partners in a company that specialized in making tapes for kidnappers.

"Do you have any new ideas?" Ramón asked him.

"Yes," he said, sitting down at the table. "Listen to this."

"We're listening," Manuel said skeptically.

"Hi," he said, addressing his constituents. "This is Jim Wyatt, and I want to tell you how much I appreciate your support for Abdullah, the Muslim religious leader who was wrongfully convicted of inciting violence. I hear that more than a million of you have called your representatives and told them to use their influence to get this man released from prison. But the government hasn't listened to you, so I'm asking you to do more. I'm asking you to gather this Sunday, July 16, and to demonstrate in front of your state capitol. Wherever you are, go to your state capitol and tell the government to release this man. If you're near Washington, go to the capitol and tell them to release this man. You have the power to change the world."

"That's good," Zoraya said with enthusiasm.

"It's all right," Ramón said.

"It's a new idea," Manuel said.

"Let's tape it," Jim said, taking charge.

When they had finished making the tape they agreed that Manuel should send it right away to the stations they were using. The more time they had to organize, the more people would show up for the demonstrations.

Back in his room, Zoraya asked: "How many people do you think will go and demonstrate?"

"Millions," he said hopefully.

"Well, if that happens, then it will justify what we've done."

"No, it won't. You could have come to me and asked me to help you."

"And you would have taken up our cause?" She shook her head, saying: "I don't believe it."

"I would have. But it's too late to prove it."

"You would have just told us to hire a better lawyer."

"I would have *found* you a better lawyer, and I would have fought for you the way I fought for other groups that weren't treated fairly."

"Maybe you would have. But I didn't know you, and we wouldn't have ever met except the way we did."

"I'm not the only person who would have helped you."

"We tried a lot of people before we decided that the only way was to use force."

"So you met me by kidnapping me. But now you know me, and you know you wouldn't have had to kidnap me."

"I know we wouldn't have had to kidnap you to get you on our side. But I still don't know that having you on our side is enough to get Abdullah released."

"But you're seeing progress."

"Yes," she sighed. "I'm seeing progress. I just hope that we'll have time to get what we want."

"You can give us time."

"No, I can't. I can't change the deadline."

TEN

DURING THAT SPRING he noticed a change in his father's behavior. When he stopped by his parents' house on the way home from work to have a drink with them, he was welcomed as usual but at times he caught his father staring at him as if he didn't know him and wondered what he was doing there.

Since his father didn't seem aware of this behavior Jim decided to talk with his mother about it. They were in the kitchen, where his mother had gone to check on the progress of a beef stew. As he watched her replace the cover of the pot he asked: "Have you noticed anything different about Dad lately?"

"Yes," she said. "His memory's not as good as it was."

"Well, sometimes when he looks at me I have a feeling that he doesn't know me."

"He didn't *want* to know you for a while," his mother told him, "after he saw our separation agreement."

"He didn't say anything to me about it."

"He wouldn't have. You know him."

"What did he say to you?"

"He said he couldn't believe that a son would do such a thing to his mother."

"But it didn't mean anything."

"It didn't to me, but it did to him."

"Then he didn't understand the reason for it."

"I tried to explain it, but that didn't help."

"I'll go and explain it."

"You can try," she said. "But he doesn't want to understand it."

He returned to the living room, where he found his father sitting on the sofa and staring across the room at a framed photograph that hung on the wall.

"I'm trying to figure out who that is," his father said.

210

"It's me," Jim said, sitting down on the sofa next to his father.

"It doesn't look like you."

"It was taken when I was three."

"Oh. It still doesn't look like you."

"Well, I've changed since then."

His father looked at him coldly. "You sure have."

"Mom just told me that you were upset by the agreement we signed."

"What agreement?"

"The one in which we agreed to change our relationship."

"I don't understand. How can a son change his relationship with his mother?"

"It happens all the time as children grow up."

"But why did you call it a separation?"

"That's a term from psychology," he said. "It means to become independent."

"Well, I'm glad you're independent now instead of DFL."

"I figured that would make you happy."

"But I don't like this idea of separation. It sounds like a divorce. We never had divorces in our family."

"We have them now. A lot of families have them."

"I still don't like it. Your mother and I had our problems, but we didn't walk away from them. We worked them out."

"I know. And I respect you for that."

"You shouldn't have let your wives leave you."

"I couldn't stop them."

"I don't understand you," his father said. "I don't understand why you needed a separation agreement with your mother."

"I'll tear it up if you want."

"You can't just tear up agreements. You have to honor them."

"Well, Mom and I can agree to tear it up."

"Are you sure that's you?" His father was staring again at the photograph.

On his next visit he brought the agreement, which he and his mother tore up in front of his father, hoping it would help.

By fall his father had lost his faculties. The doctors ruled out Alzheimer's and other common forms of dementia. They admitted that it was one of those cases they didn't understand. Without a medical explanation his mother developed the theory that his father had willfully lost his faculties in order to avoid thinking about the separation agreement. The advantage of this theory was that it gave his mother hope for recovery, which she clung to tenaciously. The disadvantage was that it made Jim feel his father's condition was his fault.

With the help of a visiting nurse his mother took care of his father at home for more than a year, until it became impossible for her to manage him. At that point his father went into a nursing home, where he had round-the-clock care. His mother visited him every day from ten in the morning until four in the afternoon, missing only a few times when there were blizzards. When Jim went with her his father didn't recognize him. Meanwhile, his mother still believed that if only they could make his father understand that the separation agreement meant nothing, then he would recover his faculties and everything would be all right.

Unable to handle the feeling of guilt that his mother's theory had aroused in him, Jim went back to see Andrew.

"It's all your fault," he told Andrew after relating what had happened.

"Now, what are you doing?" Andrew asked patiently.

"What do you mean?"

"What are you doing when you blame me?"

"I'm transferring my guilt to you."

"Right. And what is your mother doing?"

"I don't know. I guess she's transferring her guilt to me."

"Or her hope."

"Yeah. She's hoping I can bring back my father."

"You should be able to. You're her star."

"But I can't bring him back."

"I know you can't. But let me ask you—" Andrew said, tenting his hands as if he was about to pray. "Is it better or worse for her to have hope?"

"I don't know."

"You can't know."

"Then why did you ask?"

"To make sure you realize that you can't know what's better or worse for her."

"Okay. So I can't know. But where do I go from that point?"

"You go to what happens if you kill her hope and what happens if you let her keep hoping."

"I don't have the power to do either."

"Ah, you're learning," Andrew said with satisfaction. "But what if you did have the power? What would happen if you killed her hope?"

"She wouldn't have hope."

"Would you feel better?"

"I'd feel worse. I mean for her."

"Would you feel better for yourself?"

"Yeah. At least she wouldn't be making me feel it's my fault."

"You think she can make you feel something?"

"Well, I guess she can't make me, but she can enable me."

"That's different. That means you have a choice."

He considered this. "You mean a choice to feel or not to feel it's my fault?"

"Exactly. You can choose not to feel it's your fault. But let's continue. Suppose you let her keep hoping."

"Then she'll have hope," he said. "But I can choose not to feel it's my fault."

"So which is better?"

"It's better to let her keep hoping. But this is all theoretical because we agree I don't have the power to do either."

"That's the whole point. You don't have the power. Just as she can't make you feel anything, you can't make her feel anything."

"So I'm not responsible."

"You're never responsible for how other people feel. But you *are* responsible for what you do to them."

"What I did to her was I made her sign the separation agreement."

"You didn't make her sign it. She chose to sign it."

"Then she shouldn't blame me."

"She's not blaming you," Andrew told him. "She's just hoping it's why your father lost his faculties."

"What does she want from me? A miracle?"

"What would you want in her situation?"

"I guess I'd want a miracle."

Gina was in college now. She had followed in her mother's footsteps and gone to St. Catherine. Jim urged her to live in the dormitory so that she could have the experience of living away from home, but Gina wouldn't consider it, though he insisted that he didn't need her to take care of him.

The boys still came and stayed with them most weekends. Erik was twelve now, and Lukas was ten. They were still into sports, but Erik was becoming more interested in computers, which had just become available to the public. Halvar had bought them Apple computers, which they weren't allowed to bring with them, and at times it was clear that Erik really missed his computer. So Jim bought them personal computers which they could keep at his house. They tried to teach Gina about computers, but she wasn't interested, saying she couldn't imagine having any use for such a thing.

Jim was asked if he would like to teach a course on government and society in the MBA program at St. Thomas University, and having two children in college, he decided that it was a good idea. The class met once a week, and it gave Gina a night when she didn't have to worry about him.

There were about twenty students in the class, with ages ranging from early twenties to late forties. About half of them were women, who tended to sit in the front rows, while the men sat in back. In all his years of school and college Jim had never been in a class with women, so their presence was a novelty. He found that they were more serious than the men, they asked more questions, and they took more notes.

In particular he noticed a woman named Keira who sat in the front row. Her appearance was evidently designed to conceal the fact that she was attractive. Her reddish blond hair was tied back severely, and her makeup was minimal. Her green eyes were always intent, and except when she was asking questions her wide mouth was always compressed—during pauses he could hear her breathing through her nose. Though her figure was obscured by her corporate attire, the tailored suits couldn't completely hide her robust curves.

The week before the midterm exam she lingered after class to ask him some questions. Obviously concerned about the exam, she said: "This is the first course I've taken at the graduate level, and I don't know how well I'll do."

He hadn't seen any work from her, but on instinct he said: "If you review the material and understand it, then you'll do fine."

"Well, I think I understand it."

"Is there anything you don't understand?"

"No. It's just that I haven't been in school for a while. As you can probably tell," she added, lowering her eyes.

He guessed that she was in her mid-thirties, so she could have been out of school for almost fifteen years. "Well, I haven't been in school for a while either, and it looks like half the students in this class are in the same position."

"You haven't taught here before?"

"No. This is my first course."

"Well, I can't compare you with other professors," she said demurely, "but I think you're doing a very good job."

"Would you tell me if you thought I wasn't?"

"Oh, yes. I would. I'm not trying to brown-nose you."

He believed her. "Where do you work?"

"At the head office of TCH." This was the chain of hospitals that dominated healthcare in the Twin Cities, and he knew them well, having fought with them and worked with them over the years.

"And you're getting your MBA so you can advance?"

"That's right. They told me that without an MBA I can't go any further."

"Maybe someone gets a commission," he said, joking.

She smiled not only with her mouth but also with her eyes, revealing the sense of humor that had been missing. It gave him

215

an entirely different picture of her. She was an Irish girl full of life. "I wouldn't be surprised."

They might have talked longer, but a woman came in to clean the classroom.

As they walked out together she said: "I probably shouldn't tell you this, but I have to be honest. I really admire what you've done for healthcare."

"Your bosses never tell me that."

"Well, they don't get it. They're still living in an old paradigm."

Like the smile at his joke her use of this word changed the picture. She was an intelligent manager who understood the new environment in which her industry would have to operate. Having observed that she didn't wear a wedding ring, he resolved to have a drink with her and get to know her better, but only after the course was over because he believed it would be unethical for him to have a relationship with a student, just as it would to have a relationship with an employee.

Keira earned an A in the course. Applying the most rigorous standards to her work, he tried to knock her grade down to make sure that he wasn't being influenced by his interest in her, but the A held up. In fact, if he had ranked the students in his class, she would have been the number one.

Two weeks after the class was over he called her at work, and he invited her to have a drink with him. She told him okay, but she couldn't stay very long because she had to get home and feed her children.

The mention of children again changed the picture. She was now a single mother, trying to raise children and advance in her career at the same time.

They met in a bar on Selby Avenue that had been restored to its former Victorian splendor. It was convenient because she lived in a house on Lincoln Avenue.

"How old are your children?" he asked her as they waited for the bartender to bring their drinks.

"Kelly's sixteen, and Kevin's fourteen."

"Two teenagers. I know what that's like."

"Kevin's fine, but Kelly's totally out of control."

"The hormones are raging."

"They certainly are. I don't remember being like that when I was her age."

"It's different now. I think it's harder to be a kid now."

"I think it's harder to be a mother."

"Both," he agreed.

"She goes to Visitation, just as I did. But I wonder if it's worth the money. They can't control her."

"I sent my girls to Visitation. They're both in college now."

"I don't think Kelly will get that far."

"What about Kevin?"

"Oh, he's a dream. He does well in school, and he helps me at home. He didn't get it from his father."

"How long have you been on your own?"

"Since they were four and two. Their father was a drunk. He killed himself in a car accident. Luckily, he hit a tree and not another car."

"I'm sorry," he said.

"There's nothing to be sorry about. It was a blessing."

"My first wife was killed in a car accident."

"She was?" Keira looked at him with sympathy. "That wasn't a blessing, right?"

"Right. She was a wonderful person."

"Was she the mother of your girls?"

"Yes. They were six and four at the time."

"Did you raise them yourself?"

"Oh, no," he said. "My mother helped me, and my second wife also helped me."

"My mother helps me. I couldn't do it without her."

"Well, there's something to be said for extended families."

"There is," she agreed. She sipped her drink. "I read in a newspaper column that you've been married three times."

"I have," he said, restraining his feelings about the columnist.

"Are you married now?"

"No. I live with my younger daughter, Gina. She goes to St. Catherine."

"I went there. How does she like it?"

"She likes it fine. But I think she's more interested in getting married than in finishing college."

"That's what I did. I dropped out of college to get married. I had my children, and I didn't go back for ten years."

"When did you get your bachelor's degree?"

"Five years ago. And as far as I was concerned, that was it."

"I haven't had the experience, but I imagine it's not easy to go back to school."

"It's not," she said. "If I had it to do all over again, I never would have dropped out of college."

"Well, maybe you can share your experience with Gina."

"I'd be happy to." She checked her watch. "I have to get going."

"I understand. I'll give you a call."

"Please do," she said encouragingly.

Over the next year they saw each other a few times a month, just for a drink, maintaining a relationship that was potentially more than a friendship but never having enough time together to go beyond the status quo. Keira had her hands full with her job, her children, and her courses, while Jim had an election in the fall, and he not only had to organize the usual fund raising and political campaign but he also had to run for office without the support of a party. So what they had together was suitable for the time being because anything more would have put a strain on both of them and would have negatively affected their lives. In this respect, the area of greatest vulnerability for Keira was her children, in particular Kelly, because having an affair would have divested her of any authority to control her daughter's sexual behavior, while for Jim in the midst of an election campaign it would have ended his political career.

Unable to find a candidate who was willing to run against him, the DFL ended up endorsing him, and the Republicans ran a token candidate who undoubtedly had made a deal with his party for compensation in return for his sacrifice. Jim got more than eighty percent of the vote and returned to the state senate more powerful than ever.

In the early spring Carla was accepted by Harvard Law School, where she planned to go that fall. By the end of the spring Keira completed her MBA with a straight-A average, and Gina was engaged to a young man whom Joe Marchi had introduced her to. His name was Donald, he was twenty-six, and he had an MBA from St. Thomas. He worked in the finance area of Marchi's company.

Before the engagement Jim had a conversation with Gina like the one that Marchi could have had with Renata more than twenty years ago. He had talked with Donald a number of times, and he liked Donald, but he thought that they were rushing things with their plan to get married in August.

"Why don't you wait until you finish college?" he suggested. They were in her room, where she had been pretending to study.

"I don't want to wait that long," Gina said.

Remembering how she had told him she intended to save herself for her husband, he thought he understood what she meant by not wanting to wait that long, and for a brief moment he flirted with the idea of advising her not to wait to have sex with Donald and not to get married until she had finished college. But he knew that such advice would contradict the values that he and the nuns had implanted in her, which she had willingly accepted and faithfully nourished through her teens. So he said nothing.

"But I'm not going to drop out of college."

"I know you don't plan to, but it might happen."

"Well, if I did drop out," Gina said, "I could always go back. Mom went back after having two babies."

"She did, but it wasn't easy."

"It's not easy now. I have trouble concentrating on college. I have so many other things on my mind."

"Like what?"

"Like Donald. And you."

"Me? You don't have to worry about me."

"Someone has to. You never worry about yourself."

"Gina," he told her firmly, "I have a mother. I don't need another mother."

"You need someone. You can't live here all by yourself after I get married."

"So maybe that's a reason to wait," he told her, joking.

"It's the only thing that would make me wait," she said seriously. "But Donald says you're old enough to take care of yourself."

"Donald's right." Appraising her as a young woman, he could understand why Donald didn't want to wait, and he felt some empathy for the young man. "You know, your mother had trouble breaking away from her father. All her life she struggled to free herself from her father. I took her side against her father, and I tried to help her free herself. So I can identify with Donald, and I can even take his side against me."

"How did you know my mother wanted to free herself from her father?"

"By what she said, by what she did. Of course it wasn't that simple," he admitted. "She did have a conflict. She didn't want to lose her father, but she did want to free herself from him. I don't have any doubt about that."

"Well, maybe I'm different from my mother," Gina speculated. "Maybe I don't want to free myself from you."

"I think you do. You just have to understand the difference between freeing yourself from me and losing me. If you remember that there's no way you can ever lose me, it won't be so hard to free yourself from me."

After a long silence Gina asked: "Was my mother afraid of losing her father?"

"I think she was. And at times he made her feel that it was possible for her to lose him. I don't ever want to make you feel that way."

"You never have."

"If I ever do, please tell me."

"I will," she promised. After another long silence Gina asked: "Is that what killed her? Being afraid of losing her father?"

"What killed her," he said, seeing more clearly than he had before, "was not being able to resolve her conflict."

Gina took this in. "You mean not being able to believe she could free herself from her father without losing him."

"You got it," he told her.

"Well, I still don't know what I should do."

"I can't tell you, but if you don't want to wait to get married, then don't wait. For what it's worth, you already have my blessing."

"It's worth a lot. Thanks, Dad."

It was Saturday morning, and Jim was waiting anxiously for the response to his last tape when Zoraya came into his room, saying: "They're talking about you on the news. Come and see it."

He followed her downstairs to the screening room, where Ramón and Manuel were sitting in their usual places. A newcomer, a young man in a jogging outfit, was sitting on the floor. Lighter than the others, he had long hair and shifty eyes.

As usual they were watching the news about Bosnia. The camera showed a field where a survivor of a massacre claimed that hundreds of bodies had been buried. The leader of a team who had begun to examine the field avoided saying that a massacre had occurred there but confirmed that they had found human remains, which they were a long way from being able to identify.

"They'll cover up the massacres," Ramón said.

"No, they won't," Jim said. "They have no reason to."

"I don't trust them. They work for the Jews."

"They work for an international agency."

"Well, the Jews control the international agencies, starting with the UN."

"That's nonsense," Jim said. "No one controls the UN, not even its leaders."

"This is Nardo," Manuel said, introducing him to the newcomer. "He has been helping us deliver the tapes. He came back with me last night."

"What if we want to deliver another tape?" Jim asked.

"We don't have time for another tape."

"We might," Zoraya said. "And if we decide to make another tape, Nardo can go back to the city with Manuel."

"We could get an offer from the government tomorrow," Jim told them. "If it's not what you want, we'll still have time for another tape."

"Does your government work on Sundays?" Ramón asked.

"They work all the time. At least some of them do."

"Let's see what kind of response you got," Zoraya said.

Manuel turned on the video player.

An anchorman said: "We're beginning to see a response to Senator Wyatt's latest appeal in which he asked people to demonstrate and tell the government to release the Muslim cleric who he claims was wrongfully convicted for inciting violence. People not only in Minnesota but also in many other states say they're planning to demonstrate tomorrow at their capitols. Some say they're planning to go to Washington. So this could be a major event."

They switched to a shopping mall, where a reporter was talking to a gray-haired woman who held a J.C. Penney bag.

"Are you planning to demonstrate tomorrow?"

"Oh, ya," the woman said heartily. "Our whole group is going to the capitol right after church. We're making our signs this afternoon."

"And what are you going to tell the government?"

"We're going to tell them to release this man."

"You believe he's innocent?"

"We know he is. Senator Wyatt says he is."

"They believe what you tell them," Ramón said in wonder.

"Only because it's true," Jim said.

They switched to a scene that looked like New York, where a reporter was talking with two African-American women.

"Are you planning to demonstrate tomorrow?"

"Oh, yeah," one of the women said with determination. "We're sick and tired of discrimination against Muslims. A lot of our brothers and sisters are Muslims."

"It's another form of racism," the other woman said.

"If this cleric was a white man he wouldn't be in prison."

"So where are you going to demonstrate?"

"We're going to Washington," the first woman said.

"There's no point in going to Albany," the second woman said. "They never do anything there for us."

"Yeah. They never give enough money to our schools."

"And what are you going to tell the government?"

"We're going to tell them to release this man."

"You believe he's innocent?"

"He must be. Why else would a white senator from Minnesota say he is?"

"Well, maybe you haven't heard," the reporter said, "but he's being held hostage by a group of Muslims."

"I don't believe it," the first woman said. "They're probably just saying that to explain why he'd take our side."

"I asked about him," the second woman said. "And I found out that he's always taken our side, so I don't care what they say."

Jim was gratified as more scenes showed that people were responding from places far beyond Minnesota.

"You should run for president," Zoraya said admiringly.

"The press would have a field day with me."

"What does that mean?"

"It means they would tear me to pieces."

"But they're not doing that now."

"No. They have a good story, and they don't want to ruin it. Let's hope that nothing else comes along. Can we get a weather report?"

Manuel switched to the television and found the weather station. The map showed that it was expected to be sunny and clear everywhere except the Gulf Coast, where there was a fifty percent chance of rain. Temperatures were expected to be above normal, but that wouldn't prevent a big turnout. Warm weather was usually good for demonstrations.

Back in his room, he asked Zoraya: "Who's this guy Nardo?"

"He's a member of our group," she said defensively.

"Do you know him well?"

"Manuel knows him."

"There's something about him that makes me uneasy."

"I know what you mean," Zoraya admitted.

"He has shifty eyes."

"I hadn't noticed that. I just don't like the way he looks at me."

"I'm sure you can handle him. I'm more concerned about what he might do behind your back."

"What could he do?"

"He could mess up our negotiation."

"You mean by trying to make his own deal?"

"Yeah. Something like that."

"Well, I'll keep an eye on him."

When she had gone to make his lunch he admitted to himself that his uneasiness about Nardo was at least in part the typical reaction by a member of a close-knit team to the introduction of a new member. So his negative feeling about Nardo was a measure of the extent to which their fortunes had been bound together. Still, the man had shifty eyes, and Zoraya didn't like the way he looked at her.

Gina was married in August, and she moved with Donald into a spacious Victorian house on Osceola Avenue that was only a few blocks away. Joe Marchi gave them the down payment for the house as a wedding present.

Alone now, except on weekends when the boys stayed with him, Jim was open to the possibility of expanding his relationship with Keira, so when he was invited to speak in the fall at a conference in San Francisco which she was planning to attend, he accepted and booked a room in the hotel that was hosting the conference. He also made a date to have dinner with Keira the night before the conference began.

He had been to San Francisco a number of times, so Keira, who had never been there, accepted his offer to be her guide to the city. They had dinner the first night at a French restaurant on Sutter Street that he remembered from a previous trip, and they had after-dinner drinks at a nearby wine bar. Since their rooms were on the same floor of the hotel, he walked her to her door and kissed her goodnight. It was their first kiss, and it was awkward, being a tentative step beyond the comfort zone of their friendship.

"I'm sorry," Keira said. "I haven't kissed a man in fifteen years."

"Really?" he said, though he wasn't surprised.

"I haven't had the time or the opportunity."

"You've had your hands full."

"I'd like to get back into practice," she told him. "But right now I'm too tired. That flight took a lot out of me."

"Then let's resume this tomorrow night."

"Let's," she agreed.

When her afternoon workshop ended they took a cable car over to Fishermen's Wharf and had dinner there. They had after-dinner drinks in his room, and it didn't take her long to get back into practice. In bed it was as if she was trying to make up for fifteen years without sex, and by the time she finally had enough she didn't have the energy to get up and go to her room, so she spent the night with him. She didn't use her own bed again for the rest of the trip.

After that they couldn't go back to being just friends, but they couldn't see any way of maintaining the new relationship unless they lived together, and they couldn't live together unless they were married because she had to think about her children and he had to think about his career. So late in the fall they began to take the necessary steps to prepare their families for what they were planning.

The first step was for him to meet her children. They decided to take them out to dinner on a Saturday night at a place on Grand Avenue that had good hamburgers. Jim picked them up at their house and drove them to the restaurant, with Keira sitting in front and the children in back. In that configuration an observer who didn't know any better might have mistaken them for a family.

They got a booth in the restaurant, and as Kelly hung up her coat he noticed her jeans, which were so tight that it was hard to imagine how she got into them. Kelly was now seventeen, but she could have passed for a woman in her twenties, which she did everything in her power to do. She had unruly reddish blond hair, a few freckles around her nose, and insolent green eyes. In contrast, Kevin was a pleasant boy. He was fifteen, already almost as tall as Jim, and he moved with the grace of a natural athlete. He had cropped hair, the same color as Keira's, and sweet blue eyes.

They all ordered hamburgers, with varying preferences for doneness, and then Kelly began the conversation by saying: "Mom says the two of you are thinking about getting married."

"That's right," Jim said, bracing himself.

"Well, I don't understand why," Kelly said obtusely. "I mean, you don't have to be married to have sex."

"It's not about sex," Keira told her.

"Then what's it about?"

"It's about wanting to live together, to share our lives."

"You don't have to be married to live together."

"I know, but in our positions—"

"So it's really about your positions?"

"It's about a lot of things," Jim interjected. "We both have children, we both have careers, and we both have responsibilities. If we were in our early twenties, living together without being married might be an option. But for us it's not."

"Okay," Kelly conceded. "So it's not an option. Where would we live?"

"We talked about this," Keira reminded her. "We're renting our house, which we never liked, so it would be better for us to move into Jim's house."

"Where does he live?"

"On Linwood near Avon."

"Is it a big house?"

"It's bigger than ours. It has two full bathrooms."

"Two full bathrooms?" The girl looked as if she was mentally reserving one of them for herself.

"Does it have a basketball hoop?" Kevin asked hopefully.

"Yeah, in the alley," Jim said. "The kids in the neighborhood all play there."

"Cool," he said as if that was enough for him.

"But we would have to move," Kelly said, presenting another obstacle.

"We've moved before," her mother said.

"We've moved five times that I remember. We keep looking for a house we like."

"I think I'm going to like your house," Kevin told him.

"Well, I'm only going to live with you for another year," Kelly said, "so I guess it doesn't matter."

The next step was for him to meet her parents, who lived in a small house near Macalester College. They went there for cocktails and dinner the following Saturday. Her mother welcomed him as if he was the answer to her prayers, and her father ended up trying to sell him a life insurance policy. In an effort to bond with her father Jim had two martinis with him but declined the third. By then her father was sloppily referring to Keira as his princess and her mother was rushing to get dinner on the table before he had another round. Though Keira didn't comment on anything he said or did, she was obviously repulsed by her father's behavior, and when they left she hugged her mother and patted her back consolingly.

"That was a typical evening," she said as they drove away.

"At least he didn't sell me insurance."

"He's always selling, always selling." She sat there, reflecting. "I can't believe that I married someone just like him."

"Did your husband call you his princess?"

"No. He called me his goddess."

"I wonder what's worse."

"I don't know. When you're a princess or a goddess, it doesn't leave much room for development."

"Did your father make you feel like a princess?"

"He did when I was young, at least until his third martini."

"How did that affect your view of him?"

"It made me realize that treating me like a princess was his way of dealing with my sexuality. If I was a princess, I wouldn't be threatening."

"How does he feel about your career?"

"That's a good question. He never encouraged me," she said, "and whenever I got a promotion he acted like he did when he first noticed that I was growing breasts. So I guess it's just as threatening."

"Princesses don't have careers," he said, stopping for a light.

"They marry princes, and they have babies."

"Well, you're past that now."

"I hope so," she said.

They were silent, waiting for the light to change.

As they drove on he asked: "If your husband had lived, do you think he would have treated Kelly like a princess?"

"He would have tried," she said, laughing. "I hate to say it, but there are times when I really admire her for not acting like a princess."

"Maybe she wants to make sure that no one treats her like one."

"I know *you* won't. But it'll be interesting to see," she added, "how you deal with her sexuality."

"I haven't noticed it," he joked.

"You will," she said.

The last step was to introduce Keira to his mother. They had lunch at the University Club on the following Saturday. As they drove to the club he explained to his mother that he wasn't seeking her approval, he was just observing the custom of introducing a fiancée to the family. His mother said she understood.

The lunch went well. His mother got straight answers to her questions about Keira's background, and Keira didn't seem to object to being interrogated. Remarkably, the two women treated each other with respect.

As he drove his mother home she said: "Well, at least I understand where this woman is coming from."

He smiled, not having heard his mother use this expression before.

"She's Irish," his mother said. "Her parents come from the working class. We know a lot of people like them."

"You'd have to living in St. Paul."

"Have you met her parents?"

"Yes. They're fine."

"What about her children?"

"They're fine."

"Well, I counted the children," his mother told him. "If you marry her, you'll have seven of them."

"It's a lucky number."

"In craps, yes."

"Well, I'm not shooting craps with her."

"No, I don't think you are. She seems very responsible."

"You mean unlike some of my previous wives."

"Renata was responsible, but the other two—" His mother paused. "I think they used you to advance themselves."

"How do you mean?"

"I mean to get through a period in their lives when they were being held back by something."

"That may be true," he admitted. "But I didn't mind being used by them."

"Your father didn't mind being used by me. And he stayed with me. Next fall we'll be married for fifty years."

"How did you use him?"

"The same way those women used you. I had to rise above something that happened to me, and he helped me. If it weren't for your father," his mother added, "I don't know what would have become of me."

"You mean I'm like my father?"

"In that respect, yes."

"I never realized that. I thought I was completely different from him."

"You're different from him in many ways, but that's one thing you both have in common. Maybe you got it from him."

"Maybe I did. What happened to you?"

"Someday I'll tell you, but not now."

He wondered what it was. He had known about her depression after she lost her second baby, but he hadn't heard about anything that happened to her before she was married. "Are you going to have a party?"

"A party?" she said, not understanding.

"For your golden anniversary."

"Oh, yes. We are. We're going to have a big party." She acted as if they were already making plans. "It's going to be at the University Club."

"Have you reserved a date?"

"Of course. You have to book ahead."

"Well, let me know how I can help."

"You can help by showing your father that we're reconciled."

"You mean over our separation agreement?"

"Yes. If you can make him understand that it meant nothing, then maybe he'll recover his faculties."

"I'll try," he said. "But don't expect a miracle."

"I don't," his mother said. "I don't believe in miracles."

Jim had eaten dinner, and he was standing at the window looking out onto the garden. It was eight in the evening, and the tops of the trees that extended above the stone wall were still illuminated by the long light of the slowly sinking sun. It would have been a poignant moment under any circumstances, but his feeling of sorrow was accentuated by the knowledge that he might have only three more days to live. It all depended on what happened tomorrow.

His musing was suddenly interrupted by people loudly yelling downstairs. It sounded like an argument, a heated one, and then there was a commotion as if someone was being overcome by force, then a long silence, and then the slamming of a door. A few minutes later he heard someone coming up the stairs and toward his room.

It was Zoraya, who entered his room looking upset.

"What happened?" he asked.

"We caught Nardo trying to betray us."

"What was he doing?"

"He was making a phone call."

"Who was he calling?"

"We don't know," she said. "But we think it could have been the police."

"Did he talk with anyone?"

"No. We stopped him. But maybe they could trace the call."

"They probably couldn't," he assured her. "They would have had to be listening with special equipment for tracing calls."

"But they could have been listening with special equipment."

"Well, even if they were, if you stopped him right away then they wouldn't have had enough time to trace the call."

"We stopped him as soon as someone answered."

"Then they wouldn't have had enough time."

Frowning, she said: "You sound relieved. But you should be unhappy. You should want them to trace the call."

"I don't," he said. "At this point I don't want them to come here and try to rescue me. I want them to release Abdullah."

"Do you really mean that?"

"Yeah. I do. If they try to rescue me, they could kill us all."

"But you still don't know if they'll release Abdullah."

"I believe they will. I have faith in the political process."

"So will I if they release Abdullah."

The way he felt hearing this statement made him realize that converting her and saving his life had become one and the same objective.

Then she said: "We have to kill Nardo."

"What?" He was shocked. "Why?"

"Because he betrayed us."

"But you don't know who he was calling. It could have been his girlfriend."

"If it was," she argued, "he wouldn't have been so secretive about it."

"He might have just wanted some privacy."

She shook her head. "We think he was calling the police. The person who answered the phone was a man."

231

"It could have been his girlfriend's father or brother."

"Why are you defending him?" she asked as if he had turned against her.

"I'm not defending him. I want to make sure he gets a fair trial. And whatever he did, I don't want you to kill him."

"We have to kill him. What else can we do with him?"

"You can tie him up and leave him with me."

"You mean you want us to kill you but not him?"

"I don't want you to kill either of us. Where do you get this thing about killing? It doesn't come from the Quran."

"Yes, it does."

"Show me."

"I would. But I don't have a Quran with me."

"You don't carry one around with you? I thought you were religious."

"Well, you don't carry a Bible around with you."

"I don't have to. I know what it says."

"And I know what the Quran says."

"You obviously don't. There's not a word in the Quran that justifies your killing Nardo. Or me," he added.

"What do *you* know?"

"I know a lot. Remember, I could be your father."

"You couldn't be my father. My father was an asshole of the highest order."

"Where did you learn that expression?"

"In college," she said.

With a smile he said: "Then you got something out of college in return for your money."

"It wasn't my money, it was my father's money. I mean," she added, "his money paid for most of it."

"Who paid for the rest?"

"I had a scholarship."

"If you had a scholarship then someone must have thought you could make a contribution to society."

"I *am* making a contribution."

"If you kill Nardo," he told her, "you won't be making a

contribution. You'll be making a mistake, and your life will be over."

"I don't care. My life's not worth anything."

"Your life is worth a lot. And you don't have to sacrifice it to get what you want."

She shook her head, saying: "You don't understand what this is about."

"Yeah, I understand. It's about your getting back at your father for what he did to you."

"It's not about that," she said heatedly. "It's about what they did to Abdullah."

"Are you sure? Are you sure you're not using Abdullah as an excuse for acting out your anger?"

"Why do you keep questioning my motives?"

"Because they need questioning."

"Well, you make me feel like I don't know what I'm doing."

"You don't. And I'm not making you feel that way."

"Then who is?"

"You are."

"I hate you," she cried.

"I've heard that before from my daughters."

"But I really mean it."

"They did too."

She left him, slamming the door.

ELEVEN

HE AND KEIRA were married in a private ceremony attended by their immediate families. On the advice of his sister they went to Venice for their honeymoon. It was January, which according to his sister was the only time to be in Venice because there were no tourists and the people who really lived there were in town. It was chilly and damp, but it still felt warm compared with Minnesota, and the wintry mists over the canals added a layer of mystery and romance. They enjoyed the food, the art, and the ambience of the city, but most of all they enjoyed just being with each other in a place that was completely removed from their parents, their children, and their careers.

He took another week off from work to move Keira and her children into his house. Kelly was surprisingly helpful, and Kevin settled into the house as if he had always lived there. By the first weekend he was out in the alley playing basketball with Erik, Lukas, Matthew, and some neighborhood boys. He towered over them not only in height but also in talent, and Jim could tell from watching him that he would be able to play this sport in college. As a freshman at St. Thomas Academy he already had a place on the varsity team, though they weren't playing him much yet. To get more action he also played on a CYO team affiliated with St. Luke's, and Jim began to relieve Keira of the task of driving him to games. And he began to enjoy watching basketball.

On Sundays they went to Mass at St. Luke's, where they saw Gina, Donald, and the Marchis, and after church they had brunch at a restaurant on Grand Avenue, where they sometimes ran into his sister and her husband. After that the children were free. Kelly went off in a car with friends, and Kevin played basketball.

Kelly turned eighteen in April, and they had a family birthday party for her. She made a point of the fact that now she was of legal age to do anything except drink, and Jim wondered if she had anything particular in mind.

He soon found out. It was a Saturday, and Keira had taken Kevin downtown to buy him some new clothes—he was growing so fast that his shirts and pants became too short for him before they wore out. Jim was in the room that had been Gina's, which he now used as an office, and Kelly was in the bathroom that she had virtually preempted, taking a shower.

He was sitting in a chair, reading an analysis of the state's tax system when he became aware of a presence in the doorway. It was Kelly, fresh out of the shower and wearing one of his old Brooks Brothers shirts, which she had buttoned in one place.

"What are you doing?" she asked, advancing into the room. Her hair was damp and kinky, and her face was rosy.

"I'm reading. What are *you* doing?"

"I'm trying to find out if you like me."

"I like you. In fact, I love you."

She stopped about three feet in front of him. "You do? Really?"

"Yeah," he said, unable to avert his eyes from the sight of her unbuttoning the shirt and letting it slip off her shoulders down to the floor.

"What do you think?" she asked, displaying herself.

"I think you're a very attractive girl." He was getting aroused, so he changed position in the chair to hide it.

She ran her tongue around her lips, moistening them. She looked at him and asked: "Am I getting you excited?"

"Yes," he admitted.

She ran both hands over her breasts and down over her thighs, saying: "Here I am. Would you like to have sex with me?"

"As a normal male, of course I'm aroused by a naked female offering herself to me. But I can't have sex with you."

"Why not? I'm of legal age."

"A lot of females are of legal age, but I don't have sex with them."

"But are those females as attractive as me?"

"No. They're not. You're exceptionally attractive."

"Then why won't you have sex with me? I promise I won't tell my mother."

"You mean you'd have an affair with me behind your mother's back?"

"I don't want to have an affair with you. I just want to have sex with you."

"Well, I can't," he said. "I love your mother."

"You said you love me."

"I do love you. I love you as a daughter."

"Then you don't want to have sex with me?"

"I do want to have sex with you. But I can't. Okay?"

Peering at his crossed leg, she said: "I see you have a hard-on. Can I touch it?"

"No. You can't touch it."

"Can I look at it?"

"No. Kelly, stop it."

"Am I driving you crazy?"

"Yes. You are."

She smiled as if this gave her immense satisfaction. "If I ask you something, do you promise to give me an honest answer?"

"Sure. I promise."

"If you weren't married to my mother, would you have sex with me?"

"You mean if you were standing naked in front of me?""

"Yeah, if I was standing naked in front of you."

"I would be strongly tempted," he said.

"You would? Really?"

"Yeah. Really. Now, pick up your shirt and put it back on and behave yourself."

She did what he said, only this time she buttoned the shirt in several places. "You won't tell Mom I did this, will you?"

"No. It's between us."

"Thanks," she said, coming closer. "I don't know why I did that. Do you think there's something wrong with me?"

"There's nothing wrong with you," he told her. "You're just bursting with sexual energy. It's perfectly normal at your age."

"You mean other girls hide it?"

"They do all kinds of things with it."

"Mom says I flaunt it too much."

"You could tone it down a little. But don't repress it."

"You know," she confessed after a moment. "I wouldn't have done that with a man I didn't trust."

"That's reassuring," he said with a smile.

She bent over and kissed him purely on the forehead, saying: "Now you can be a father to me. Okay?"

"Okay."

As the time approached for the golden anniversary party his mother talked more and more about it. She had denied believing in miracles, but she acted as if whatever she might call the recovery of his father's faculties, she expected it to happen at this party. She had invited everyone they knew, which turned out to be a very large number of people, and by early September more than two hundred had accepted. He pointed out to her that they would have to take over the entire club in order to accommodate them all, and she told him not to worry, she had already done this.

Stephen and his wife Marya came from New York, having rented a Lincoln Town Car at the airport. Stephen had convinced their mother that this arrangement would be better than having a driver, who wouldn't know how to handle their father. Stephen, who drew a minimal salary from the neighborhood center he ran in the Bronx, had offered to help pay for the party, but their mother had declined, insisting that it was her party.

The event was optional black tie, and most of the men took the option, a notable exception being Patrick, who refused even to wear a tie because it was a symbol of the bourgeoisie. But he was an asset at the family table because Jim's father recognized him and enjoyed his company.

"Are you still teaching?" Jim asked his brother.

"Yeah," Stephen said. "I teach one course a semester."

"I taught a course at St. Thomas, and I really liked it. Keira was a student in my class. But I don't have time for teaching now."

"I can understand that," his brother said.

"Where do your students come from?"

"Mostly from Yonkers, the Bronx, and Manhattan."

"Do you have a lot of Latinos?"

"Yeah. Almost forty percent of them are Latinos, and that percentage is rising. They think I'm from Argentina."

Stephen had lived for ten years in Argentina, working for a bank and then serving a non-profit organization that helped poor people start businesses. When he returned to New York he used money from a foundation that a friend of their mother's had set up to create the center in the Bronx, which he and Marya ran together. Marya was his third wife. His first wife had left him, and his second wife had been killed by a drug gang to make sure she didn't talk about what she had witnessed in Colombia. So his personal life had been complex.

Between the appetizer and the main course their mother got up and asked Jim to dance with her. As he led his mother out onto the floor she told him: "Stay in front of our table where your father can see us."

"Are we trying to make him jealous?" he joked, guessing what she was up to.

"We're trying to show him we're reconciled."

"Okay," he said, going along with her.

The band was playing a song from his mother's era, probably written by George Gershwin or Cole Porter, which was perfect for her purpose. She was a good dancer, and he moved her around the floor respectfully.

"Hold me closer," his mother said.

He held her as if she was his date at a junior prom.

"That's right. Now, let's go over in front of him."

He guided his mother over to a spot that was right in front of his father, who stared at them as if he was trying to figure out who this man was dancing with his wife. He leaned forward and finally got up and walked over and tapped Jim on the shoulder, saying: "I'm cutting in."

Jim obligingly handed his mother over to his father and sat down.

As he watched them Stephen said: "He hasn't forgotten how to dance."

"No. He hasn't," Jim said, admiring the way his father led his mother around the floor. Except for professionals, no member of Jim's generation could dance like that.

Noticing them, the bandleader swung into the "Anniversary Waltz," and their parents amply demonstrated that they could waltz as well as foxtrot. By then the other couples had stepped to the side of the floor, leaving it all to the couple who had been married for fifty years. With the floor to themselves they showed what they were capable of doing as the band played a medley, giving them samples of the waltz, rumba, swing, tango, and finally again the foxtrot.

"Wow," Stephen said as they applauded. "He still has it."

"They should enter a competition," Jim agreed.

When they finally returned to the table his father looked happy and his mother at least looked content. Though his father hadn't recovered his faculties, they still had something they could do together well after fifty years.

A month later his father died of undetermined causes. From the expression on his father's face his mother concluded that he was at peace.

In the spring Kelly, who had improved her grades significantly, was accepted at Colorado College, where she planned to major in marketing. Gina, in her final semester at St. Catherine, announced that she was pregnant and made a point of the fact that the baby was due after she had finished college.

By fall Kevin, now seventeen, was the only child in the house, though he was still joined most weekends by Erik, sixteen, and Lukas, fourteen. The boys were mainly interested in sports and computers. So far they had all managed to avoid girls who could teach them anything about sex. They relied on magazines for their education on this subject, but it was still theoretical.

In early October Gina had a baby boy, whom they named Joseph. Marchi was ecstatic because none of his daughters had given him a grandson. Angela, now forty-four, had produced three girls, and Bianca, now forty-one, had produced two girls. Gina was the one who had finally come through for him, and she had put the icing on the cake by naming the boy after him. The extended family attended the baptism, with Carla flying from Boston to serve as a godmother, and afterward Marchi had a party at his house to celebrate the blessed event, with champagne flowing.

At one point he took Jim aside and told him: "You did a good job raising those girls. I never told you that before, but now I can tell you."

"Now that they're out of danger?" Jim said.

"Well, you know what it's like raising girls. Anything can happen."

"Yeah. I know. But why should we worry about them more than we worry about boys?"

"I don't know. I never had a boy."

"You have one now."

"I don't have to worry about him with Gina as his mother and Donald as his father."

"So you can enjoy him and let them worry about him."

"Yeah. Well, what's different about raising boys?"

"It takes them longer to get into trouble."

"How are your boys doing?"

"They're doing fine. They've had good mothers, who have done most of the job of raising them."

"You think mothers are more important for boys?"

"I think boys need their mothers more. I think they would have had a harder time than Carla and Gina losing their mother."

"You think so?"

"Yeah. But I don't know."

"Well, then maybe it was a good thing you had girls with Renata."

"Maybe it was. Maybe it was by design."

"Maybe. When you reach my age," Marchi said, "you want to believe it's by design."

During that winter Keira had an opportunity to apply for a big job in her company. They were doing a search for the position, implying that there was no one inside who was capable of filling it, but in a double message they said they would welcome applications from insiders.

"So is this a game?" Keira asked him. They were sitting in the kitchen, where they had eaten a late dinner.

"They have to let insiders apply. It's a legal requirement."

"You mean they're hoping no one will apply."

"Not necessarily. They might be doing it to find out if anyone inside the company wants the position."

"Well, people could want it but not know if they're qualified."

"The search committee will decide if they're qualified."

"But shouldn't the company already know if anyone inside is qualified?"

"Yeah. They should," he agreed.

"Then if I'm qualified, why don't they tell me?"

"If they did, it would look like they're giving you an inside shot at the position."

"And they don't want to do that because it would give me an advantage?"

"It would make you think you have the job," he said. "But what if you didn't get it?"

"I guess I'd feel that they misled me."

"So they want you to apply if you think you're qualified."

"Do you think I am?" She had shown him the job description. It was the vice president for administration, the position she now reported to. And he could see from her résumé that she had all the required skills as well as the years of experience.

"I know you are. But you have to believe you are."

"I believe I am—until I start thinking about the fact that they've never had a woman in this position."

"It's time they did."

"The board may not think so."

"What's the board got to do with it? I thought they only selected the president."

"This is the number two position," she explained, "so if anything happens to the president, the person in this position will take over."

"It's time they had a woman president."

"The board may not think so."

"You said that before."

"Well, that's the obstacle."

"It's only an obstacle in your mind," he said. "If you're the best candidate, the board will select you."

"That's easy for you to say."

"Yeah. It is. But I'm not just saying it. I know your board, and I know they're okay with the idea of a woman running your company."

"Are you giving me inside information?"

"In a way, yeah."

"How did you get it?"

"By listening to them. They're painfully aware of the fact that there's a shortage of qualified people in your industry, so they're not going to rule out half the potential candidates for this position."

"So you think I should apply."

"Do you want the position?"

She gazed through him. "I want it more than I've wanted anything in my life."

"Then go for it," he told her, "and don't look back."

When Zoraya brought his breakfast the next morning she made no reference to their conversation the previous evening. It was as if she had never told him she hated him, as if she had never slammed the door.

"Manuel bought the paper this morning," she told him, putting it down on the table. "I thought you might want to read it."

"Thanks. Is there anything about us?"

"No, but there's a lot about Bosnia."

"Maybe I should say something about it in my next tape."

"You're not going to make another tape."

"Well, I might not have to. In any case, I'll say something about it at a press conference when this is all over."

"You mean if you're still alive."

"Yeah." He scanned her face, looking for a hint of flexibility.

But she was impassive, and she left him abruptly without saying another word.

In the paper he found several articles about Bosnia. One article covered the military advances of the Serbs against the Bosniak cities and towns, stating that the European Union was unlikely to intervene. Another article said that France had threatened to pull its four thousand soldiers out of the peacekeeping force in Bosnia unless the UN agreed to take stronger action. The British foreign secretary questioned whether military action could save the Bosniaks. Jordan said it would pull out its troops if nothing was done to stop the Serbs from killing the Bosniaks. Another article focused on the plight of the Bosniak refugees and estimated that about twenty thousand people who had fled from the Serbs were unaccounted for. An op-ed article addressed the issue of ethnic cleansing and bluntly called it genocide.

After reading the stories Jim wasn't proud of being a politician. His colleagues were all looking for someone else to blame or trying to prove that there was nothing they could do about the situation. Zoraya was right: no one in Europe or America cared what happened to the Muslims in Bosnia. Politicians weren't going to win any votes or raise their approval ratings by intervening in Bosnia.

Zoraya returned an hour later and took him to the screening room. As they sat down at the foot of the bed he noticed that Nardo was missing.

The television was on, live, and a reporter was describing the situation at the capitol in Minnesota. "People began arriving here early in the morning, and we expect them to keep coming until early in the afternoon, when church is out. We guess there are about two hundred thousand people here now. The city is prepared for a crowd of three hundred thousand, but it looks like there could be a lot more."

The scene changed to Chicago, where a reporter explained that instead of going to the capitol, which was down in Springfield, people were gathering on Michigan Avenue and filling the park along the shore. Similar scenes were reported for New York, Boston, Philadelphia, Baltimore, Atlanta, and Miami, while in Washington people were filling the Mall, holding signs that said: "Release Abdullah!"

Summarizing, the anchorwoman said: "It's still early, but it looks like this could be one of the largest demonstrations in our history. It probably won't reach the scale of the civil rights demonstrations, but it could surpass everything else."

"We have a lot of people on our side," Jim said, pleased by the response.

"Are you on our side?" Ramón asked.

"I think I've proved that."

"You have? How? You're only doing it to save your life."

"I'm doing it to save your lives too."

"What you do you mean?"

"If you kill me, they'll kill you."

"No, they won't. They don't know who we are."

"They'll find out, and they'll track you down."

"They'll never find out who we are," Manuel insisted, though he didn't really sound confident.

"When do you think they'll make another offer?" Zoraya asked.

"When they know how many people demonstrated."

"That won't be until the end of the day."

"It might not be until tomorrow."

"I thought you said they work on Sundays," Ramón said.

"They do, and they're busy now counting the votes."

"The votes? Oh, I see. If they don't release Abdullah, then these people will vote against them."

"That's right. You're learning."

Back in his room, he asked Zoraya: "Where's Nardo?"

"In a room down the hall. We locked him up."

"Well, I think you'll want to accept the next offer. But if you kill him, you'll lose everything."

244

"I thought about what you said last night," she told him after a long silence. "I mean about my motives."

"And what did you conclude?"

"I concluded that I *am* acting out my anger against my father."

Encouraged, he waited for her to elaborate.

"That's what drove me to violence. That's what makes me want to kill people. But it's not what makes me want to get Abdullah released."

"I understand," he said. "I wasn't talking about your goal but about your method."

"Then you agree that there's nothing wrong with my goal of getting Abdullah released."

"Yeah, I agree."

"But if there's nothing wrong with my goal, then how could my method be wrong?"

"There's no connection between your goal and your method," he explained. "So right goals don't justify wrong methods."

"What if I have to kill someone to achieve my goal?"

"You're not in that kind of situation."

"You mean I don't have to kill Nardo or kill you in order to get Abdullah released."

"That's right. If you kill either of us, it will be an admission of failure."

After a moment she asked: "Are there situations where you *would* have to kill someone to achieve your goal?"

"The only one I can think of," he said, "is to save your life. Or to save the life of another person."

"Would you kill to save your life?"

"I think I would. But I don't know because I've never been in that situation."

"Then it's not always wrong to kill people?"

"It's almost always wrong."

She looked at him as if he had given her more than enough to think about, and she left him, saying: "I'll talk with you later."

Keira got the position, and from then on she worked more than seventy hours a week, coming home after eight at night and going into the office on weekends. But she was happy, and her absence gave Jim a chance to spend more time with Kevin, who needed direction at this stage in his life.

Having grown to a height of six feet four, Kevin was the star of the basketball team as well as a straight-A student, so he had choices on where to go to college. After talking with the coach Jim realized that as good as Kevin was at the sport, he wouldn't be recruited by top basketball colleges like Duke, Indiana, or North Carolina, and he wasn't likely to make it as a professional. So with the support of a guidance counselor he got Kevin to start thinking about a top academic college that appreciated basketball talent, namely Princeton. Since he had legally adopted Kevin, he could claim a legacy spot for him, but as things turned out Kevin didn't need it. His SAT scores placed him in the top five percentile in the country, and Princeton accepted him for early admission. Jim's father would have been happy to see another generation of the family going to Princeton, though he might not have understood how Jim had become the father of a teenage boy named Kevin.

Whether or not they approved of it, his constituents didn't seem to have a problem with his personal life. He was reelected in 1988 with more than eighty percent of the vote. After the election the party strategist who seven years earlier had told him that people wouldn't accept his being married three times invited him to rejoin the DFL. Jim declined the invitation, feeling that the party might have done him a favor by not supporting him for the U.S. Senate. If he had gone to Washington he would have had to take Gina with him or leave her with his mother, and he would have been removed from the lives of Erik, Lukas, and Matthew, not to mention the fact that he would never have known Keira and her children, in whose lives he had made a difference.

With Kevin gone, Jim focused his attention on the three remaining boys, who spent most weekends with him. Erik, who was seventeen, wanted to go to MIT and study engineering. Lukas, who was fifteen, wanted to be an artist like his mother, either an actor or a musician. They were both going to St. Paul Academy, where Erik was getting excellent grades and Lukas was involved in the drama group as well as a band. Matthew, who was eight, wanted to be like his older brothers, from whom he absorbed information and misinformation like a sponge.

After playing together for more than ten years the New Granada band had broken up, and Inga was doing solo recordings and concerts. She was in a position to pick the times and places of her concerts, so she didn't travel as much as she used to, and Jim saw her more often. She also had a solo personal life, having broken up with Danny when she dissolved the band. For the first time in years they did things together with the boys, and they developed a friendship that was held together by more than their mutual interest in the boys.

"I went back to Granada," she told him one Saturday as they were walking along Grand Avenue with the boys.

"How was it?" he asked, not having been there in a while.

"I loved it. I want to live there as soon as the boys are both in college."

"In the Albaicín?"

"Oh, ya. I have an agent looking for a house. It has to have a well in the patio," she added.

"An *aljibe*," he said.

"That's an Arabic word, isn't it?"

"Yeah. Words that begin with 'a-l' are usually Arabic."

"Like Alhambra," she said. "I'll never forget our time in Granada."

"I won't either," he said, putting his arm around her shoulder.

Erik and Lukas were walking ahead of them, conversing with animation while Matthew listened attentively.

"They get along pretty well," he said, referring to Erik and Lukas.

"They have different interests, so they're not competing."

"I guess that's why my brother and I didn't get along so well. We had a lot of interests in common."

"The only interest they have in common is computers, and they do argue about that. Erik insists that Apple is better, and Lukas prefers the PC."

"When they talk about computers I don't understand half of it."

"I don't understand any of it. But that's okay. Kids always have something that their parents don't understand."

"Yeah. They're always ahead of us in something."

"Well, that's why I broke up the band. We weren't keeping up with things."

"Are you keeping up with them now?"

"I'm ahead of them," she said confidently.

She did buy a house in Granada, and she moved there as soon as Lukas went to acting school in New York. For the time being she kept her house in St. Paul so she would have a place to stay when she visited and so Erik, a junior at MIT, would have a place to stay that summer when he worked for her father.

Meanwhile, Carla was trying to make partner in a Boston law firm. In her words she was working like an animal. Gina now had three children, two boys and a girl. Kelly had graduated from college and had a job with a marketing firm in Denver. She loved her work, and she had a serious boyfriend, though she wasn't yet ready to move in with him. And Kevin was a junior at Princeton, majoring in international relations. For the past two years he had been the leading scorer on the basketball team.

With his other children gone, Jim focused on Matthew, who was now twelve. Matthew knew a lot about computers, and he played the guitar very well, but he no longer wanted to be like Erik or Lukas. He wanted to be his own person, though like most boys his age he had no idea who he was. Since he liked sports, as a spectator but not as a participant, Jim took him to Twins and Vikings games, where he enjoyed analyzing the situations and of course seeing his teams score runs and touchdowns. Afterward they went to the restaurant on Grand Avenue that still had good hamburgers. At one of these meals Matthew said: "Mom's not doing too well."

Thea and the doctor at the institute had split after three years—they had never married—and she was living with Matthew in a rented apartment on Grand Avenue. She had lost her job at the institute and had never gotten into medical school. She now had a low-level job with the city health department. "How do you know?"

"She cries a lot."

Jim could empathize with the boy's feelings because he remembered how his mother had cried during her period of depression, making him feel that the bottom had dropped out of the world. "Is she seeing a doctor?"

"You mean a shrink?"

"I mean any kind of doctor."

"Yeah," Matthew said skeptically. "She's taking pills, but they don't seem to be helping much."

"Well, I'll see if I can find another doctor," Jim said, wondering who among all the doctors he knew might be able to help Thea. He remembered their very first conversation, in which she enlightened him about treatment of mental health problems, explaining that now they had medications to help people with depression.

The following Monday he called Thea and asked her how she was doing.

"I'm doing fine," she said as if it were none of his business.

"Well, that's not what our son says."

"What did he say?"

"He said you cry a lot."

"I do. So what?"

"So maybe you should try another doctor."

"Oh, you're going to tell me which doctor I should see?"

"I'm going to recommend one." He gave her the name of a psychiatrist who had been strongly recommended by his mental health expert.

"I wouldn't go to that guy if my life depended on it. He doesn't know shit."

He told her who had recommended the doctor.

"He doesn't know shit."

"For Matthew's sake I think you should try him."

"I know what you're doing. You're using Matthew to control me."

"I'm not using him. I know how he feels."

"You don't know how anyone feels."

"Okay. But I can imagine how he feels."

"That's what you do. You imagine how other people feel, and then you exploit them. You use their feelings to control them."

"I'm trying to help you," he said patiently.

"No, you're not. You're trying to control me. You're trying to get me to see a doctor who doesn't know shit."

"Does the doctor you're seeing know anything?"

"That's a good question," she said after a long silence. "I thought he did, but he can't seem to find the right medication."

"Well, then try this other doctor."

"I'll think about it," she finally said.

It was after ten when Keira came home looking as if she had spent the evening digging her way out from under an avalanche. She said that she had eaten but could use a drink, which he made for her, a Dewar's on the rocks.

They sat at the kitchen table while she sipped her drink, gazing at nothing in the cold fluorescent light. She finally said: "I can't go on like this."

"You're working too much."

She shook her head. "It's not the work."

"Then what is it?"

Hiding her face behind her hand, she started to cry.

He waited with a feeling of doom.

"I can't live two lives," she said, sobbing. "I can't be married to you and have a relationship with someone else."

He was bowled over. "Someone else?"

"Yes. Someone else."

"You haven't been spending all this time on work?"

"I've been spending most of the time on work, but not all of it."

He couldn't believe it. Of all people, he couldn't imagine Keira having an affair. "Is this really happening?"

"I'm sorry, but it is."

"Well, who's the guy?"

"It's not a guy."

"What do you mean?"

"I mean it's a woman."

"You're kidding."

"I'm not."

"You mean you're having an affair with a woman?"

"It's not an affair, it's a relationship."

"What kind of relationship?"

"Like the one we had."

"The one we *had*? What happened to it?"

"We still have it. But it's not what it was. It's all my fault," she said, beginning to sob again. "I'm not the person I thought I was."

He tried to understand. "You found out that you prefer women?"

"That's part of it, but not all of it. I found out that I prefer a relationship in which the partners are equal."

"We're not equal in our relationship?"

"No. We're not. You have more of everything. You're the one who gives, and I'm the one who takes."

"You've given me a lot."

"I don't feel like I have. I feel like I have nothing to give you."

"You have a lot to give me."

"Well, I have more to give her."

He paused, trying to calm himself. "May I ask who she is?"

"She's a consultant. She's done some work for the company. She's never been married, and she's never had children."

"Do you know her background?" he asked, conscious of sounding like his mother.

"I know enough. We have the same values."

"So what are you planning to do?"

"We're planning to live together. We're going to buy a farm."

"What about your job?"

"I'm going to keep doing it. I need the money. But I'm going to start working more reasonable hours."

"That's a good idea. You don't want to burn out."

She wiped her eyes and then looked at him expectantly.

"What do you want from me?" he asked.

"I want you to say it's all right."

"Do you need that from me?"

"No. I don't. I want it from you."

"Then it's all right. I'm not happy about it for myself, but I could be happy about it for you. I mean, if this will make *you* happy."

"Thanks," she said, touching his cheek with the tips of her fingers. "I'll always be grateful to you."

Jim was partly consoled by winning yet another election. He had served twenty years in the state senate, but he still had a lot of things to do, and he was only fifty-three so he still had time to do them. He was also still young enough to pursue his career at the national level. Bill Clinton had just been elected president, which proved that you could come out of nowhere and get elected to the highest office.

In January, which was always a good time to get away from Minnesota, he went to a conference in New York. He had been to New York a number of times in the past few years, sometimes just to get away, and he always had dinner with Stephen and Marya at a Spanish restaurant. They arranged to have dinner on Friday, so he was on his own until then. He had dinner at the hotel on Tuesday, and he spent the evening in his room, reviewing his speech for the next morning.

The speech went well, though as usual he had the feeling that one person in the audience hadn't applauded.

That evening he went to the hotel bar. He was sipping his drink and shooting the breeze with the bartender when a young woman stepped up to the bar and ordered a glass of white wine. She had straight brown hair that was tied behind her head, and she wore the narrow designer glasses that had become popular. She was dressed in a gray business suit with a frilled shirt and paisley tie.

After sipping her wine for a while she turned to Jim and asked: "Do you know a good place to eat around here?"

"The restaurant in the hotel is good."

"I've eaten there. I want to try someplace different."

"Well, what kind of food do you have in mind?"

"Anything," she said, "except Mexican and southwestern."

"Do you like French cuisine?"

"Oh, yeah. I love *fois gras* and *coq au vin*."

"Then I have just the place for you. Would you like some company?"

"I'd love it. It's no fun eating alone."

"Are you here on business?"

"Yeah. I live in Tucson, and I work for a bank that's owned by a bank here in New York. They brought me here for training."

"What kind of training?"

"How to cross-sell the bank's products. You know," she explained, "if a person has a checking account, you sell them an investment product."

"Is that what you do?"

"That's what I do. Consumer banking."

"It sounds interesting," he said.

"It's not. It's the last thing I wanted to do, but I'm stuck in this job. And I'm stuck in Tucson."

"I've never been to Tucson. What's it like?"

"It's boring," she said. "Nothing ever happens there."

"Why don't you leave?"

"I have to stay there and take care of my mother. We moved there from Ohio seven years ago because of her health."

"She has respiratory problems?" he guessed.

"Yeah. She was better for a while, but now she's worse. She's on oxygen."

"Does she have emphysema?"

"Yeah. She was a chain smoker."

"That's rough," he said sympathetically.

"Oh, by the way," the young woman said, extending her hand, "I'm Stephanie."

"I'm Jim," he said, shaking it. Her skin was very soft.

"What do you do?"

"I'm a private investigator."

"Really?" She was very interested. "What kind of cases do you work on?"

"Kidnappings, money laundering—" He knew something about these activities because Stephen had been involved in trying to stop them when he lived in Argentina during the 1970s. "When someone gets kidnapped nowadays it's usually by terrorists who are trying to raise money to overthrow some government. They launder the money, and my job is to find it and have their bank account frozen."

"It must be dangerous. I mean, if the terrorists find out what you're doing, they could kill you."

"They could. They've tried to," he added for good measure.

"Wow," she sighed, gazing at him with admiration. "If I could ever get out of Tucson, that's the kind of thing I'd love to do."

He took her to Cote Basque, where she ate as if she was fueling herself for a long trip without food stops.

They went back to the hotel and had drinks at the bar, brandy for him and port for her. And then she went with him to his room, where she started by taking off her glasses and ended by liberating herself from her boring life in Tucson as a consumer banker.

"Any news?" he asked when Zoraya opened the door to his room.

"The crowds are getting bigger and bigger," she told him. "Millions of people are demonstrating."

"That's great."

"Yes. But that's not what I came to tell you."

"What did you come to tell me?"

"We're going to kill Nardo."

"Oh, no. That's crazy."

"Come with me."

"No, I don't want to witness it."

"You're not going to witness it. You're going to do it."

"What?" he said, outraged. "You know I'm against killing people."

"Yes. I know. But you said it was okay to kill someone to save your life."

"I didn't say it was okay," he told her. "I said you might have to kill someone to save your life."

"Well, you have to kill him to save your life. Come with me."

He went with her if only to have more time to talk her out of it. He followed her to the production room. Ramón and Manuel were standing over Nardo, who was sitting in a chair with his hands tied behind his back.

"The executioner has arrived," Ramón said.

Nardo was obviously terrified.

"Ramón will explain," Zoraya said, standing back from them.

"I'm going to give you the gun," Ramón said, "and you're going to shoot him in the back of the head. Manuel will make a video tape that will show you killing him. We'll keep the tape to make sure that you don't tell anyone about us."

"You mean if they release Abdullah and you let me go."

"That's right. If they don't release him, we don't need the tape."

"Because we'll kill you," Manuel said helpfully.

"Well, I'm not going to kill him."

"If you don't," Ramón told him, "we'll kill you no matter what they do."

"You promised to release me if they released Abdullah."

"We didn't promise to release you. We only promised to kill you if they didn't release Abdullah."

"You implied that you would release me."

"But we didn't promise to release you."

He looked at Zoraya, who refused to meet his eyes. Suddenly, he had a desperate idea. "Okay. Give me the gun."

Ramón handed him the gun. "You know how to use it?"

"I've never used a gun before."

"Well, this is how you release the safety," Ramón said, doing it for him. "Then you point it and pull the trigger."

He walked around behind Nardo, who began to plead with them.

"I was only calling my girlfriend," he cried in anguish. "I wouldn't ever betray you. Please don't kill me, please don't kill me."

Jim stood behind him and pointed the gun at the back of his head. If Nardo had been pointing a gun at him, he probably could have pulled the trigger. But under these circumstances there was no way he could justify it. Crucially, he couldn't believe that killing Nardo would save his life. If they intended to kill him whether or not Abdullah was released, then they could kill him whether or not he killed Nardo.

"I can't do it," he finally said, pointing the gun at the floor.

"Not even to save your life?" Zoraya asked.

"No. Because it isn't necessary."

"It *is* necessary," Ramón maintained.

"But I have no problem killing you," Jim said, pointing the gun at him.

Ramón put his hands up and said mockingly: "Please don't kill me, please don't kill me."

At that point he realized that the gun wasn't loaded. They wouldn't have been so stupid as to hand him a loaded gun. He aimed it at the ceiling and pulled the trigger. There was only a click.

For a moment it looked as if he had a chance to escape because they didn't have the gun, but Manuel immediately produced another gun and pointed it at him, saying: "Don't get any ideas, *hombre*. This one's loaded."

Back in his room, he asked Zoraya: "Whose idea was that?"

"Mine." She had stopped by the door as if she didn't intend to stay long.

"Well, it was a stupid idea. What was the point?"

"To find out if you would kill Nardo to save your life."

"But it wouldn't have been to save my life. He wasn't pointing a gun at me."

"If we had a video of you killing him, we wouldn't have to kill you. So killing him would have saved your life."

"But the gun wasn't loaded, so I wouldn't have killed him."

"You thought it was loaded, didn't you?"

"Yeah. And you thought I'd pull the trigger?"

"I wasn't sure what you would do."

In a flash he understood. "So it was a test to see what I'd do?"

"That's right. It was a test."

"Did I pass or fail?"

"You passed," she said tensely. "You proved to me that you wouldn't kill someone even to save your own life."

"I shouldn't have had to prove it," he told her.

"Maybe you shouldn't have had to, but I'm glad you did."

He welcomed this admission of a feeling about him, but he still had a question for her. "Are you going to kill Nardo?"

"We have to," she said definitely.

"You don't have to do anything. You always have a choice."

She stood and looked at him as if he wasn't making her life any easier.

TWELVE

LIVING ALONE, EXCEPT for the company of Matthew on weekends, Jim dropped by his mother's house more often after work to have a drink with her and talk. She was still living in the house on Goodrich Avenue, still going up and down the stairs, and still driving. In July she celebrated her eightieth birthday at a party he gave, attended by his brother and sister as well as Carla and Gina, but she had no major health problems, only a minor case of arthritis.

They sat in the living room, where his mother had always joined his father to have cocktails before dinner while the children were upstairs doing homework. His mother had her usual bourbon on the rocks, and Jim had a red wine. He had more than once suggested that his mother sell the house and move into an apartment because it would be a lot easier, but his mother was determined to stay in the house as long as she was able to cope with the stairs. As she explained, she had lived in the house for fifty-six years, and it harbored memories of her marriage, her children, and her grandchildren.

During these visits Jim learned more about his mother than he had ever known or imagined. She revealed things she had kept to herself and lived with. She eventually told him what had happened to her as a young girl—the thing his father had helped her to rise above. She was twelve when it started. Her family was living in a house on Summit Avenue, and it was the Twenties, a time of prosperity and immoderation. Her parents, who were very social, gave a lot of parties because the house was perfect for entertaining, with two living rooms, a large dining room, and a room that was dedicated as a barroom. There were always about fifty guests at these parties, which ended only when the last people left or

258

collapsed on sofas around dawn. And the only people up before noon were maids and children.

Her mother had an uncle who was still a bachelor. He was attractive, and he had money, so there was no shortage of young women with their eyes on him, but he preferred a life without responsibilities, a life of social engagements and parties, and he never missed a party at her parents' house.

Around ten o'clock, when he knew she was in bed, he would come upstairs and talk to her and kiss her goodnight. It wasn't long before he was touching her and getting her to touch him, always warning her not to tell her mother because if she did then something bad would happen to her. Afraid and believing that the whole thing was her fault, she didn't tell her mother, and she let her uncle do what he wanted with her. Eventually, he penetrated her. It hurt and made her bleed, but the next day when the maid saw the sheets she assumed that the girl had started having periods.

Her uncle abused her for three years without anyone knowing or guessing, and he only stopped because his company transferred him to Chicago. The next time they saw each other they both acted as if nothing had happened, though when he kissed her on the cheek in public she shuddered at the thought of what they had done, and she still felt it was her fault.

"Did you ever tell your mother about it?" Jim asked when she had finished.

"No. I never did."

"Why didn't you tell her?"

"Because I felt it was my fault."

"But it wasn't your fault," he said. "It was your uncle's fault."

"I know that now, but I didn't know it at the time."

"Did you ever tell anyone?"

"I told your father—after we were married. I should have told him before, but I wasn't sure if he could handle it."

"How did he handle it when you told him?"

"He cried for me. It was the only time I ever saw him cry."

After a silence Jim said: "You said he helped you rise above it."

"He did. You may not believe it, but I was very shy as a girl. All through high school and college I stayed away from boys."

"I don't blame you."

"Before I met your father I had only one boyfriend. Well, he wasn't exactly a boyfriend, but I went out with him a few times."

"How old were you then?"

"I was just out of college at the time, so I must have been around twenty-one."

"What was he like?"

"Oh, he was very attractive. A lot of girls were in love with him, but for some reason he wanted to go out with me."

"Maybe because *you* were attractive."

"I didn't think I was. I thought I was a leper."

"What happened with him?"

"One night after a party he took me for a drive on the road that runs through the Yacht Club golf course. He stopped the car, and he wanted to kiss me, so I let him. I hadn't ever kissed a boy."

He listened intently, imagining the scene.

"Then he wanted to do other things, and I wouldn't let him. I remembered what my uncle had done to me, and I freaked out." She had evidently learned this expression from Carla. "After hitting him I jumped out of the car and ran away."

"Did he come after you?"

"I don't know. I ran across the golf course and never looked back. I reached the road that goes around the lake. I walked along the road to the caddy house, and luckily the cop was there, parked in front of it. He took me home."

"Did you ever see the guy again?"

"Oh, yes. You can't avoid people in this town. I saw him at a party a week later. He came up to me and apologized. But he never asked me out again."

"So how long after that did you meet Dad?"

"Not long. My cousin fixed me up with him on a blind date."

"You mean you didn't know him?"

"He was older. He ran with a different crowd."

"I assume," Jim said, "that he didn't attack you the way that other guy did."

"No. He was very gentle, very understanding, even though he didn't know what had happened to me. I guess he must have sensed something."

He looked over at the three photographs that were hanging on the wall over the floral loveseat. They showed his parents on their honeymoon in Bermuda: his mother in a white one-piece bathing suit standing on the beach, his father posing on a sand dune, and the two of them together under a palm tree. They looked so young, they looked so happy.

"Your father was probably the only man who could have helped me," his mother said, smiling with tears in her eyes. "He was such a lamb."

That night, lying awake in bed, Jim remembered the nights when he was a child unable to sleep because he could hear his mother crying in his parents' bedroom. He was about six at the time, and he didn't understand why she was crying. Later, he learned that she was suffering from extreme postpartum depression because her baby after him was born before his father could get her to the hospital, and it came out in their bed, lifeless. That had happened four years ago, and even though she had safely delivered another baby two years ago she was still suffering from depression. But all those nights while he lay awake hearing his mother cry in anguish, he felt that the bottom had dropped out of the world. He didn't know about the lost baby. He only knew that if his mother was unhappy, it must be his fault. So he kept trying to make her happy: by being a good boy, by doing well in school, and by being a good older brother to Stephen.

In particular, he remembered the time when he came home from school and found his mother lying in bed with the shades drawn. Unable to get her attention, he went downstairs and out into the backyard and picked a bunch of daffodils, which were in full bloom. He brought the bouquet back to his mother and offered it to her, saying: "I love you." When his mother saw the flowers she burst into tears and rolled over away from him, making him feel utterly rejected.

In his bedroom he found the toy walkie talkie that his uncle had given him last Christmas, and in the kitchen he dumped the flowers into the garbage. He went out into the backyard and lay down on the lawn, where he pretended that he was a spy who had swum from his ship onto the island of Iwo Jima and was radioing his fleet, giving the positions of the Japanese so that they could be bombed by planes from the carriers before the marines landed. He was the only American on the island, taking a risk that no one else was willing to take, and he would be responsible for the American victory. He imagined that he was in a movie with an audience watching him, though deep down he had a feeling that one person wasn't watching him.

Now, as he lay awake reflecting on what his mother had revealed to him that day, he understood that when he came home from school and found her in bed with the shades drawn and when he heard her sobs during the night she was crying not only for a lost baby but also for a lost girl. And his heart went out to her.

Two years later she fell on an icy sidewalk and broke her hip. In the hospital she caught pneumonia, and a week later she died. It happened so fast that his sister, who lived in southeastern Minnesota, and his brother, who lived in New York, were unable to make it to her deathbed. So he was the only child with her, holding her hand and praying for her soul when she passed away.

It took months to deal with the things in the house: the silver, the china, the furniture, and all the stuff that had accumulated over almost sixty years, including things from the grandparents. Stephen stayed for two weeks, and Anna made several trips up to St. Paul to help him, but ultimately it fell upon him to make decisions on what to keep and who should get what. Among the photographs that weren't framed he found one of his mother that must have been taken when she was around twelve. If he hadn't known it was his mother, he might have assumed from her dark hair and her dark eyes and her tan skin that she was a girl from southern Spain. There was something about her—a look of sadness in her young eyes—that made him recall the beggars he had encountered in Córdoba, Sevilla, and Granada.

On Monday morning after breakfast Zoraya led him downstairs to the screening room to watch the news and wait for the government's next offer. They saw the report on Bosnia, where survivors were verifying stories of Serbian atrocities. The report focused on a town where the men had been hauled away in trucks and shot in a field, while the women—many of whom had been raped—were herded into buses and removed from the area. Meanwhile, the Serbian forces were advancing on another safe haven, preparing to attack it. And the world was watching, doing nothing.

The next story was about the heat wave. Temperatures in many regions of the country were breaking records, supporting the theory about global warming. Leaders of economically advanced countries, whose pollution was the main cause of the problem, were urged to do something about it.

Finally there was a story about Jim. An anchorman showed scenes from Sunday's demonstrations and then cut to a press conference where a spokesman was reading a prepared statement. "The government has noted the public support for the Muslim cleric convicted of inciting violence. While the government is not willing, and will never be willing, to negotiate with the captors of Senator Wyatt, it's willing to review the trial of the cleric and, if any errors in the process are found, to order a retrial. That's all I can tell you at this time."

The spokesman then left the podium without answering any questions.

"We're not getting anywhere," Ramón said, scowling.

"We are," Jim argued. "With every tape we get a better offer."

"So what will they offer next time?"

"A retrial. I mean, they've already offered it."

"They haven't. They've only offered to review the trial."

"It's the same thing. They've already decided to have a retrial, but they don't want to look like they're overruling the legal system."

"Why not? They can do what they want."

"They can't do what they want. Not in our system."

"Then how can they offer a retrial?"

"They can get some judge to find a reason."

"Why haven't they already done this?"

"Because they don't want to look like they're yielding too easily."

"I don't understand your culture," Ramón said, shaking his head. "All you care about is what things look like."

"Appearances are important."

"Well, we won't accept a retrial. We want them to release Abdullah."

"Give them time. If we make another tape today, you'll get what you want. But you'll have to give them more time."

"You mean extend the deadline?" Zoraya asked.

"Only to give them enough time."

"Enough time for them to find you," Ramón snarled.

"How stupid do you think we are?" Manuel said.

"If we extend the deadline," Zoraya said, "then we'll be yielding, and they might think they don't have to make a better offer."

"Give them a chance. Give us all a chance."

Zoraya frowned as if she had doubts but she finally said: "We'll think about it. But if you're going to make another tape, you better get started."

He followed her back to his room, where he worked on another speech. There was nothing more he could ask his constituents to do. They had responded beyond all expectations. So with his last tape he had to try something different.

A half hour later he called Zoraya, yelling through the door. She came promptly and led him to the production room.

He sat at the table and rehearsed his speech. "Okay. I'm ready."

Manuel turned on the video recorder.

"Hi," he said, looking into the camera. "This is Jim Wyatt. I want to thank all of you who responded to my appeal. Because you showed your support for the rights of minorities, the government has informed me directly that they're going to release the Muslim religious leader who was wrongfully convicted of inciting violence. They're going to let him return to his mosque in

New Jersey where he can resume preaching the gospel of peace. You've demonstrated once again that people have the power to correct the government's mistakes, and to promote understanding between different races, religions, and cultures. I thank you from the bottom of my heart."

"That isn't true," Ramón said, looking indignant.

"The government didn't agree to release him," Manuel said.

Zoraya frowned, saying nothing.

"Look," he explained, "I've put the government into a position where they either have to confirm what I said or they have to deny it. If they deny it, they'll look like they don't know what they're doing. And that'll cost them votes."

"You're betting," Zoraya said, "that people will take your word over the word of the government."

"It's a safe bet," he said confidently. "And the government knows that people will take my word over theirs."

"Okay. So send them the tape."

Back in his room, Zoraya sat down in one of the chairs and stretched out her legs. She looked as if she was finally relaxing.

He sat facing her.

"I have a better feeling now," she told him.

"I do too. With that tape I changed the game on them."

"Why didn't you do that before?"

"I didn't think of it," he said honestly. "But it wasn't the right time before. We had to move them closer to releasing Abdullah."

"You mean so people would believe they had agreed to release him."

"That's right. Before, they probably wouldn't have believed it."

She was silent for a while. "You know, I've been thinking about what you said in our last conversation. I mean about having choices."

"And what did you conclude?"

"We might have done this another way."

"You mean without kidnapping me?"

"Yeah," she said. "We might have found you or someone like you who would listen to us and take our side."

"But now you have a lot of people on your side."

"Yeah, we do, thanks to you."

"You have to do something with it," he told her, "while it lasts."

"Well, I don't know what to do with it. I've never been in this position before."

"I can help you. I've been in this position many times."

"So after they release Abdullah will you help me?"

"Of course I'll help you," he assured her.

"You know," she said, gazing at him peacefully with eyes that had once narrowed with suspicion and flared with hatred, "I finally believe you."

In the afternoon she led him downstairs to the screening room, where they watched the news and waited for an announcement. Around four a government spokesman met with the press and fielded questions.

"Can you tell us when the cleric will be released?" a reporter asked.

"No, I can't tell you," the spokesman said.

"Can you confirm the statement by Senator Wyatt?" another reporter asked.

"No, I can't."

"Are you saying it's not true?"

"No, I'm not saying that. I'm only saying I can't confirm it."

"You mean you don't have authority to confirm it?" another reporter asked.

"That's what I mean. I don't have authority."

"Then what can you tell us?"

"I can tell you that we're doing everything possible to bring this situation to a peaceful conclusion."

"Did someone in the government talk directly with Senator Wyatt?"

"I can't answer that."

"Do you have any information on where he's being held?"

"I'm sorry, but I can't answer that."

"He doesn't know much," Ramón said.

"He's holding them off. It's his job," Jim said.

"I wouldn't like to have a job like that," Manuel said.

"They pay him a lot," Jim said.

"Well, then maybe I wouldn't mind doing it."

For the next hour they watched the news on Bosnia, which kept getting worse. Then the spokesman reappeared and read a prepared statement. "The government has confirmed its willingness to release the Muslim cleric whose cause is being supported by Senator Wyatt. As soon as possible arrangements will be made for the release of Senator Wyatt as well as the release of the cleric."

The spokesman retreated, declining to answer any questions.

"Does that mean what I think?" Ramón asked.

"Yes," Jim said, though he suspected that the government was playing the same game he was. "It means that they'll release Abdullah."

"So what do we do now?" Manuel asked.

"We have to find a way of communicating with the government," Jim said, "so that all the details can be worked out."

"We have a way of communicating with them," Ramón said.

"We can't keep using tapes. It'll take forever."

"We can't use the phone," Zoraya said.

"Zoraya could meet with them," Jim said.

"They would arrest her," Manuel said.

"Not if you keep holding me."

"So how would that work?" Ramón asked.

"She would make sure that Abdullah is released, and then she would call you and tell you to release me."

"They could trace the call," Manuel pointed out.

"It won't matter then. It'll all be over."

"But won't they do something to us for kidnapping you?"

"The deal will include amnesty for you."

"Amnesty? Is that what we want?"

"I think you do. If you settle only for safe passage out of the country, you'll never be able to come back."

"We want amnesty," Zoraya said definitely.

"Okay," Ramón agreed. "So when should Zoraya meet with them?"

"Tomorrow morning," Jim said.

"All right." They were in agreement.

Of course they were still holding him, and they still had to lock him in the room, but it felt different. He couldn't imagine how it would take more than a day or two to release Abdullah, and then it would all be over.

That evening Zoraya brought dinner for both of them, and they ate together, sharing a bottle of French wine.

"Where did you get this?" he asked.

"From the cellar. They have hundreds of bottles of wine there."

"This isn't your uncle's house."

"No. It belongs to the people Manuel works for. He's their chauffeur, and when they're away he watches the house."

"He's done a good job of watching it. Where are they?"

"They're in Mallorca. They have a house there."

"What if they'd come back?"

"They wouldn't have. They go for a month every year at this time."

"They must have a lot of money and a lot of time."

"They do," she said. "The guy's retired. He used to work on Wall Street."

"Well, it's an ideal place to hold a hostage."

"That's what we figured. The neighbors are so far away that they can't see what happens here. And they don't care anyway."

"I imagine they don't. These houses must be owned by people with a lot of money."

"Yes," she agreed. "What kind of house do you live in?"

"A normal house in a normal neighborhood."

"How many bedrooms?"

"Five," he told her.

"Do you live there alone?"

"I have since my last wife left me."

"I wouldn't like to live alone in such a big house."

"It's all right. I have a lot of good memories."

After a long silence she asked: "What's it like in Minnesota?"

"It's a nice place to live. The winters are too long and too cold, but other than that there's not much to complain about."

"Are there any Muslims?"

"Yeah. There are. I don't know how many."

"Could I come and visit you?"

"Any time. You can have one of my daughter's bedrooms."

"That would be nice," she said, smiling.

She stayed with him until almost midnight. When she got up from her chair to leave, she approached him and said: "Can I ask you to do something for me?"

"Sure. What?"

"Give me a hug."

He took her in his arms and held her the way he had held his children so many times for so many reasons.

"Thanks," she said. "I needed that."

"I needed it too."

Before closing the door she said: "You know, it's amazing how we got here from where we started. Don't you think?"

"It's beyond amazing." He looked at Zoraya, seeing how she had evolved in his mind from an alluring creature of fantasy to a real live young woman who had the traits that make a leader. "It's nothing short of a miracle."

It was the first good night's sleep he had gotten since arriving there last Tuesday. He was still deep under when he was awakened by the sounds of gunfire. Alarmed, he sat up and listened.

The shots were coming from the second floor, and they were from automatic weapons as well as from handguns. After a while the shots from the handguns stopped, and there were only a few last rat-a-tat-tats, followed by sounds of men shouting to one another between rooms, between floors.

He jumped out of bed and got into his clothes, assuming it was a swat team from the FBI. He was debating whether to remain silent or call out to them when a battering ram broke through the door of his room and an arm in a dark shirt reached through the hole, groping for the knob.

"I'm Jim Wyatt," he yelled to them, not wanting them to shoot. "Can you help us open this door?"

"No. It's locked with a key."

"Then we have to break it down. Stand clear."

He stood clear while they battered the door to smithereens.

A young man in uniform lunged into the room, asking: "Are you okay?"

"I'm fine," he said, concerned about what they might have done to his captors. "Are all the other people okay?"

"You mean the people who kidnapped you?"

"Yeah. There were two men and a woman. Three men," he said, remembering Nardo. "Are they okay?"

"We had to take them out," the young man told him bluntly. "They fired at us."

"Oh, God," he said. "Did you kill them?"

"We killed the people who fired at us. If you want to be helpful, you can come with me and identify them."

He followed the young man out of the room. Down the hall three men were battering through the door of another maid's room. From inside, someone who sounded like Nardo yelled: "Don't kill me! Please don't kill me!"

When he reached the bottom of the stairs Jim saw the bodies in the hall. Ramón, who had fallen forward, still had a gun in his hand. Behind him lay Manuel with a gun nearby, and then Zoraya, just outside the door of the bedroom she had used. She was curled up like a sleeping child.

"Are these the people who kidnapped you?"

"Yeah," he said hoarsely. "You didn't have to kill them."

"They fired at us."

"The girl didn't fire at you."

"Well, we couldn't tell if she had a gun. She came out into the hall after they started firing at us."

"She was trying to stop them."

"You don't know what she was trying to do."

"No. I don't. But I think I know." He walked toward her, avoiding the pools of blood from the two men. When he reached

Zoraya he knelt down and cleared the hair from her forehead. At least they hadn't damaged her face.

Her mouth was open as if in surprise and her eyes were staring without light. He closed them tenderly. Then he leaned over and kissed her forehead, which was still warm. "I love you," he said in Arabic as if he was saying goodnight to a daughter. "I would have liked to see what you did with your life."

"What's that?" the young man asked suspiciously.

"Nothing," Jim said, rising to his feet.

"It sounds like you got close to these people."

"They say it often happens between captives and their captors," he muttered. "I want to get out of here."

The main floor of the house was occupied by the swat team, and he was detained by the man in charge, who asked him to go into the kitchen with him and answer a few questions. They sat at a table where the help probably ate.

"I'm Captain Lamonica," the man said. "Are you okay?"

"Yeah. I'm fine." He could still see Zoraya curled up on the floor like a child.

"Can you tell me anything about your captors?"

"They were kids," he said sadly. "Except for the chauffeur."

"The chauffeur? Was his name Manuel?"

"That's right. How did you know?"

"We talked with the people who own this house."

"How did you find us?"

"We traced a phone call."

"So he did betray them."

"You mean Nardo? Yeah, he was working for us. We caught him delivering a tape, and we got him to change sides."

He was impressed, but he didn't feel grateful. In fact, he blamed them for how things had turned out. He probably shouldn't have believed what the government spokesman had said in his last press conference, but he had thought they were making progress.

"Can you tell me the names of the other two people?"

"Ramón and Zoraya. I don't know their last names. They were brother and sister," he added, still seeing them sprawled on the hall floor.

"Do you know where they were from?"

"They were from Ceuta. It's a Spanish enclave in Morocco."

"Do you know how long they've been here?"

"They came here as students. They both finished college, so they must have been here at least four years. Probably longer."

"Their visas must have expired by now."

"I guess they must have."

"Well, we have to crack down on these international students," Lamonica said as if that was the problem.

Jim said nothing, not wanting to prolong the conversation. All he wanted now was to be alone in a room at the hotel.

They eventually drove him back to New York. A crowd of reporters was at the hotel waiting for him, but he put them off, promising to talk with them after he had a chance to recover. They asked him for a specific time, and he finally agreed to hold a press conference at noon.

In his room he sat down at the desk and phoned each one of his children, beginning with Carla and ending with Matthew. Surprisingly, he was able to reach all of them. It was as if they had been waiting for his call.

Then he undressed and took a shower. They had let him take showers, and they had even provided him with clean underwear, but he felt he needed purification, and he stood under the warm water with his eyes closed for a long, long time. At home he would have run out of hot water.

After drying himself with the ample hotel towel he put on clean underwear, which he found in his suitcase—of course the hotel had held it for him—and then he shaved.

At least feeling physically clean he lay down and wept.

As promised, he met with the press at noon in a hotel conference room. He read the following prepared statement: "First of all, I want to thank the media for covering my story and reporting it accurately. You've been terrific. And I want to thank all the people who responded to my appeal and asked the government to release Abdullah ibn Hasim al-Qahtani, the Muslim cleric wrongfully convicted of inciting violence. I'm proud of the American people for recognizing injustice and trying to rectify it. But I'm not proud of our government for ignoring you and for killing three people unnecessarily. I'm not proud of our government for allowing thousands of Muslim men and boys in Bosnia to be rounded up like cattle and slaughtered. I'm not proud of our government for allowing thousands of Muslim women and girls in Bosnia to be brutally raped in a campaign of terror. I'm not proud of our government for standing by and allowing these atrocities to occur only fifty years after we ended the Nazi genocide. The same thing is happening in Bosnia, only now we call it ethnic cleansing, which doesn't sound as bad as genocide. But what's happening in Bosnia *is* genocide, so we have to stop it now as we did then. Muslim men are human beings like our fathers, our brothers, and our sons. Muslim women are human beings like our mothers, our sisters, and our daughters. Muslim children are human beings like our children. They have a right not to be tortured, not to be murdered, and not to be raped. They have a right to live in peace. So we must stop what's happening to them."

The room exploded in applause. As usual he had the feeling that one person hadn't applauded, but it didn't bother him.

"I'll answer some questions," he told the reporters.

"How did they treat you?" a reporter asked.

"They treated me well. The food was so good that I gained weight."

There was laughter like the kind you hear in a grim situation when people are hoping to have something to laugh about.

"They say that hostages often get close to their kidnappers," a reporter said. "Did that happen to you?"

"Yes. I came to understand their perspective."

"Was your statement influenced by this understanding?"

"Oh, yes. Like a lot of my colleagues I wasn't focusing on the situation in Bosnia. I was focusing on domestic matters."

"What do you think our government should do in Bosnia?"

"We should take military action, preferably through NATO. After all, this is happening in Europe."

273

"Tell us more about the kidnappers. What were they like?"

"Two of them were recent college graduates." He looked around, noting the ages of the reporters. "They could have been your kids."

"What made them resort to violence?"

"Their lack of trust in our system. Their feeling that we don't care what happens to Muslims."

"You say your captors changed your perspective. Did you change theirs?"

"I changed one of them enough so we had a meeting of minds. I think they would have made a deal with our government."

"So why did it end in violence?"

"Because our government wasn't negotiating in good faith."

"Are you planning to run for president?"

He smiled. "That's an easy one. No."

"Why not? You have national recognition now."

"I think I can do more good in my present position. If I ever change my mind about that I'll let you know." Deciding that this was the right note to end on, he thanked them and stepped back from the podium.

That afternoon the government announced that Abdullah would get another trial. They had found a technical error in the process.

Six weeks later NATO airstrikes on Serbian positions in Bosnia helped to bring an end to the war. By late November a peace accord was signed in Dayton, Ohio, and sixty thousand NATO troops were deployed in Bosnia to maintain the fragile ceasefire. Meanwhile, there was growing evidence to confirm the alleged massacres of civilians as well as captured soldiers at Potočari, Sandići, the Jadar River, the Cerska Valley, Kravica, Tišća, Grbavci, Orahovac, Petkovići, Branjevo, Nezuk, Baljkovica, and Meces. It was estimated that more than eight thousand Bosniak men and boys were killed in the ethnic cleansing. An increasing number of commentators were calling it genocide.

A year after his kidnapping Jim took Matthew on an extended trip to Spain. Matthew was sixteen now, old enough to get something out of the trip. They started in Madrid, where among other attractions of the city he introduced his youngest child to tapas, flamenco, and the Prado. Interestingly, Matthew wasn't thrilled by flamenco, but he loved the tapas. Unlike most kids his age he was willing to try anything that his parents ate, and he discovered that he loved stuffed mushrooms, fried eggplant, mussels, squid, and other dishes that he had never eaten at home. He also loved the Prado, especially the later Goyas, which he asked to go back and see again.

They rented a car and drove to Córdoba and Sevilla, stopping for a few days in each city, and then over to Granada, where they stayed at the hotel inside the walls of the Alhambra. Matthew was fascinated by the Alhambra, and he bought a book from which they learned a lot about its history. As they strolled through the gardens Matthew told him things he hadn't known about the Alhambra, and even though Matthew had taught him a lot about computers, this exchange about a matter that touched his heart was a milestone in their relationship.

He had a phone number for Inga, and hoping she would be in town he called her one morning. She answered, saying: "*Hola?*"

"Hi. It's Jim. I'm here in Granada with Matthew."

"Why didn't you tell me you were coming?"

"Oh, I don't know. Anyway, I'm here, and I'd like to see you."

"I'd like to see you. Come right over. I just finished doing a recording."

She gave him directions, and they took a taxi to the Albaicín, where the driver left them at the bottom of a street that was really an extended stairway. They climbed the street, turned a corner, and found her house.

Like most of the houses in the old Arab quarter the house was surrounded by a wall. In front there was a heavy wooden gate, with a door within it that Inga opened to let them in. She was wearing jeans and a loose green top, with her hair in a ponytail. She was in her late forties now, but she looked much younger.

She gave Jim a warm hug, and then hugged Matthew, whom she had met at family occasions but didn't really know. She showed them around her house and her recording studio, which occupied one side of the house. She demonstrated her sound equipment, and Matthew was enthralled.

They had lunch in the courtyard, which of course had a well in the middle. Fed by the well, a fountain plashed from one of the walls. The table was shaded by lemon trees that were beginning to bear fruit. An old almond tree stood in a corner.

She served them *salmorejo*, a chilled Andalusian soup that blended the flavors of roasted red peppers, roasted tomatoes, almonds, and vinegar.

"This is dynamite," Matthew said. "Will you give Dad the recipe?"

"Sure. I got it from a food magazine," Inga said.

"You have a nice place here," Jim told her.

"I'm happy here."

"I can see that." It was in her eyes, which made him feel that she had matched her dream with reality.

"I have everything I want. I even get visits from Erik and Lukas."

"So they tell me. They love it here."

"It's a long way for Lukas to fly here from LA, but he claims he can sleep on a plane, so he doesn't mind it."

"If he gets that part in the play then maybe he'll go back to New York."

"I wish he would. It would be closer. And I think he'll have a better life in New York. There's more for him to do."

"Did Erik bring his fiancée here?"

"Oh, ya," she said, sounding like a Minnesota Swede. "I like her. I think she's just perfect for Erik. He's so serious. She makes him laugh."

"I like her too."

"Mothers are supposed to feel that no woman is good enough for their son, but I didn't feel that way about her."

"What about fathers?"

"They're supposed to be jealous of any man who comes near their daughter."

"I never had that problem with *your* father," he said, deadpan.

She laughed. "Ya, sure. Remember when he caught us in the basement?"

"He wanted to kill me."

"What were you doing?" Matthew asked, interested.

"Nothing. She was singing, and I was listening to her. I'm sorry to disappoint you," he kidded, guessing what his son had imagined. At that age they assumed that everyone had sex at every opportunity.

"It's funny now," she said, still laughing, "but it wasn't funny then."

They hugged each other for a long time before he left with Matthew. She urged him to come back again, and he intended to.

After leaving her they wandered through the narrow streets of the Albaicín with no particular destination. They were passing the entrance of a church when a girl in a tattered blue dress stepped out in front of them.

"Money?" she said in English.

They stopped, and Jim looked at her. She was probably about twelve. Her light brown face and her long dark hair needed washing, and her body emitted the odor of the homeless. But her dark eyes were full of hope, if only for money.

"What's your name?" he asked in Spanish.

"Luz," she said shyly.

"Do you have a home?"

"No. I live on the streets."

"Where are your mother and father?"

"My mother's dead, and I don't know where my father is."

"Do you go to school?"

"Not anymore."

"Are you here at the church every day?"

"Yes. Except on Sundays."

He took out his wallet and gave her enough pesetas to feed herself for at least a week. He almost told her that he would be back, but he didn't want to raise her hopes in case he decided not to do what he had in mind.

"*Gracias*," she said, her eyes lighting up when she saw how much money he had given her. "*Que Dios le bendiga, señor.*"

As they walked on, Matthew said: "What a nice girl."

"So you didn't see a beggar. You saw a girl."

"Well, how could I not have seen a girl?"

"That's a good question," Jim said, putting his arm around Matthew's shoulder. "And the answer is, you'd have to be blind."

Book Club Guide

Blind in Granada

Tom Milton

Introduction

Jim Wyatt, a prominent state senator from Minnesota, is kidnapped on a visit to New York City by an Islamic human rights group who mistakenly believe that he is a CIA agent. They hold him hostage in return for the release of a Muslim cleric who was convicted and imprisoned for inciting violence in connection with the bombing of the World Trade Center in 1993. Through a series of video tapes addressed to the public and aired on television, Jim urges people to support the cause of releasing the cleric, who he believes was wrongly convicted. Between the tapes, while locked in a bedroom, Jim examines his relationships with his four wives, his seven children, and his parents. He also develops a relationship with Zoraya, the leader of his captors, who is young enough to be his daughter. Out in the world Muslims are being killed daily in the ethnic cleansing of Bosnia, which his captors use as justification for what they are doing. Since they have set a deadline by which time if the government doesn't release the cleric they will kill Jim, his life depends on his efforts to gain the trust of Zoraya and persuade the government to release the cleric.

Jim is happy in his career, and he's successful, but whenever he gives a speech and the crowd applauds he imagines that one person among them, an unknown spectator, does not applaud, which leaves him feeling invalid and empty. He has a complex personal life. For some reason he marries women who in one way or another have been abused by their fathers, and he tries to help them rise above what happened to them. To some extent he does help them, but whatever he does it's not enough, and they eventually look elsewhere to satisfy their needs. As long as he's married, Jim is always a faithful husband, but after a wife has left him alone he reverts to a fantasy in which instead of being a state senator he's a CIA agent, a mercenary, a war correspondent, or a private investigator. In fact, he worked for the CIA right after college but reluctantly abandoned that career to satisfy the needs of his first wife. So between marriages he plays a role to impress women he meets in bars, who don't know who he is, and his one-night stands with these women at least temporarily validate him and fill the emptiness inside of him.

Playing a role to impress a woman is what gets him kidnapped. Unknown to him, the woman he meets this time in a bar is also playing a role, pretending to be an heiress from Granada on a visit to New York to learn about historic preservation. Jim is especially susceptible to her because of his lifelong love of Spain. According to a family tradition his mother, though Irish, had a Spanish ancestor, which explained her dark hair, her dark eyes, and her perennial tan. In college he majored in Spanish, with a minor in Arabic, and he did his junior year abroad in Spain, where he saw the wonders of Granada. So while he's looking for a woman to impress in order to fulfill his needs, this woman is looking for a man to kidnap in order to get the government to release the Muslim cleric who was her mentor, and when he pretends to be a CIA agent she decides that he will make a perfect hostage.

As sometimes happens in these situations, the hostage and the kidnapper develop a relationship, and during the period of confinement they learn a lot about themselves from their interactions with each other. Jim, who has always been an advocate for social justice, adopts the cause of his kidnappers, and Zoraya, who has never experienced love, begins to see its possibility. Though his primary goal is to convince the government to release the cleric and thereby save his life, his emerging goal is to help Zoraya rise above what her father did to her. So all the issues of his life converge in his relationship with Zoraya.

A conversation with Tom Milton

You've developed several themes in this novel. Some are familiar, and I'll get to them, but now I'd like to talk about the theme of appearances versus reality. I don't remember this theme from any of your previous novels. So why now? Is something happening in the world that brought it to the surface?

For one thing, we have the issue of real news versus fake news, or however you want to phrase it. But that's not new. As one of Jim's captors points out, Americans often care more about appearances than about reality. Of course, as a politician Jim cares about appearances, but unlike many politicians at least he's honest with his constituents.

Still, as a politician he must have to play a role.

He does, and at times he gets tired of that role and wants to escape from it.

He escapes into a fantasy world in which he plays the role of a CIA agent, a mercenary, a war correspondent, or a private investigator. Why those roles?

They give him a mystique that he doesn't have as a politician. I mean of living in a world where his life is in danger.

Ironically, by playing the role of a CIA agent he falls into the hands of a woman for whom he's a perfect target for kidnapping. And she just happens to play a role that lures him into a clever trap.

In more than one sense he meets his match in Zoraya.

I think it's ironic that pretending that his life is in danger actually puts his life in danger.

Yes, so appearance becomes reality.

Well, I wonder if he really wanted his life to be in danger, at least subconsciously.

I won't pretend that I understand him, but he does have needs that aren't met by his success as a politician.

So let's talk about his personal life. All four of his wives were in one way or another abused by their fathers, so evidently one of his needs is to help women rise above what their fathers did to them. I can guess where that comes from, but he doesn't seem to know until late in the novel. Did you place him in captivity so he would have time to reflect on his life?

Oh, yes. He was always so engaged in his career and in his relationships that he never took the time to reflect.

As I watched a relationship develop between him and Zoraya I felt that he was finally beginning to understand his life.

The issues of his life converge in Zoraya, who offers him an opportunity to integrate his personality.

It was interesting how his relationship with her evolves from a one-night stand with a woman he met in a bar to something like a father-daughter relationship. I could even imagine him adopting her as he adopted the children of his fourth wife.

I could imagine that happening.

There's a lot about father-daughter relationships in this novel. We talked about how all of Jim's wives were affected by the negative relationships they had with their fathers, but we haven't talked about Jim's relationships with his daughters. He has three daughters, including an adopted daughter, and they all present him with different challenges. Yet somehow he deals more or less successfully with those challenges.

I think it's a matter of necessity. I mean, he realizes that with his daughters, especially the two who lost their mother at an early age, he's all they have, and if he doesn't watch out for them they could go off the deep end.

Are his daughters more challenging than his sons?

They are for him, and maybe they are for other fathers.

Well, let's talk about the theme of being blind. The title comes from a poem written about Granada. The poet sees a woman encountering a blind beggar in Granada, and he tells her to give alms to the man because there's nothing in life like the pain of being blind in Granada. Does the poet mean the pain of not being able to see the wonders of Granada?

There are a lot of wonders in Granada, especially in the Alhambra. But I think the poet also means the pain of not being able to see the wonders of the world. And that goes back to the theme of appearances versus reality. Too often appearances blind us to the wonders of the real world.

You mean like seeing a beggar and not a human being.

Exactly. Or seeing terrorists and not human beings when we encountered Muslims after the attack on the World Trade Center in 2001.

That's the springboard for the action in your novel Milos and Amira, *but in this novel the springboard of the action is the bombing of the World Trade Center in 1993. The year is 1995, and the war in Bosnia is always present in the background. The issue of what's being done to Muslims in that situation provides a context for what his captors are doing to Jim. Did you get the idea to write this novel during the war in Bosnia?*

I did, though it took a long time to germinate.

You wrote about refugees from that war in Milos and Amira. *Did the ethnic conflict in that story help you to develop this novel?*

It moved things along. But almost everywhere you look in the world today, you can see an ethnic conflict. I think what made this novel come together was the character of Zoraya, who like my other heroines has a passion for justice.

Returning to Jim, I found his relationship with his mother fascinating. Her ancestors are from Ireland, but according to a family tradition she has a Spanish ancestor, which explains her dark hair, her dark eyes, and her tan skin. With his love of Spain and dream of pursuing a career there, Jim embraces that tradition. Yet he also has a need to separate from his mother, which at one point he tries to do with a formal separation agreement. In doing that is he for real, or is he playing a role?

I don't know. I let my characters do what they feel like doing.

Whenever Jim wants to marry a woman he introduces her to his parents. His father usually likes the woman and has no problem, while mother always warns him about the risks of marrying someone from a different social, ethnic, or religious background. But these differences don't cause problems in Jim's marriages. It's always something else, and it's always the same thing: the woman needs something that he can't give her. So after four marriages he must be carrying a heavy load of failure.

He's carrying a heavy load of something, but he doesn't understand what it is. Like many people he keeps doing the same thing over and over, hoping for a different outcome.

Isn't that a definition of insanity?

If it is, then I must be insane. I mean you could say that I keep writing the same novel over and over, hoping for a different outcome.

I wouldn't say that. Your novels all have something in common, but they all have different characters and different stories. But I have one last question. What about the one person in the crowd who never applauds Jim's speeches? Is it his mother?

I don't know. It could be anyone.

Well, reading this novel raised a lot of questions in my mind, as your novels always do. And it made me conscious of how at times I'm blinded by appearances and don't see the wonders of the real world.

It's always good talking with you. I think you're my ideal reader.

Discussion questions

1. What impels Jim to play a role when he meets a woman in a bar who doesn't know who he is?

2. Why does he play the roles of CIA agent, mercenary, war correspondent, and private investigator?

3. Why does he fall for the story that Zoraya is an heiress from Granada visiting New York to learn about historic preservation?

4. Why don't his captors detain him as soon as he enters the house with Zoraya?

5. Why does Jim have such a hard time convincing his captors that he's not a CIA agent?

6. What is the origin of Zoraya's passion for justice?

7. Apart from trying to save his own life, why does Jim support the cause of his captors?

8. What is the purpose of having the war in Bosnia present in the background of this story?

9. Why did his captors ask Jim to kill Nardo?

10. How effective was Jim's campaign to get the government to release the Muslim cleric?

11. How is the theme of appearance versus reality dramatized in Zoraya's experience in Granada with the American tourist?

12. How does seeing the photograph of his mother as a twelve-year-old girl advance our understanding of Jim?

13. How does the ending relate to Jim's experience with Zoraya?

14. If Jim had met Zoraya when he was younger, what kind of relationship might they have had?

15. What does Jim have in mind when he encounters the girl as a beggar in Granada?

www.ingramcontent.com/pod-product-compliance
Lightning Source LLC
Chambersburg PA
CBHW030804210726
48290CB00002B/425